BURNING FOR AUTUMN (POLICE AND FIRE: OPERATION ALPHA)

ON CALL SERIES BOOK 1

FREYA BARKER

Dear Readers,

Welcome to the Police and Fire: Operation Alpha Fan-Fiction world!

If you are new to this amazing world, in a nutshell the author wrote a story using one or more of my characters in it. Sometimes that character has a major role in the story, and other times they are only mentioned briefly. This is perfectly legal and allowable because they are going through Aces Press to publish the story.

This book is entirely the work of the author who wrote it. While I might have assisted with brainstorming and other ideas about which of my characters to use, I didn't have any part in the process or writing or editing the story.

I'm proud and excited that so many authors loved my characters enough that they wanted to write them into their own story. Thank you for supporting them, and me!

READ ON!

Xoxo

Susan Stoker

ACKNOWLEDGMENTS

I am beyond fortunate to have Karen Hrdlicka and Joanne Thompson to keep me on the straight and narrow. These two ladies are part of the development, the execution and the grooming my work and I don't know what I would do without them. I love you girls so much!

I also have a fabulous crew of beta readers who pour over every book: Debbie Bishop, Pam Buchanan, Sam Price, and Deb Blake. Ladies, your input is so important!! Love you!

My Barks&Bites group, a small but growing group of readers, who are so generous in their support and enthusiasm for my books. You ROCK!

Stephanie of SBR Media, my agent and my voice of reason in this industry, is literally a crutch I can lean on for anything! She patiently listens while I have a melt down or freak out and calmly guides me back to sanity. I absolutely adore you!

To my publicists, Debra Presley and Drue Hoffman of Buoni Amici Press, you ladies have the patience of saints. You work your fingers to the bone and still you indulge my daily list of questions. Already I have no idea how I ever managed on my own..

To all the fabulous bloggers—some of whom have been there since my very first book—thank you for your support, your valuable time, your enthusiasm and your incredible loyalty.

And last but never least, my gratitude to you, my readers. I cannot express enough how amazed I still am with every new reader who finds my books. Your kind notes, your awesome reviews, and in some cases your wonderful friendship, are beyond special to me.

Love you all.

CHAPTER 1

Autumn

"Bad day?"

I look around as I'm coming out of the small waiting room. I just had to tell the parents of a four-year-old their child is not eligible for a clinical trial we were hoping might benefit her. The little girl's injuries are simply too severe. The lower part of her face, her neck, her chest, down part of her back, and the upper part of her legs were hit with hot oil when she pulled the fryer off the counter. She'll surely face years of surgery and that's the best-case scenario.

Oil burns are awful and often result in third-degree burns. Close to fifty percent of this little girl's body has sustained damage and about two-thirds of it are full-thickness burns.

"You can say that again." I recognize the man from one of the presentations I did for the local fire stations. A good-looking, tall man with bulk in all the right places, who'd easily stood out with his red cropped hair and beard. Being a redhead myself, I'm not usually attracted to fellow gingers, but this guy was not hard on the eyes. "Station Two, right?"

"Good memory," he says with a wide grin.

Damn, the strong white teeth peeking through that soot-stained facial hair bump him up another notch on the hot scale.

"You kinda stand out," I confess with a shrug. "If I had a brother, I imagine he might look like you."

"Ouch." The firefighter slaps a hand to his chest and feigns stumbling back a few steps. That's when I notice the bandage on his other hand and automatically step forward, reaching out.

"Did you get that looked at?"

"It's fine, just an occupational hazard. Only one of the reasons I'm here."

"What's the other?" I ask, with an eyebrow raised and he grins again.

"I could lie and say I came to see you, but I have a feeling that wouldn't fly even if it were true."

"Astute observation."

I'm doing my own grinning now, enjoying the silly back-and-forth, but in the next moment the full weight of the day settles back on my shoulders.

"Actually, I thought I'd check on a burn victim from a call we answered last night. A little girl, Missy Fraser?" He must've seen my face drop, because he immediately followed it with, "Shit, don't tell me—"

"No," I quickly stop him. "She's hanging on. I'm not supposed to...you should probably talk to her parents. They're in here." I step aside and motion at the waiting room's closed door.

He takes a long look at the door before turning back to me. "Listen, I don't know what you do to wind down after a difficult shift, but there's a place out on Main Street, The

Irish Embassy Pub, where you can find a drink and a willing ear. On any given night, you'll find a good number of first responders there, doing exactly that. Folks who get the stress of the job. In fact, I'm planning to head over there tonight after my shift ends. You should pop in."

If I thought he was asking me for a date, I'd shut him down right away, but this feels more like a friendly invitation. I can handle that. I've been in Durango almost eight weeks and too busy to strike up any friendships. I miss my friends back in San Antonio. Especially on days like this, where it would've been nice to be able to talk to someone who understands. That's what this guy is offering me.

"I don't even know your name," I suddenly realize out loud.

"Evan Biel," is his instant response, as he holds out his good hand.

"Autumn McCoy," I return, shaking it firmly.

"I knew that." The cheeky grin is back. "I paid attention in class."

"Good to know. I should get going, though, I have a patient waiting in my office. It was good to meet you."

"Likewise, and keep The Irish in mind," he repeats his offer.

"I might pop in." I nod a smile and take off down the hallway. I'm already ten minutes late.

I certainly have hit the floor running since taking on this one-year project at Mercy. It's not that I wasn't happy in San Antonio at the Burn Center Annex, but I was starting to feel stuck in a rut. Not just my work, but in my personal life as well: the same routines, the same environment, the same friends. Don't get me wrong, I adore my friends, but always being the oldest in the group was starting to make me feel like the spinster aunt, always living vicariously through the others. I'm only forty-two and not quite done kicking a few cans myself.

When I was approached to help set up a brand-new burn center at a level III trauma hospital, I was intrigued. The work would be much broader, and definitely more involved than my position as clinical researcher at the Annex had been. More hands-on with patients, which is something I didn't have much of before. I'd mostly been at the receiving end of data—processing information—but with this new position, I'd be able to follow it all the way from the source.

My role here is more of a liaison between the patient and what is available in terms of new treatment options and clinical trials. The case numbers I've been used to working with suddenly have become living, breathing people.

The fact the job meant moving to Durango, Colorado for a year only made the decision easier. A memorable trip with my parents—before Dad up and left us when I was just ten—had introduced me to the beauty of the Rocky Mountains, and I'd always wanted to return.

"Hey, Jeff, sorry to've kept you waiting."

The man jumps up when I walk into the small sitting area outside my office.

Jeff Youngman was the first patient at Mercy I'd been able to successfully enter into a new clinical trial. He'd been caught in a barn fire and his neck, shoulder, and upper chest on his left side had sustained second and third-degree burns. Mid-to late forties, and in otherwise good health, he'd been a prime candidate for the promising post-grafting treatment.

"No problem," he mumbles, following me inside. A soft-spoken man, Jeff is also painfully shy.

"You know the drill, right?" I gesture to the open door of the small examination room off my office.

While he gets ready, I pull his file up on the computer and scan last week's observations to orient myself. He's already lying back on the table, his upper body exposed, when I walk in.

"Let's see how we're doing," I offer with a smile, heading straight for the small sink to wash my hands before donning a pair of gloves.

My role is simply to record progress and changes, but that still requires me to touch the patients. He closes his eyes when I carefully remove his dressings, which makes me feel bad. I know all too well how uncomfortable that can be.

"It's looking good. Let me take a few pictures for your file." I grab the digital camera, snap off a few close-ups of the burns, and go through the whole hand-washing routine again before grabbing fresh gloves to redress his wounds.

I'm already feeding the updates into his digital file when he walks in.

"Same time next week?"

"Actually, that won't work for me." I flip open my planner to find an unfilled spot. "I have some friends from back home coming down for a visit, and I'm taking a few days off." It will be the first days off since starting here eight weeks ago. Sophie was a colleague at the lab in San Antonio, and one of my good friends. She's coming down with her boyfriend, Roman—or Chief, as most everyone calls him. He's a firefighter as well. Good guy. I'm looking forward to their visit.

"You're not from Durango?"

"Nope. I'm a Texas girl. San Antonio, born and bred," I inform him with a smile. "Don't get me wrong, I love it here, but Texas will always be home."

Keith

"Any news on a new chief?"

I hold back the mayor after another long, tedious committee meeting I was forced to sit through. Last April, a few of the town's council members had voiced some concern about the apparent rise in major crimes in recent years, and to appease them, the mayor had called a committee into action to examine the role and effectiveness of policing in Durango.

Yeah. It gives me a headache too.

For eight fucking months I've had to sit and listen to a bunch of yahoos who love nothing more than hearing themselves talk. They discuss ways in which the Durango PD—my department—can improve on their efficiency in combating rising crime. Nothing but a bunch of cackling hens, unhampered by any expertise on the subject. Today's topic had been how to better integrate police into the community, and one idiot suggested a police float at the annual parade.

What the fuck? Like pulling a group of officers to spend valuable time building a goddamn float is gonna put a halt on rising crime? Jesus, if I ever had aspirations to go into politics, this committee crap has cured me for life.

Who's got time for this shit?

I wouldn't even be here if our former chief of police hadn't been put away for a slew of felony charges, close to a year ago. Before I knew it, Mayor Stan Woodard had appointed me interim chief. Except I don't consider eight months *interim*, which is why I'm stopping him on his way out the door.

"Things are moving along." The smile he gives me, along with the friendly hand on my shoulder, are meant to placate. They only piss me off.

"What does that mean? Moving along. Have you got any

interviews lined up? Do you have suitable candidates? Heck, are you even looking?" I don't even attempt to hide my irritation.

I know Stan wants me to take on the job permanently—he told me so himself—but I thought I'd made it perfectly clear there is no way in hell I'll do it. I was perfectly happy in my job before the chief's responsibilities landed in my lap. These days, I hardly have any time for real police work, I'm buried in bureaucracy and politics. No thanks.

"Are you telling me how to do *my* job now?"

I'm not about to let him divert attention by pretending to be insulted.

"You know damn well I'm not. Just as you know damn well, because I've mentioned it a time or two, if you try to prolong this any more than is necessary, you're gonna force me to quit. And don't make any mistake," I hammer home when he rolls his eyes disbelievingly. "I'm *this* fucking close to throwing in the towel. Goddamn parade floats—you've gotta be kidding me."

I'm still muttering in frustration when I walk out of the boardroom, out of City Hall to the Durango PD office right around the corner.

"I take it that didn't go well?"

Tony Ramirez, one of my detectives and a friend, saunters into my office and flops down in one of my visitors' chairs.

"Understatement of the fucking century," I groan, rubbing my hands over my face. "I'm afraid he's going to push this right to the edge. He's gonna force me to put my money where my mouth is. I'd better start looking for openings elsewhere."

"Bullshit. I'm not used to you being Mr. Negativity."

"Can you blame me? Look at this fucking office." I wave an arm at the disorganized stacks of paperwork the secretary adds to religiously on a daily basis. "I'm getting buried under administrative and procedural shit, and I'm about to drown."

"Well snap out of it. You've been a miserable son of a bitch for months. Since when do you let life dictate you? Take fucking control."

There aren't many people who have the guts to talk to me like that, even less I'd accept it from. Lucky for Tony, he's in the last group. "How do you suggest I do that?"

"By finding your own replacement and introducing him or her in front of the entire council at next month's committee meeting. You'd have to make sure this person is beyond reproach, has a stellar policing record, is an accomplished leader, and knows how to play the political game."

My snort is loud. Even if such a person existed, chances they'd want to relocate to Durango to handle its relatively small police department would be slim. I'm still chuckling when I notice Tony's not laughing.

"Fuck me. You know someone?"

"Possibly." He smirks, getting up. "Get your cranky ass up. Time to get out of here, grab a bite, I'll tell you all about it."

* * *

A few familiar faces greet us as I follow Tony inside The Irish. He picks a booth near the bathrooms, I'm assuming for privacy.

"So? Care to enlighten me?" I prompt after we've placed our order for a couple of beers and burgers.

"You know I spent six years with the Denver PD before signing on here, right?" I nod my confirmation. "Joe Benedetti was my commander in the Major Crimes Division. We've stayed in touch over the years."

The waitress interrupts with our beers. Tony waits until she leaves before he explains how his former commander has indicated he might be in the market for a smaller department and a smaller community to raise his kids in.

"Okay, so he's an experienced leader, and I assume he has a solid record, but does he have the stomach to deal with the politics of the job?"

This time it's Tony's turn to snort. "We're talking about thirteen years as division commander in the Denver PD. Trust me, he knows how to play the game."

From the corner of my eye, I catch a glimpse of a wild mop of red hair passing by, but when I turn for a better look —all I see is the door to the ladies' room swing shut.

Shortly after, the waitress appears with our burgers and hungry as a horse, I dig in. I'm feeling a fuckload better with a full stomach and a plan. Tony is going to talk to his former commander to see if he's interested enough to come down to Durango for a weekend, so he and I can meet.

"I'm heading out. I've got to hit the gym," Tony announces, getting up and pulling out his wallet.

"On me." I wave him off, and with a chin lift he tucks his wallet away and heads out.

I'm not ready yet. Feeling a lot lighter than I have in a long time, I head over to the bar to see if I remember how to socialize. I chat with a few guys from the firehouse and have just ordered my third beer when a sexy, almost hoarse voice sounds behind me.

"Is this seat taken?"

CHAPTER 2

Autumn

"Be my guest."

The dark brooding man I'd been watching for the better part of an hour has a voice like silk. Deep, dark, smooth, and totally in character with his appearance. Nothing like my raspy smoker's voice—even without the habit—sounding more like the morning after a rough night on the town.

Evan Biel never showed.

I'd gone home, walked into my house, and was struck by the utter silence suddenly threatening to drown me. So instead of the quiet night at home I'd decided on, I rushed into the bedroom. Stripping out of my 'work' clothes, I pulled on a pair of yoga pants and an oversized T-shirt, and shoving my feet into a pair of flip-flops, hauled right back out of there. It's all about the comfort. The pub Evan had suggested sounded like a place that could handle my sloppy attire. It's not like I was going on a date, where there'd be certain expectations on my wardrobe.

I liked The Irish the moment I walked in. A little dark, a

lot worn, but with that laid-back atmosphere you only find in a real pub. Anyone could come in and feel at home, and I can see why folks would come here to wind down after a stressful day. The food wasn't exactly gourmet fare, but nothing says comfort like a heaping plate of fish and chips.

I first noticed the two men sitting in the far corner when I got up to use the facilities. Law enforcement was the vibe I was getting. Good-looking guys, both of them, although the quiet one—the one who seemed to be doing the listening while the other talked—held my attention. Not sure why, maybe just the reserved silent intensity that rolled off him. It would be interesting to see if he could be riled up.

I don't usually walk up to a stranger in a bar, and even if I did, I'd probably make sure I was wearing something a little less sloppy. But I came here for a little social interaction, which I haven't seen because my new firefighter friend left me hanging. I'd been eyeing this guy since he sat down at the bar after his friend left. So when I saw him order another beer, I put my big girl panties on.

"Can I get you another beer?" I offer, even as I'm looking at his mostly full pint.

"I'm good, thanks."

I catch him doing a quick scan of me before turning back to his glass. *Yikes.*

He's a little older than I initially thought. I'd pegged him for mid-thirties, but I may have been off by a decade. His hair is dark, but with a hint of silver, and the striking angular face, with high cheekbones and square jaw, sported a web of fine lines around the eyes. Those were remarkable. I'd expected dark brown, but his are a very light hazel.

"Could I have another Guinness?" I lift my empty glass to the bartender.

"On me," my handsome neighbor says when the glass is set in front of me.

"Oh, no," I protest. No way in hell I'll let him buy my beer. "I don't let strange men pay for my drinks, thank you very much."

His head slowly turns to me and he looks me over again, from the bottom of my flip-flopped feet up. They come to rest on the bright red frame of my glasses. "I thought red was a fashion faux pas for a redhead." Automatically I reach up and push them back up my nose.

"I wouldn't know what constitutes a fashion faux pas if it bit me in the ass," I counter, resisting the urge to smooth the wrinkles I know cover my shirt.

"You don't say."

The dry, drawn-out comment delivered with a poker face should probably upset me, but it has me barking out a laugh instead.

"Hey, comfort is the name of my game." There it is, a little twitch at the corner of his stern mouth, hinting at a smile that promises to be a stunner. "Autumn. My name, it's Autumn," I clarify when he looks at me funny at first.

"Hello, Autumn—who sits next to strangers, but buys her own drinks, and lives for comfort—the name's Keith." He holds out his hand, and I'm pleased to note the shake is strong, not holding much back because I'm some weak female.

"That's not the name I would've picked for you," comes flying from my mouth before I can check it. His eyebrow rises sharply.

"No? Why not?" I hear the sharp undertone telling me I've unearthed a wee chip on his shoulder, but I ignore it.

"Don't get me wrong, I like it. It's a handsome, strong name, which by definition suits you perfectly. I don't know, I could be wrong, but you strike me as law enforcement. More a rough-and-tumble kinda guy, and Keith almost seems too sedate and proper."

This time I get a full on grin. "Rough-and-tumble?" he echoes, that dang eyebrow still somewhere up in his hairline, but at least I have him smiling. Sort of.

"Just calling them as I see them." I shrug, taking a deep swig of my beer. I note he neither confirms nor denies my assumptions around his career.

In my peripheral vision, I see him turn his upper body completely toward me, leaning his elbow on the bar.

"What is it you were looking for tonight, Autumn?" he inquires softly, his voice dropping even lower and his words ripe with innuendo.

Despite the tingle running over my skin, and the flutter in my belly, I'm disappointed in his blatant come-on. I swing around sharply. "Oh, I don't know, a friendly face? Some lighthearted banter? A bit of normal interaction to get me out of an empty house at the end of an extraordinary crappy day?"

I'm already off my stool, and heading for the door, when it occurs to me my reaction is way out of proportion. I don't even know why his assumption I was looking for a quick hookup hit a chord with me. It's not like I've never done exactly that before. In fact, I'd been the one to sit next to him and strike up the conversation that, at closer scrutiny, might well have suggested as some kinda come-on.

The truth is, I've discovered a long time ago those quick meaningless fucks never make you feel better in the long run. I should know—I tried often enough.

I would've been happy just shooting the shit with this guy —he intrigues me—and I'm disappointed he just sees me as a walking, talking vagina.

Shit. Great way to make new friends, moron.

I may be an idiot but I'm not a coward, so instead of barreling out the door, I turn on my heel, square my shoulders, and walk right back to him.

"Didn't mean to take out my crappy day on you," I apologize, holding out my hand, which he cautiously takes. "New in town, the last thing I wanna do is piss off the locals. I'd be grateful if you'd just forget this entire unfortunate encounter. Y'all have a good night now."

This time I calmly turn and head for the door, only mildly disappointed when he doesn't say a word in response.

* * *

Keith

Unfortunate encounter, my ass.

My eyes follow the slight sway of her hips under the shapeless shirt covering her ass. Her whole getup screams don't come close. I resist going after her, because frankly, I'm having a hell of a time reading that woman.

I noticed the fiery red hair when she'd slipped by me earlier, and her voice sounded sinful. When I finally got a good look at her, it was her body language—as well as her appearance—that threw me off. The whole package was confusing as hell.

Then she opened her mouth and out came this acerbic wit in that husky voice, and I noticed the ridiculous glasses that somehow looked cute on her, all of which piqued my interest. Fuck, I thought she'd been flirting. In fact, I'm pretty damn sure she was, but she turned on me so fast, my damn head was spinning. Two seconds later, she's back apologizing.

Now I've had a long and frustrating day—and may not be at my sharpest, especially after a couple of beers—but I'm smart enough to know when to hold off for another day.

There will definitely be another day.

I got enough to know her name's Autumn, she's a Southern girl–just new in town—lives in a house, hasn't made a lot of friends, if any, and is brutally honest. She also has balls, a spunky attitude, and some physical attributes that make for a sexy package, but she likes to hide her light under a bushel. She's not one to go unnoticed, and since I'm still the fucking interim chief of police, and a heck of a detective if I say so myself, I'm sure it won't be difficult to find her.

I slide off my stool and turn to the bartender, Jay. "Settle my tab?"

"You taking care of the lady's too?" He leans against the bar with a knowing smirk on his face, clearly having witnessed her rather dramatic exit.

"Sure. Why the fuck not." I pull out my wallet and drop enough bills on the counter to hopefully cover both our bills.

I'm still grinning when I slip behind the wheel of my truck. She'd been pretty adamant about paying for her own beer, and I'm sure she'll be back to The Irish when she discovers forgetting to pay at all. If I were to take a wild guess, she's gonna be pissed to discover I ended up taking care of her whole tab.

"Blackfoot," I answer when my phone rings, just as I pull away from the curb.

"Boss, you home yet?" Mike Bolter, the station's desk sergeant, wants to know.

"Not yet. What's up?"

"What started as a trailer fire at the park on Animas Drive, just turned into a two-alarm. You may wanna go have a look. It looks like it might jump the railroad tracks, an electrical pole went up like tinder and the box is sparking."

"You talking about Durango Fountain? That place behind the rafting outfit?"

"Yup. Conley's at the scene. Sent him out when the call first came through."

"I'm on my way. Send two more units to help with possible evacuation of the surrounding buildings. If the fire chief calls, tell him I'll be there in less than ten."

Pole fires are a bitch, especially when the lines start burning. They become unpredictable projectiles, and it's safest to clear the immediate surrounding area. Considering fires also make for cheap entertainment, there's sure to be a crowd watching.

Flashing lights are visible through the trees and an occasional flame shoots up over their tops. The acrid stench of smoke filters into the cab of the truck. An ambulance rushes past me, heading in the opposite direction, when I turn off Main by the rafting outfitter.

I park my truck behind the patrol unit and make my way over to where I see Officer Conley trying to move back the gathering crowd. Farther down are the smoking remnants of one trailer, a second one burning, along with a row of brush separating the trailers from the tracks behind. A single electric pole between the damaged trailers and a double-wide on the other side is engulfed in flames.

"Talk to me," I order Conley as I walk up to him.

"Fire chief just told me he wants this whole cul-de-sac evacuated. The wait is for La Plata Electric to cut off the juice."

"Any injuries?"

"They pulled a middle-aged man from the first trailer. That's all I know."

"Okay. Two more units are en route, you need more to get this area cleared, radio Bolter."

"Will do, Boss."

I roll my eyes at the unwanted title my guys were quick to bestow on me, and head over to where I see the fire chief standing by one of his rigs. Not a lot of love lost between Curtis Buxton and me, but on the whole we manage to stay civil. He was a friend of Tom McMahan, and wasn't happy I broke the so-called code of honor when I instigated the investigation into our former chief, even though he'd publicly denounced the man shortly after his arrest. Still, he runs a tight ship at the DFD and his men respect him.

"Need that crowd gone, Blackfoot."

"Extra units should be here any minute. We'll get it done. What have we got?"

"Other than the one victim my men pulled from that first trailer, and that it's clear the fire started there before spreading out, I've got nothing concrete yet, just suspicions. We've gotta get this under control before I call an investigator in. Likely won't be until sometime tomorrow."

"Fair enough. The victim gonna live?" He gives me a dirty look. I know he's not a doctor or a medic, but he's got enough experience to be able to tell me whether the guy even has a fighting chance. He may not have said it in so many words, but it's clear to me he believes it may be a case of arson, which would make this the third such case in the past couple of weeks. This is the first one leaving a victim, making me even more eager to get a handle on this.

"Talk to Biel. He's over by Engine 11."

I catch him on a break. He's sitting on a step on the side of the large truck, tossing back a bottle of water.

"How's it going, Evan?" I ask, clapping him on the shoulder.

"Just peachy. Never mind I should've been celebrating the end of a twenty-four hour shift, not pulling a damn drunk from a burning trailer."

"Guy was drunk?"

"The alcohol was strong enough to notice over the thick smoke."

"He gonna make it?"

"Probably," Biel acknowledges. He pours the remainder of the water over his head.

"Talking?"

"Nothing coherent. If you're looking to question him, I suggest you wait until tomorrow. Let him sleep it off."

CHAPTER 3

Autumn

It's ridiculous.

I've been here two months, and I haven't unpacked half my boxes. If I wait any longer, I might as well not bother—it'll be almost time to move back.

I wonder if that's been my issue; if that's why I haven't tried harder to find another posse. I miss my girls: Quinn, Tory, and Sophie. Instead I find myself hanging out on the couch holding conversations with my cats. I'm starting to live up to the 'cat lady' epitaph my friends tease me with.

Last night's attempt to 'mingle with the natives' can't exactly be called a success, but it was a start. Today I'm tackling those boxes, come hell or high water. Not that I really have a choice, they're stacked in the spare bedroom where Sophie and Roman are supposed to sleep.

I spend the next few hours unpacking, and with each box I empty, I feel a bit lighter and my house starts looking a little more like a home.

Gizmo and Jack—my pretty tortoiseshell and the playful tabby who goes wherever she does—are checking out the last empty box, while their less nosy siblings are snoozing on the couch. Ziggy, a calico girl and the most asocial one of the bunch, is perched high on the backrest. The other two, Boots and Panda, are barely distinguishable, curled together in a black and white ball of fur on the seat.

Five cats. *Christ,* what was I thinking? If anything screams lonely spinster, it's a house full of cats.

Armed with a bucket of cleaning supplies, I tackle the bedroom and attached bathroom. Finding this place was a stroke of luck. The owners were sent overseas for work and had put their furnished place up for a one-year lease. It's technically half of a duplex. An older gentleman, Mr. Bartnik, whom I've seen all of a handful of times, lives next door. The nice mature area and two-bed and bathroom suite, had made this an easy decision. I wanted the space so my friends could come and stay. The rent was steep, but I can afford it—the one-year contract pays well.

I'm just scouring the closet for clean linens for the bed, when my phone rings.

"Hey, girl," I answer, seeing Sophie's name pop up on my screen.

"Hey back. S-so are you ready for us?"

"Getting there. I was just looking for sheets to put on the bed."

Sophie snickers. "You m-mean you were able to find them under all those boxes?"

"Hush up. I'll have you know every last one of them is unpacked."

"Progress," she teases, knowing me all too well. "Have you m-met any new people yet?"

I shake off the mental picture of teasing hazel eyes in a striking face, before answering. "A few. Mostly through work, though. I did go out for dinner last night." I don't tell her that I'd been so rattled by a handsome cop; I completely forgot to pay my bill. Nor that when I returned half an hour later to settle my bill—completely mortified at the discovery—apparently said cop had settled up the tab for me. How fucking embarrassing.

"On a date?"

"No, by myself. Pub grub. It's a cool place, actually. Apparently a hangout for local first responders. Roman will get a kick out of it. I'll take you guys there, they've got decent food and they have Guinness on tap."

"S-sounds good to me, although I'll take a pass on the Guinness, that's m-more your s-speed."

Ever since I've known Sophie, she's stuttered, but she's grown more confident over the years, and—although I hate to admit such a thing—having Roman in her life has brought her out even more. I doubt she even notices her stutter herself these days. "No worries, I'm sure your man is willing to toss a few back with me."

"His arm won't need twisting," she confirms with a chuckle. "Anyway, reason I'm calling is to give you a heads-up that we'll be on the road tomorrow morning. We're aiming to s-stop in Roswell for the night. Roman wants to get his geek on and have a look around. Then the plan is to get to S-Shiprock the next day, m-maybe s-stay a night there or in Farmington, and we s-should hit Durango s-sometime on Wednesday, if that's s-still okay."

"Of course! Can't wait, girl." I grin ear to ear.

They're planning to stay until Saturday. I've already cleared my afternoons for the second half of this coming week. That way I can get some work done in the mornings while they do their own thing, and have the rest of the day to do fun stuff.

I've been so busy, I haven't had much of an opportunity to

explore Durango myself. I'm looking forward to that.

* * *

"No luck?"

Jen, one of the nurses on the burn unit, stops me as I pass by the nurses' station. She's the one who'd left a message this morning, alerting me to a possible new candidate for the program. The patient had been in a fire over the weekend and had sustained burns to thirty percent of his body. He's scheduled for his first skin graft surgery this afternoon.

"Not a good match, I'm afraid. Not with his history of substance abuse. I'm sorry."

"I was afraid of that," Jen admits. "I had to try, though. I feel for the guy."

"Of course," I quickly respond. "And I appreciate it. I wish I had the freedom to accept everyone into this trial." I don't have to say more, she knows I'm not just talking about this patient, but the little girl down the hall. She's remains in a medically induced coma and continues to fight for her life. "How is Missy?"

"Still hanging in. Hurts my heart to see those parents struggle to cling onto hope."

It is sad. I've seen them a few times in passing since I've had to give them the bad news, but have given them their space. No matter how much I want to show my support, it doesn't do them any service.

"I hear ya." I smile at her sympathetically. "I best be heading back upstairs. Talk to you later."

With a wave I head for the stairwell—the only kind of exercise I'm willing to engage in. Already focused on my next appointment, I'm not paying particular attention to my surroundings.

"Looking for Doug Boynton. I have a few questions."

It's not just the mention of the patient I just left, but the sound of the voice, that has me turn around.

Casually leaning against the counter at the nurses' station is none other than the man from the pub. *Keith*. Fucking hell, if possible, he's even more striking in daylight. I, on the other hand, am like freaking Cinderella. Daylight is not my friend. Every freckle, frown line, wrinkle, and blemish stands out like a beacon on my face, screaming 'well past expiration date.'

To avoid him seeing me, I quickly swing around and reach for the stairwell door, but his voice stops me.

"Running?"

* * *

Keith

I noticed that mop of red hair right away, even tied back in a stern ponytail looking like it might hurt. Instead of calling out, I turn to the desk and ask for the patient I'm here to see. I'm very aware when she spots me, and then promptly turns her back.

Against better judgment, I call after her. "Running?"

That does the trick. Funny, somehow I knew challenging her would have a better chance of succeeding than simply calling her name. She not only stops in her tracks, but also swings around and marches right up to me, shoulders back, head high. Oh yeah, she does not like being accused of cowardice.

"Keith? Was it?" she snaps, forced to look up at me at such close proximity. She doesn't fool me, she remembers, as well as I recall those big green eyes behind the red-rimmed glasses and the abundance of freckles covering her face and upper chest. I want to bet they don't just stop there. "Can I help you?"

"You work here," I state the obvious. I hadn't really pegged her for a doctor, but I could be wrong. She's dressed better, albeit moderately so, in a plain white dress shirt, gray slacks, and a pair of flats. Barely noticing the presence of the nurse I'd been talking to, I focus on those eyes, betraying she'd at least spent a passing thought on me these past couple of days, regardless of what comes out of her mouth.

"I do. Therefore there is nothing for me to run from." She layers on the bluster. *Liar.*

"Good to know." Too bad I don't have the time right now to challenge her. I get the sense I might enjoy chipping away at that tough, confrontational exterior.

She visibly bristles at my grin before grinding out, "Did you come to collect? I believe I owe you a dinner."

"Actually..." I turn a raised eyebrow to the nurse, who is obviously following the interaction with intense curiosity.

"Yes, of course. Right," she mumbles. "Mr. Boynton is in room three twenty-four. Second on your right."

Looking back at the prickly redhead, I tip an imaginary hat. "I'm afraid I'll have to take you up on that invitation to dinner some other time...duty calls. Good seeing you again, Autumn." Her barely suppressed snort, and the dramatic roll of her eyes, has me chuckle all the way to the unfortunate Mr. Boynton's room. I'll be collecting on that dinner at some point, I now know where to find her.

I'm eager to get some answers from Doug Boynton. Yesterday the fire inspector confirmed arson, which makes it my case. It's on the board as Ramirez's—since I'm not technically on the rotation anymore—but as I mentioned to Tony, I need to get my teeth into something or I'll go fucking insane. Crime analysis was sent in as soon as we found out fire inspection was done with the scene, and a preliminary report was on our desks this morning.

By the time I was done questioning the victim, I was convinced he didn't set the fire. I was also convinced someone had targeted the man specifically. Doug mentioned he'd come home to find a bottle of Jack on the trailer step. An alcoholic, among other things, he didn't question too closely where his poison of choice came from. He can remember drinking that afternoon, but little else.

The moment I walk out of the hospital, I call Ramirez.

"Was a bottle of Jack found at the scene?"

"Daniels? Let me check the report. I'm pretty sure there was mention of bottles, but I don't know if they were specified. Hang on."

I find my Tahoe and climb behind the wheel while I wait for Tony to dig up the information. "Any time now."

"Hold your horses, Blackfoot. There's an itemized list that was just added to the report. They found thirty-nine liquor bottles: thirty-eight empties, and one with some residue."

"Tell me that's the Jack Daniels."

"Sure is. What's the significance?"

"Our alcoholic vic found a surprise bottle on his doorstep the afternoon of the fire," I enlighten him.

"The Jack."

"You've got it."

"You're thinking the arsonist dropped off a present," Tony clues in right away.

"Bingo."

"And I take it you want it analyzed—stat?"

"A gold star for the grasshopper."

"Kiss my ass, Blackfoot."

"I'll take a pass, Ramirez."

I'm still grinning when I hang up the phone. Feels fucking great to be using my mind for something other than administrative and procedural shit.

* * *

Autumn

With a frustrated expletive, I toss my purse on the couch, sending my poor cats scattering.

I have not been able to concentrate on a damn thing since that embarrassing encounter this morning. What annoys me most is once again he had me flustered, and I don't fucking *fluster* for anyone. It didn't stop me from checking out his ass in those well-worn jeans as he sauntered down the hall, though.

Then Jen's questions started, which I tried to evade, but she was persistent and I ended up walking away without a word. Guess I didn't make any friends there either. Serves me right for striking up a conversation with a stranger in a goddamn bar.

I offer the cats an apology by way of scratches and dinner and scrounge through the fridge for my own. Not that I feel like cooking, with my luck I'd start a fire.

Grilled cheese it is. Works well with the massive glass of wine I poured.

I'm just licking the crumbs from my fingers when a ping on my phone announces an incoming text. Probably Sophie letting me know they've arrived in Roswell.

It's not.

It's him.

Unknown number: *I like your gorgeous hair better loose.*

Before I have a chance to check myself, I've fired off a text of my own.

Me: *I'm cutting it off tomorrow.*

CHAPTER 4

Autumn

"You stood me up."

It was easy to spot Evan, with Durango Fire Department printing on the back of his navy T-shirt and the short-cropped russet hair.

I stopped in to pick up a few last minute things on my way home. Sophie texted me this morning that they expected to hit Durango late afternoon, giving me a couple of hours to put a decent meal together. I was just about to grab fixings for salad when I see him picking through avocados in the produce section. He swings around at the sound of my voice.

"I did?" He looks genuinely surprised.

"Last Saturday night," I explain, "I got all dolled up…" That's a lie. "…Little black dress, makeup, killer heels—ready for a night on the town—but guess who didn't show? Bullshit play, dude."

His mouth starts working, but no sound comes out. "I was…I thought…*shit*." I suppress a chuckle, but he catches it and his eyes narrow. "You're pulling my leg."

"Mostly," I confess, grinning. "I did show up at The Irish. Ended up having dinner alone and tried to make nice with one Durango's finest." He picks up on the sarcasm too, lifting an eyebrow in question.

"Call came in right at shift change. Was well into the night before I got home," he explains. "I'm going on call again, but maybe we can try for tomorrow night? I wasn't lying, I usually do drop in for a few beers at the end of my shift."

"No can do. I've got friends arriving from out of town today. They're staying until the weekend."

"We'll have to do it next week then. Maybe you should give me your number, so I can get in touch with you."

He holds out his phone and it takes me a minute to take it from him. I don't want to create expectations. "Just friends, right?"

"Promise." He lifts his hand in a Boy Scout salute. "You look too much like my sister."

"Shut up." I punch him for good measure, but I have to admit I'm relieved and put my number in his contacts. "And don't bail on me, you'll kill my self-esteem. Turns out I'm not that good at making new friends."

His eyes narrow at my reference to my first pub experience. "Durango's finest, huh? Who'd you try to make nice with?"

I shrug. "Dark moody guy, name of Keith. You know him?"

"Blackfoot?"

"I wouldn't know, he never said. Are there more guys named Keith on the force?"

"Nope, just the chief."

"That's hardly a creative nickname," I point out. "Just because he's Native American."

"Not a nickname," Evan says, smiling. "He's the chief. Chief of Police."

"Get the fuck out the door—*him*?" There's no way I can reconcile that sexy voice and fine ass in faded jeans with my mental image of what a Chief of Police should look like. A cop, yes, I could see that—one who'd probably like to push boundaries—but chief?

"Relax, it's only temporary. Not a position he exactly chose to be in." He tilts his head, a smile playing at the corner of his mouth. "But now I'm curious, you say you *tried* to make nice?"

"It was nothing," I try to evade, waving my hand, but Evan isn't going to make it that easy.

"Oh, I bet it wasn't nothing," he teases, nudging my shoulder with his. "Knowing Blackfoot, and what little I've seen of you, guaranteed there would've been some kind of fireworks."

I'm still thinking about his words when I pile my groceries in the car. Not sure what Evan was implying, but I can't deny even thinking about Keith Blackfoot causes my blood pressure to rise.

When I walk into the house, I pick up the few flyers shoved through the mail slot, drop them along with my groceries on the counter, and quickly change out of my work garb into something more comfortable.

My original plan had been to cook a big piece of meat, but Evan changed my mind. He'd been picking up supplies for the firehouse and mentioned he was doing tacos tonight. I'm not a big fan of tacos, just because they're so damn messy. I do, however, have an awesome taco pie recipe somewhere that can be prepped beforehand and then just tossed in the oven for half an hour before dinner.

Twenty minutes later, I have chicken breasts and thighs simmering in a mix of stock, lime juice, palm sugar, cumin, and a few chopped jalapeño peppers. That'll sit for a couple of hours until I can pull the chicken apart. I check the recipe sitting on my counter, when I spot the corner of an envelope sticking out from between a couple of flyers.

I hardly get mail here. The only things coming through that slot with any regularity are the wasteful amounts of flyers from local stores, restaurants, and car repair places. I don't even look at them.

It's a plain white envelope with my name on it. No address, no sender. Just my name handwritten in print. Curious, I slip my finger under the flap and tear it open. The note inside looks to be torn from a notebook.

ENJOY!

Only the single word is written on it. I flip over the note, check the envelope, but there's nothing else. Maybe just some weird advertising gimmick I don't get. I toss it aside, and turn back to my taco pie recipe.

Close to five, the doorbell rings. The house is clean—and smells amazing, if I say so myself—the table is set, I just need to toss the flyers in the blue box. That's when I notice the note again. On a whim I shove note and envelope in the kitchen drawer, before jogging to the front door.

"You're here!"

Gorgeous Sophie with her shiny blonde hair is a perfect contrast to her dark and ridiculously handsome boyfriend. I barely get a chance to open the door all the way before she pulls me into a tight hug. With at least a few inches on me, I have to lift my chin not to get smooshed against her shoulder, but I can just roll my eyes at the man behind her. I'm not usually one for public displays of affection, but I willingly let Sophie have a moment. Roman shakes his head, grinning, as I try to dislodge from her hold.

"It's s-so good to s-see you!"

I step aside and urge her inside. "You too, girl. Get in here."

"Nice place," Roman mutters as he steps through the door, giving me a brief one-armed side hug in passing. "Smells great too."

"That's because it's food," Sophie points out before turning to me. "I s-swear, fancy lingerie and fine perfume is wasted on the m-man, but wear a ratty old s-shirt cooking bacon, and next thing I know he's having m-me for breakfast."

The man in question doesn't seem in the least insulted, and is already lifting the foil off my taco pie.

"Don't touch," I warn, slapping his hand. "And don't even think about eating anything other than pancakes in my kitchen for breakfast."

* * *

"So how are you liking Durango?" Roman asks after dinner.

"Love the hospital. State-of-the-art facility and the staff is top-notch. I really enjoy working there, but I miss my girls."

"Awww, we m-miss you too." Sophie leans over and squeezes my hand. "We were out for girls' night last week and Tory pointed out drinking just isn't as m-much fun without you there. We all agree."

"I'm sure you guys managed drinking without me just fine. Besides, we can go have a drink at that place I mentioned on the phone before you guys go."

"I'm out if you guys want to go tonight." Roman looks at his watch. "I'm supposed to meet up with an old friend in twenty minutes."

"I thought we'd catch up here tonight," I suggest. "I

stocked up on wine and beer and picked up a few munchies. We can go another night."

"Then m-maybe you can ask your buddy to come," Sophie directs at her boyfriend. "Wouldn't hurt Autumn to m-meet s-some new people."

"I can do that."

Neither of them seems to notice my eyes rolling. "It's not like I need help, guys." Both sets of doubting eyes settle on me and I look from one to the other. "Well, I don't."

* * *

Keith

Crap.

Analysis came back on the dregs in the whiskey bottle.

Aside from Jack Daniels, they found benzodiazepine. The drug combined with the alcohol alone could've been lethal, even without the fire. Doug Boynton didn't escape just one, but two bullets.

It also confirms that whoever is setting these fires, fully intended for the victim to be in that trailer, which makes this a case of attempted murder, not just arson.

Grabbing the report, I kick back my chair and head over to Ramirez's cubicle. He's still at his desk, eating a sandwich over a fast food wrapper.

"D'you see this?" I slap the report on the desk next to his dinner.

"Yup," he says, taking another bite before he turns, tilting his head at the computer screen. "I also just pulled up the detailed lab report on the accelerant. Have a look."

"What am I looking at?" I lean over the back of his chair

and try to decipher what I'm reading, but I wouldn't even know where to start.

"See that?" he says, pointing at something I can't pronounce. "That's kerosene, and this here is a compound found in anti-freeze: methyl alcohol. Those are the two predominant components. All readily available, but what is interesting is the burn pattern. The report suggests, according to the burn pattern, the cocktail may have been sprayed instead of poured."

"How does that match up with the earlier fires?"

"To a T. Same components, spray pattern, the whole bit."

"A firebug."

"Looks that way. Hey, by the way." Tony peeks over the walls of his cubicle before he changes subjects. "My buddy, Joe Benedetti."

I do a quick scan of the office myself, but there's no one within hearing distance. "Yeah? What about him?"

"Coming to visit his old friend the weekend after next. You should keep your calendar open."

I grin and clap him on the shoulder. "I will." I take a quick look at the clock. "Shit, I should get out of here. I was supposed to meet up with someone five minutes ago."

"Hot date?"

"Fuck no—a buddy visiting from Texas."

I call Chief the moment I get behind the wheel to let him know I'll be a few minutes late.

He's already sitting at the bar of the Diamond Belle Saloon when I walk in. Since he took me down to the River Walk when I was in San Antonio a few years ago, I figured I'd give him a taste of Durango history in return.

Roman Proudfit and I met at a US First Responders Association (USFRA) Emergency Preparedness Conference about five years ago. He'd stuck out because he wasn't hiding his heritage, but didn't flaunt it either. He carried it proudly.

Even then, in his mid-twenties, he was very composed, which surprised me. I had expected the cocky sense of entitlement you often see in his generation, but that wasn't him. He was a leader, he was smart, he was spiritual, and he quickly earned my respect.

We've stayed in touch over the years, but this is his first visit to Durango.

"Nice place you've got here," he says, when I pull out a stool.

"Can't do Durango without doing the Diamond Belle." I point at his glass. "What are you having?"

"Something Pinstripe? All I know it's a red ale and it's pretty decent."

"Ska Pinstripe, that's a local brew."

"So I'm told."

"Want another?"

Instead of answering, he sucks down the rest of his draft and slams the glass back on the counter with a grin. I hold up two fingers for the bartender, who needs no more instruction and starts filling glasses.

"So where is your girl? I thought I was going to meet her?"

Chief's otherwise stoic face softens at the mention of his woman. "She's hanging with her friend, but they were talking about going out another night. Sophie told me to invite you."

"Sounds good to me."

Chief starts grinning. "I don't think you get it, Keith. Sophie's looking to get her friend hooked up."

Well, shit. If he asked me this two weeks ago I probably wouldn't have thought too hard about it.

"I don't know, Roman. Don't get me wrong, I'd love to meet this girl, who was able to drag you on the first vacation since I've known you, but I'm not really in the market for some kind of blind date."

"I hear you. I did my duty," he says taking a sip of his draft. "To be honest, I don't think Autumn was up for the idea either."

My ears suddenly perk up. "Autumn?"

"Yeah, Sophie's friend? She moved here about two months—"

"Friday night's good for me," I interrupt him, wearing a grin. "What time?"

His head swings around and his confusion is almost comical. "What the fuck?"

Before I have a chance to explain, my phone rings.

"Blackfoot."

"Boss? We've got another one."

CHAPTER 5

Keith

"This guy have a hard-on for trailers or what?"

Apparently so.

When I mentioned I had to go, that a local firebug apparently had struck again, Chief followed me out and hopped in the passenger seat of my Tahoe. This trailer fire was on the north side of town again, except along the river this time.

"And why at this time of night?" Chief ponders out loud.

"That's a good point. Why not overnight when there's less chance there'll be witnesses?"

I don't really expect an answer and it's quiet the rest of the drive, until we see the flashing lights and a small crowd gathering in the glow of the flames.

"Unless..." He points a finger at the crowd. "He's looking to be seen. This is not for his own gratification, he's doing it for someone else's."

The only difference from last week is that this trailer backs onto the Animas River instead of the railroad. Apparently the crew got here early enough to douse a neighboring trailer, to prevent it from going up as well. In every other way this scene is eerily similar. Behind the fire engines, one of my guys is trying to back up a nosy crowd, only partially successful, and I spot Evan hacking down some brush surrounding the trailer. It's been bone-dry here since the beginning of May, that low brush will go up like tinder and act like fuel for a hungry fire.

The only person I don't see is the fire chief, until I spot him standing with what looks to be a woman with several small children, all huddled together next to an ambulance. I head straight over there with Chief beside me.

"Blackfoot." Curtis sees me coming and steps away from the small group, throwing a curious glance at my company.

"Buxton," I respond in kind. "Roman Proudfit, San Antonio Fire Department. Roman, meet Chief Buxton."

"Sir." Roman nods respectfully.

Buxton all but ignores him, which sets my teeth on edge, now's not the time to get into it.

"Single mom, three kids under five. EMTs have the baby in the ambulance."

He gives me a brief synopsis of the situation. From the sounds of it, the family was lucky. Mother had fallen asleep on the couch watching TV. Her kids were already down for the night on the far side of the trailer, and the baby was in a cot in the mother's bedroom on the opposite end. She woke up when she heard glass break. Her two oldest started screaming, so she ran for them. The small bedroom had already filled with thick smoke and flames were leaking in from the window, but she managed to grab the two kids and hurried out with them. The first engine rolled up just as she was going to run back inside. Apparently she fought tooth and nail as they tried to restrain her, while one of the firefighters went in. By the time he came out carrying the baby, both ends of the trailer were already engulfed in flames.

The implications are chilling.

"Bastard," Roman mutters under his breath.

"Psycho is more like it," Buxton contributes. "Fucker lit that thing from both ends."

I'm about to ask the woman a few questions when Ramirez shows up. Making sure he's up-to-date, I leave him to question witnesses and manage the scene. I tilt my head, letting Chief know I'm ready to get out of here, and he follows me to my vehicle.

"It's not just about the fire," he says when we pull away from the scene. "This guy intended for there to be victims. Fucking babies."

His angry vibes fire up the already charged atmosphere in the truck. I'm fucking furious myself. And frustrated. The first couple of fires were just structural, but whoever this son of a bitch is, he's just upped his game.

"I hope to Christ he left some incriminating evidence. Anything we can put our teeth into, because right now we've got nothing concrete to go on."

"Maybe one of her neighbors saw something," Roman suggests.

"Here's to hoping, but I'm not holding my breath." Without thinking, I pull into my slot at the police station. "Shit. I'm sorry. I'm gonna be busy for at least a few hours. Can I drop you off somewhere?"

"I can walk. We're actually staying just down the road. Autumn's place is on East 3rd." I file that snippet of information away as we get out. "Invitation for Friday stands," he says clasping my hand. "Provided you can get away."

"I plan to be there. I'll be in touch."

"Sounds good." He starts to walk away, and I move toward the station when I hear him call out. "Hey, Blackfoot!"

"What's up?" I turn to find him standing on the edge of the parking lot.

"You've heard of hero syndrome, right? Don't be blind to whatever might be under your nose."

Well, fuck.

* * *

Autumn

"Isn't that nuts?"

I look up to see Jen sliding into the seat across from me. I'm just having a quick bite at the hospital cafeteria, since I overslept this morning. Not sure if it was the bottles of wine Sophie and I killed last night, or the sore muscles, after those crazy kids hoisted me up on a zip line before that.

They'd been ready and waiting for me when I got home at around one yesterday, just telling me to prepare for an adventure. I never bow down to a challenge, but I had to swallow damn hard when we drove up on the parking lot of Zip Line Durango.

I don't do heights. Not if I can avoid it anyway.

I almost backed out, then Chief raised his eyebrow at me. Cocky bastard. He knows how to get me going and I was first in line to get strapped into a harness, determined to show him. I showed him all right. When I had solid ground under my feet again, my body felt like it had just been hauled through a cement mixer, and I had no voice. I'd left that behind in the treetops—where I screamed so loud—I'm pretty sure I scared the bird population clear into New Mexico.

Sophie suggested the wine was celebratory, but for me it had been purely medicinal.

Either way, the overindulgence coupled with the aching body kept me in bed too long, and I'd had no chance for breakfast before my first appointment. Hence, my desperate grab for hospital food. I have two more patient appointments, and a weekly report to write before I can get out of here.

"Isn't what nuts?"

"Those fires. There was another one set on Wednesday night. They brought in a nine-month-old baby in respiratory distress with some second degree burns."

"I know about the baby, I have an appointment with her mother in fifteen minutes, but what do you mean 'set'?"

"Just like Mr. Boynton's. That hot firefighter I saw you talking to last week?" She waves her hand in front of her face. "That guy can rescue me any day of the week. And he's so sweet—he showed up to check on that baby this morning —I about melted."

"Are you talking about Evan?" I ask, mildly amused at her 'high school girl with a crush' dramatics. Gives me something to fire back with next time she grills me about Keith Blackfoot.

"The guy with the red hair? Is that his name?" I see her make a mental note before she continues, "Anyway, he mentioned something about this being the fifth fire in the past month and a half."

I'm still thinking about that when I walk into the little girl's room ten minutes later. A large teddy bear dressed in firefighter's gear is tucked at the feet of the sleeping baby. Evan's doing, most likely. He really is a good guy and part of me wishes I could feel something other than purely platonic sentiments toward the easygoing man. Instead, my traitorous mind seems stuck on a brooding, complex cop instead.

Shannon, little Brooklyn's mom, readily agrees to enroll her daughter into one of the active clinical trials. She doesn't have insurance and the prospect of free care and treatment for her little one is a major incentive. Although the baby's injuries are limited to second-degree burns, they are on one side of her scalp and forehead, and will at least, in part, be visible. This new treatment promises to minimize scarring and I really hope it works for Brooklyn.

It's pretty sobering to hear all Shannon's belongings have gone up in flames. She tells me her other two kids are in the care of her folks, who live just south of town, and she feels fortunate she and her children at least have a temporary roof over their heads at her parents' place.

Given that Brooklyn will likely be released in the next day or two, we end up setting a schedule for Shannon to bring her daughter in. I do my best to schedule around her work hours, even if that means an occasional appointment at night. It's the least I can do for this poor woman.

When I finally get home, it's already after three. An hour later than planned, because on my way out the door after my last appointment, Jeff—the barn fire victim—showed up. He happened to be at the hospital and popped in with some concern about the graft on his chest. He complained about itching and, even though that's a normal part of the healing process, I offered to take a quick look.

The house is quiet. I guess Sophie and Chief aren't back from their hike up Perins Peak yet. That's an activity I was glad to beg off, especially with muscles I never even knew I had still aching from yesterday's outing. A bath might be nice, actually. A slow soak to ease my body and relax my mind.

It takes me a few minutes to figure out the damn jets on the tub—it's my first time using it—but I get them going. I set my phone on the windowsill where I can reach it, and sinking down in the water, groan out loud when the bubbles hit all the right spots. *Bliss*. With my eyes closed, I let my thoughts drift.

I may have dozed off, because when my phone chimes with an incoming message, I scramble upright in the tub, almost knocking it into the water with me.

***Sophie:* Home in 30. Need anything? Food?**

I wipe my hand on a towel and quickly message back.

***Me:* Nope. All good. We'll grab a bite at the pub.**
***Sophie:* K.**

My eyes catch the message just below from *Unknown*—the comment about my hair—and a small charge ripples over my skin. *Keith*. I never got a reaction to my threat to cut it off. To be honest, I'd half expected him to show up at the hospital. Ridiculous, I've had all of two run-ins with him, three if you count the text, and none of them particularly pleasant, but I can't get the man out of my head.

I shift slightly in the tub, trying to decide whether to come out, when forced bubbles skim an area of my body that hasn't seen a lot of activity lately. Another slight shift has the spray of water hit right on target. A tingle starting at the apex of my thighs spreads a warm wave up my belly. A hand smoothing over skin chases the sensation to the tip of my breast where the hot rush of blood peaks my nipple. My mouth falls open and my eyes close, imagining the rough scrape of deft fingers driving me toward climax. The memory of an assessing hazel gaze, and the amused twitch of strong lips, is enough to trigger a deep, bone-melting release.

Damn him.

* * *

"Nice place," Roman comments, looking around with approval.

We managed to secure a booth along the wall and take a seat. The Irish is a busy place on Friday nights: almost every table is taken. Other than the bartender, who nods when he spots me, I only see one or two familiar faces.

"You know what, I'll go grab us some drinks from the bar." Chief's ass barely hits the seat when he's up again, weaving his way to the ancient copper and oak bar. Within seconds, he's chatting with a guy at the bar wearing a DFD shirt.

"We'll be lucky to s-see him back tonight," Sophie observes, and I turn at her words. The warm smile as she looks at her man's back allays any worries there might be trouble in paradise. She clearly doesn't begrudge him his fun. "This place is right up in his wheelhouse."

"I thought it might be."

"I'm just s-sorry his buddy is caught up with work and can't m-make it."

I don't respond. I don't want to let Sophie know I was relieved when I heard there would just be three of us.

A waitress stops by the table, and since Chief doesn't look like he'll be back with those drinks anytime soon, we place an order with her. Over a loaded platter of nachos and drinks, we catch up on friends and a bit of gossip from back home.

We're on to our second drink when Sophie's attention shifts to me. "Tell m-me truthfully, how are you doing?"

"Good. Like I said before: the hospital is fantastic, the people are great, and I love my work. I really enjoy being able to see the actual impact of the work I've done in the lab for so many years."

Sophie puts her hand on my arm. "I'm glad for you, but that's not what I m-meant, and you know it."

I know exactly what she meant to ask; it's just that I'm not sure how to answer it. Am I doing okay? I've buried my nose in work because I love it, but if I'm honest with myself, I've also been hiding from life. Even in San Antonio, most of my social life revolved around my small select group of friends. When Sophie met Roman, I watched as she started broadening her horizons and actively living. Maybe that was a catalyst for me. Maybe I came here looking for an opportunity to see what more was out there for me. You can't sit around waiting for life to land in your lap. I know that, but I haven't done much about it.

"I'm not sure. I like it here; it's not that. Remember when you were in school and the prospect of starting a new year, with new teachers and friends would be as exciting as it was terrifying? This is like that. As much as I think I could love it here, I'm also afraid of leaving the safety of the life I knew behind. What if I like it better here?"

"What if you do?" Sophie bounces back at me. "What if you can turn that job you love s-so m-much into s-something permanent, and you end up s-settling here?"

"But I'd miss you guys."

She gives my arm a squeeze. "I'm here now. I'm s-sure the other girls will be coming up for a visit s-sometime s-soon as well. There's nothing keeping you from flying down for a weekend, every now and then. And besides that, who knows where I'll be next year. Or Quinn, or Tory? Wasn't it you who told m-me to go for it, who pushed m-me to s-step out of m-my comfort zone? Time to practice what you preach."

"Shit, girl. You're not pulling punches, are you? It's not that easy. For one, I'm a lot older than you guys are."

Sophie leans over the table and gets in my face. "Bullshit."

Hearing one of my own go-to retorts flung back at me, from sweet little Sophie's mouth, has me snort out a laugh. Before you know it, we're both bent over the table, giggling with tears running down our face.

"Whoa," Chief interrupts, walking up to the table. "How much did you guys have while my back was turned?"

The laughter sticks in my throat when I hear someone clear their throat from behind Chief's back. It sounds oddly familiar.

"By the way, guess who decided to pop in after all." He steps aside to reveal his friend. "Girls, I'd like you to meet Keith Blackfoot."

CHAPTER 6

Keith

I have to admit, it gave me no small rush of satisfaction seeing the stunned blush on Autumn's face.

I could only see the top half of her over the table, but by the looks of it, she had put some effort into her appearance. A light touch of makeup on her lips and behind those red-rimmed glasses, her flowy top showing a hint of enticing cleavage, and the mop of hair tamed with a healthy luster.

She barely manages to nod primly when I slide onto the bench beside her, making sure my leg is pressing the length of hers. Fuck, I shouldn't enjoy taunting her so much, but I do. Leaning in, I whisper only for her to hear, "Glad to see you wore your hair down for me."

I can feel her reaction in the stiffening of her body beside me, and grin.

"Hardly," she bites off between clenched teeth.

"Do you two know each other?" Sophie, Roman's pretty girlfriend, asks, her face a mask of confusion as her eyes flit between her friend and me.

"No."

"Yes," I say, at the same time. This causes more confusion from Sophie, but Chief squints his eyes when he looks at me.

"So that's why you changed your mind on a dime," he concludes with a grin.

Now it's Autumn who looks confused. "How so?"

"Like you, our friend here didn't feel much for the setup he could smell a mile away," Chief answers her before shooting a telling look at Sophie, who pretends to study her nails. "Until I mentioned your name."

"Drinks anyone?" The waitress provides a welcome distraction from my turn on the hot seat.

The next half hour or so, Chief, Sophie, and I talk, while Autumn tosses back her Guinness. They describe their trip to Roswell, I answer questions about my job and the arson case, and Sophie describes in hilarious detail their visit to the zip line. I occasionally glance beside me, where Autumn silently broods—throwing daggers at her friend—who doesn't seem in the least bothered.

"S-she rose to the challenge, though," Sophie concludes, with a smile at her friend. "Even if it was s-screaming at the top of her lungs."

"Oh, look," Autumn says, eager to change the subject as she points to the other end of the pub. "Darts. Let's play." She shoves at me to get out of her way, and I get up to give her room.

She looks a little unstable, like she's already half in the bag, and I have to grab her arm to steady her. She surprises me by grabbing my hand and pulling me to where a couple of older guys are throwing darts.

I never had a chance to check out her bottom half, but I'm looking now. With her ass encased in tight jeans, I get my first real glimpse at the body she's been hiding under men's clothes. It's fucking spectacular. Narrow waist but substantial lush curves round out a ripe hourglass figure. I was already attracted to her, but a good look at her bounty has my cock stand up in salute.

The two men—a couple of former firefighters I happen to know—get their own eyeful as we approach, and I can't stop the inadvertent growl in my throat when I see their appreciation of the view. I curb my impulse to drag Autumn straight out of the pub. With introductions out of the way, along with a little negotiation—a couple of beers from the bar—the dartboard is ours. I never noticed Roman and Sophie followed us until they sit down on a couple of stools at this end of the bar, matching amused looks on their face.

"Have you played before?" I ask Autumn. She throws me a smartass look, before squaring her shoulders and hitting the triple twenty with her first dart. Single twenty with her second and another triple with her last. She walks to the board to collect her darts in a surprisingly straight line.

I have a feeling I've been had. The woman is clearly a shark. Not only that, but my so-called friend sitting at the bar doesn't even try to contain his fun at my expense. He knew.

"You playing?" I offer him my darts, but he raises his hands defensively.

"Fuck no. She tricked me into letting her emasculate me once, I'm not giving her another shot."

"Thanks," I grumble. "Some friend you are." That comment leads to more hilarity from the peanut gallery. "Okay." I turn to a grinning Autumn. "Challenge accepted—but let's make it interesting, shall we?"

"What do you propose?" she asks, an eyebrow raised.

"Remember that dinner you owe me? Best of five. I win—I choose the time and place. You win; I pay and let you pick when and where."

"Done," she answers right away.

Before she clues in this is a win-win bet for me, I take my turn. Triple five, twenty, and triple twenty. By the time I turn back, she's done the math and is squinting her eyes at me.

"Did you just trick me into going out with you?"

"Hey..." I shrug innocently. "Wasn't me who dragged you into this, Red. That was all you."

I can't quite distinguish her disgruntled mutterings, but they clearly provide more entertainment for our friends.

By the time we've played a couple of rounds—Autumn took the first two, but to her chagrin I won the third—Sophie and Roman get up.

"We're heading out. Sophie's tired and we want to get on the road early," Chief announces.

"Oh shit, I'm so sorry," Autumn apologizes. "I've been a horrible friend. Let me just get—" She drops her darts on the bar and looks around for her purse.

"S-stay. You're having fun. We're just going to pack up and go to bed. You can't leave Keith hanging halfway through a bet."

Chief tries to hide a grin and catches my eye. "*Good luck,*" he mouths. I have no doubt my keen attention on Autumn has not escaped his notice.

"But..." One last feeble objection from Autumn, but it falls on deaf ears, she's already being hugged by them both.

"If we don't s-see you in the m-morning—"

"I'll be up," she interrupts Sophie.

"Stay in touch." Chief grabs my hand. "And call me if there's any way I can help."

I know he's referring to the arson case and I nod my gratitude. My mind has not shut down since he suggested the possibility those fires were started by someone looking for some limelight. A first responder. It almost sickens me to think of it, but it's not that far-fetched. I researched: the numbers were fucking disturbing.

A gentle hug from Sophie drags me from my thoughts. "*S-she's good people, and s-so are you,*" she whispers, before her man drags her out the door. I have a feeling packing is not all that's on Chief's itinerary.

"This is just wrong," Autumn announces the moment the door closes, and snatches up her purse. "They're my guests, I can't let them—" I hold her back by the arm when she threatens to stalk out the door after them.

"Red, I think you're missing the point. They *want* some time alone."

It takes a second for my words to sink in, but when they do, she tosses her bag on the bar and snatches up her darts. "In that case, best of seven," she deadpans.

Autumn wins game four, but I take five and six, mostly because by that time she's lost some of her edge. But even under the effects of Guinness, she still manages to take me down in game seven.

"Well, that was fun," she announces, coming back from the washroom while I quickly pay the tab. "But if you pay my tab one more time, we're going to have problems." I grin when she tries to wag an admonishing finger in my face, which seems enough to throw her off balance.

"Come on. I'll take you home."

"But has it been enough time for them to—"

"It's been two hours," I remind her.

"Chief likes to take his time."

I'm pretty sure that's information I could've done without. Still, I mumble, "Good to know," making her snicker as she leans into me, her hand on my chest. Now I know for sure she's more than a little tipsy. Autumn's laugh is raspy, rich, and sexy as all get out, but combined with her body plastered against me, and her hand drawing circles on my chest, the woman is downright lethal. "Let's go, Cinderella. Best get you home before midnight."

I purposely leave my car at the bar. The night air is nice and crisp, and I'm pretty sure a walk will do both of us good. That, and maybe I'll be less tempted to put my hands all over those curves that have been teasing me all fucking night. I'm mostly successful, just with her arm tucked in mine, until she stumbles and I steady her, wrapping an arm around her waist.

"Where did you learn to play darts like that?" I ask, trying for some conversation to draw attention from the hand I leave resting on her hip. It moves enticingly every step she takes.

"I was in a league in college. It was either that or some sport requiring athletic ability, of which I have none, to get me out of my dorm room a few times a week. I was rapidly becoming the scary resident hermit. It was a way to socialize. Something I've never been particularly talented at either."

"Oh, I don't know." I squeeze her hip as we turn onto a narrow path leading to a beige brick, two-story house. "You seem to do pretty well. And from where I sit, the only thing scary is how fucking sexy you are."

She stumbles on the first of the three steps leading up to a porch with two front doors. I barely manage to hook my arm around her middle to prevent her from going down.

"Don't say stuff like that when I'm trying to concentrate on walking," she snaps, making me grin.

She turns in my hold, her green eyes shooting fire behind those glasses, and suddenly I don't find anything funny. She's standing on the first step, her head almost level with mine. It's like all the air disappears, along with rational thought, leaving us standing in a vacuum. All I can see is her face in the diffused glow of the porch light. She feels it too, her eyes blinking and her soft lips parting. It's an invitation my body recognizes before my brain registers, and my mouth is already taking hers when I realize what is happening.

Fuck.

Her taste is spicy like her attitude, and her hunger matches mine as fingers weave into the long hair brushing the collar of my shirt. The sharp sting of her fingers twisting elicits a growl from the back of my throat. I pull her closer, her breasts flattened against my chest, and my hand kneads the plump swell of her ass. I pull back when she whimpers, afraid I may have hurt her. One look at her flushed face and darkening eyes tells me she's far from hurting. This time it's her who reaches for me with her mouth, while her hands pull me down by my hair. I'm this fucking close to laying her down on the steps when the sound of a squeaking porch door stops me in the nick of time.

"Autumn? Is that you?"

A stooped older gentleman in pajamas steps out on the porch, as Autumn pulls from my hold and swings around.

"It's me, Mr. Bartnik." She takes the last few steps and puts an arm around his hunched shoulders. "I'm just getting home. You should go back to bed. It's late."

She leads the man back to his front door under a wave of disgruntled protests, which she appears to ignore. When he's safely inside, she turns back to me, but stays at the top of the steps, looking a little uneasy.

"I'm…that was…"

In two steps, I'm at her level and take her face in my hands, pressing a hard kiss against her mumbling lips. "You'd better get inside too," I whisper. "And I believe the word you were looking for was *fucking incredible.*"

"That's two words," she corrects me, when I let go of her and head back down the steps.

"Smartass," I throw over my shoulder, not stopping. All I hear is her snort behind me.

I'm still grinning when I reach my truck and get behind the wheel.

CHAPTER 7

Autumn

The second time I wake up it's because Gizmo is taking up residence on my face.

The first time was to say a head-throbbing goodbye to a grinning Sophie and Roman, who left at the butt-crack of dawn. Assholes. They derived way too much pleasure from my pain. It being a Saturday, and me with nowhere to be, I crawled straight back into bed the moment their SUV pulled away from the curb.

The two ibuprofen and glass of water I swallowed down earlier provide a modicum of relief, as I blink my eyes open and shoo Gizmo away. Seems every single one of my cats found their way onto my bed, only temporarily on board with sleeping the day away. The moment they notice I'm awake, I'm regaled with a concert of complaints, varying from Ziggy's hoarse little mewls to Jack's loud yowls for attention. Food is what they're after, and given my alarm clock reads eleven fifteen, I suppose breakfast is a little late in coming.

I stumble out of bed, do what I need to do in the bathroom, and dressed in my favorite uniform—yoga pants and men's T-shirt—try not to trip over cats on my way downstairs. The animals quieted with their mouths full of tuna paté, I get coffee going. I'm not one for the convenient machines that take barely seconds to brew. My coffee needs some time on the stove. An old-fashioned stove-top percolator, filled with fresh coffee grinds and water in the reservoir, needs at least ten minutes to bubble before it even gets close to my desired taste. To kill time, I grab my phone from my purse, only to find three missed messages.

Sophie: **Just wanted to thank you again. Had such a great time.**

XOX

Also, get laid. He's hot.

My eyes roll in my head and although tempted, I'm not going to respond to that. I don't want to encourage her.

Unknown: **You won. Pick a place.**

Without the aid of caffeine in the morning, my mood is questionable at best. Add hungover, and you'd best be cautious in your approach. Ordering me around via text is not a good idea. I don't care how hot you are, or how fantastic you can kiss.

Unknown: **Shit. That didn't come out right.**

. . .

Ya think?

Apparently he cut his losses, since there's nothing after that. A smart man knows when to keep his mouth shut. I'm not going to respond to those messages either. Not now. Instead, I save his contact information before setting the phone on the counter facedown, and go see about my coffee.

Armed with my travel mug, I head up to get the laundry. One of my least favorite chores. Luckily, Sophie apparently already stripped their bed and stuffed their sheets in the washer. I quickly gather up my bedding and toss it on top of my laundry basket, perch the whole thing on my hip, and walk back down the stairs.

I'm halfway down when a loud bang on my door startles me, causing my precarious hold on the basket to slip and my laundry goes flying the rest of the way. Well, shit.

Fuming by the time I get to the front door, I'm ready to tell off the persistent Jehovah's Witness folks who seem to think it's a good idea to knock on my door every weekend since I moved here.

"I told you already, I'm not interest—" I fire off, as I'm opening the door, only to find Keith on my step.

"That kiss last night tells a different story," he returns dryly, rendering me momentarily mute. "I see my timing needs work." His eyes slide over my shoulder to the pile of laundry at the bottom of the stairs.

"What are you doing here? You scared the crap out of me." Always better to go on the attack when you feel at a disadvantage. I most definitely feel at the short end of this stick, wearing slop clothes, sporting hungover hair and face, and my dirty laundry all over the damn floor.

"Let me give you a hand." Completely disregarding my question, he steps around me.

Before I have a chance to react, he's already recovered my basket and is picking my sheets off the floor. When he lifts up a handful of my undies, I jump into action.

"I've got it." I snatch up any stray bits of clothing as I go and yank my basket from his hands.

Why is it, whenever I'm around this man, I feel discombobulated. Off my game—not that I have much of one to begin with. Rattled, I stomp into the laundry room and start stuffing things in the washer, taking a moment to settle myself down, and half hoping he'll be gone by the time I get out.

I know it was too much to ask for when I find him checking out the pictures I hung on the wall, just last week. Mostly vacation shots I took over the years—scenery—but some featuring friends, and even a few with me. Of course he gives close attention to one of the few childhood images I have left. In it, my hair is in pigtails and the glasses perched on my nose are far too big for my face. I'm about nine and I'm smiling. It was one of the last times I remember being happy and carefree. I have this particular photo on the wall to remind myself to focus on those sometimes all too rare moments of happiness. I've wasted too many years letting negative circumstances dictate the quality of my life.

Having Keith scrutinize the picture suddenly feels like too much exposure.

"Coffee?" I blurt out as a distraction, not thinking about the consequences until he makes himself comfortable at the kitchen table.

"Sure."

Fuck.

I turn my back and pour him a cup from the pot, still simmering over a warm flame on the stove.

"Perfect," he says, when I hand it to him without bothering to offer cream or sugar. For some reason, he strikes me as a purist. Something he confirms when he takes his first sip of my strong brew and appears to enjoy it.

I sit down across from him. "So aside from rescuing my laundry, what *are* you doing here?"

"Have you looked at your messages yet?" I answer his question with a snort. "Right," he continues. "I figured that didn't go over well, which is why I'm here."

"You couldn't have called?"

"I hate talking on the phone, much prefer texting, but I tend to shorthand everything. It makes me sound like an asshole."

This time I bark out a laugh and get up to fetch my phone. I find my latest entry and show the screen with his contact information to him.

"I deserve that." He chuckles, shaking his head when he sees 'ASSHOLE' in capital letters next to his phone number. "Give me a chance to redeem myself." I shrug. Truth be told, I'm curious what he has to say. "I'd like to take you out for dinner. I was hoping for tonight, but since you fairly won the right to pick time and place, I won't push it."

"And?" I tease, being a bit of an ass myself. He seems to consider my prompt for a second, but then he gets up and rounds the table.

"Good morning," he mumbles, lifting my chin with his finger and pressing a gentle kiss on my lips. "You look good enough to eat, but I'll take dinner. To start."

His suggestive words, delivered in that dark rumble, have heat flush my body. Fuck, he could crook his finger right now and I'd strip naked. Which is exactly what freaks me out.

"The only reason I'm agreeing to this is that I never back down on a bet," I start, defenses firmly in place. "So I'll go out for dinner with you, and I'll even let you pay, as promised."

"Why do I get the sense there's a 'but' coming?"

"*But*, not tonight. Or tomorrow night, for that matter. In fact, I think I might have to put it off for most of this week." I'm lying through my teeth, but I'm on a roll now.

"Pushing your luck, Red," he warns, squinting his eyes.

I blink mine innocently. "I'll need some recovery time. It's been a busy few days." He just shakes his head.

"Walk me out. I have to get back to work."

"It's Saturday," I point out, but follow him anyway.

"Aware of that, sweetheart. Unfortunately crime doesn't take a day off."

"Gotcha."

He turns around at the door, and despite myself, I walk straight into his arms. His kiss is deep, wet, and so hungry I can taste it. It doesn't appear to matter how many barbs I throw up, this man isn't fooled for a second. I may not want to admit it, but he affects me as much as I appear to be affecting him, judging by the hard length pressing into my stomach. *Yikes*.

When he releases my lips, a regretful moan escapes me.

"Tomorrow night. Be ready at six," he growls, and I don't even have the fight to object. He kissed the starch right out of me.

"Okay," I meekly mumble, immediately irritated with myself for being a pushover.

Another quick peck and he takes a last look at my disheveled appearance before grabbing for the door. I'm not sure I even want to know what he's thinking, suddenly aware I never even brushed my hair and I probably have crusties in the corners of my eyes. The fact it would suddenly bother me has me bristle, but before I can lash out, he takes the wind right out of my sails.

"Good fucking coffee."

"I know," I agree without a hint of false modesty. If there's anything I'm sure of, it's my coffee.

My answer puts a grin on his face as he turns and walks out the door.

"I'm going to be fifteen minutes late."

I've spent most of the afternoon fussing over what to wear. Not sure why it matters, when I usually don't give a crap, but for some reason I feel the need to show Keith I clean up okay. At least I think I do. I'm a mess. So much so I just realized ten minutes ago I haven't even figured out what restaurant, let alone made a reservation. I'm sweating buckets, and at this rate, I'll need my third shower of the day.

"You called," I point out the obvious, blurting out the first thing on my mind. "You don't like calling." His deep chuckle curls my toes. *Damn*. I'm a disaster.

"Texting wasn't working out. Thought I'd turn a new leaf."

"You know we can do this another night. Or if you'd rather just forget about it altogether, I'm good—"

"Fifteen minutes, Red. Be ready."

He doesn't even wait for an answer, just interrupts me and then hangs up. The nerve.

Fifteen minutes later, I have managed to get a reservation at what looks to be a nice restaurant, when there's that sharp knock on the door.

"Hey," I mutter opening the door. He looks really good. The dark jeans make his legs look even longer, and his white dress shirt, sleeves rolled up to his elbows, contrasts nicely with his dark skin. He's even tied his hair back, accenting the sharp lines and angles of his face.

Without losing eye contact, he walks me back into the house, closing the door behind him. One arm snakes around my waist, pulling me flush against his body, while his other hand slides up my back, tangling in my hair. I left it loose, which he seems to appreciate; given the tight hold he has on it.

"You have reservations?" he asks, his face so close I can feel his breath stroke my skin.

"The Ore House," I tell him, my voice raspy.

"Fuck." He closes his eyes and leans his forehead against mine. "Sweetheart, you're killing me with this hair. And that dress should be outlawed."

"This thing?" I push back and look down at myself. Sure, the simple black wrap dress fits nicely, but it's nothing to lose your head over.

"That *thing* clings to every damn curve." His voice sounds almost pained as he runs a hand from my waist, down over the curve of my hip. "What time is our reservation?"

"Seven. When you said you'd be late, I—"

"It's fine," he cuts in, backing me up against the wall. "We'll have appetizers here."

I don't have to ask what he means when his mouth takes mine in a voracious kiss. His hand slides up to cup my breast, and my breath hitches when his fingers find the hard peak of my nipple through the sleek fabric. His knee inserts between my legs, and with his thick thigh he rubs along my core.

"Jesus," he mutters, pulling his lips from mine and dropping his head in my neck. "I can feel your heat through my jeans, and you have no idea how badly I want to explore that." Catching my breath, I'm about to tell him to go right ahead, when he takes a step back and grabs my hand. "Let's get you fed."

"Wait. I forgot to lock the cat door. I need to make sure the cats are all inside."

"Cats? As in plural?" He looks around, but my guys are probably in hiding. "How many?"

"Five." I chuckle when both his eyebrows disappear in his hairline. "You're not allergic, are you?"

He hesitates a moment before answering. "Not in the literal sense of the word."

CHAPTER 8

Keith

The Ore House is a landmark restaurant in Durango. She picked well.

I put my hand in the small of her back when the hostess leads us to our table. My hand has been on her in one way or another since she opened the door for me. Backlit in the doorway, she looked like some kind of siren: a halo of red hair and lush curves on display in that formfitting dress. A walking wet dream, and I can barely keep my eyes off her, even as we're handed menus and order drinks.

I spent most of the weekend working. Something I've been doing for the past eight months, in an attempt to stay on top of things. If I've discovered anything, it's that I'm not cut out for the position of Chief of Police, no matter how much Stan Woodard wants me for the job. Dealing with committee members, wanting an update on plans put in place for the damn DPD parade float, had about done my head in. Shoving that aside I focused on trying to get a bead on whoever is setting fires around town, but we have little to go on.

Tony interviewed Shannon Payne, the single mom, but she had nothing to offer. No bottles of laced liquor left on her doorstep, which might suggest a pattern for us to follow. That this may be someone who is looking for some recognition with each fire he sets has been eating at me. I finally pulled Tony aside this afternoon and shared Roman's warning with him, only to discover the idea was not new to him. We spent a few hours behind the closed door of my office, making a list of possible candidates. All first responders, and all people we both know, making it all kinds of fucked up. It had been a relief to walk out of the station.

"Holy shit," Autumn stage-whispers, flipping through the leather binder. "I had no idea this place was so expensive. If I'd known—"

"It's fine." I grab her hand and give it a squeeze.

"We'll go Dutch."

"Over my dead body." Her eyes shoot up at my statement, and I can almost see the bristles go up.

"I'm more than capable paying for myself, you know." Her tone is snippy and I can't help grinning. I'm slowly starting to figure out this woman, and every thing I discover only increases her appeal.

That doesn't mean I'm going to let her near the bill.

"I have no doubt you are, but you won't be tonight." I don't bother telling her, if she's with me, she won't be paying any other night either. She'll find out and we'll probably have another face-off over some bill, but I'm hoping eventually she'll figure me out too. The small huff she responds with is cute.

The waitress returns and we place our orders. I throw Autumn a sharp glance when she chooses the cheapest entree on the menu, but I'm not about to fight with her on it. I get the feeling there will be plenty to argue about with this woman, so I'll pick my battles.

Instead, I set out to get to know her better. "Explain to me what you do. I know you work at the new burn center but little else."

Her annoyance forgotten, a light comes on in her eyes when she talks about her work. Although interesting enough, I could've found that information on my own, but in listening to her talk about it I learn a shitload about who she is. For all of her sometimes thorny exterior, the woman has great empathy for the patients she works with and shows deep passion for what she does.

I also learn she doesn't like talking about her parents, who are apparently both gone, and she has no siblings. She doesn't get out much and aside from the friends she left in San Antonio; those cats of hers are the only family she has. I would've much preferred those to be dogs—cats are arrogant assholes—but fuck, if they make her happy, I can handle a bunch of asocial felines.

"All we've done is talk about me," she semi-accuses when the waitress drops a small folder with the bill on the table. "I still don't know much about you."

"We have to save something for next time," I tease, checking the total and pulling out my wallet. "Besides, I like listening to you talk."

"Spoilsport," she mumbles, as I slip a few bills in the folder and pull her up by the hand.

"Come on. I want to show you something."

"Where are we going?" she wants to know, when I head up the mountain drive to Fort Lewis College.

"Wait and see. You mentioned not having had much of a chance to see Durango, which gave me an idea."

It's pretty chilly up on the ledge by the college, so I grab a windbreaker from my back seat and drape it over her shoulders. At nine forty-five at night, the sky is dark but the town of Durango below is completely lit up. It's been ages since I've been up here just to enjoy the view.

"Ohhh, I wish I'd known about this when Sophie and Roman were here. This is such a pretty spot." I lead her to a bench at the edge of the lookout. Sitting down next to her, I drape my arm around her shoulder and tuck her close. "I'm not that cold," she says, as if that would be the reason I want her close. "Your jacket keeps me comfortable."

"Maybe I'm cold," I tease her. "Or maybe I just really like the feel of you against me." Her eyes flit to mine, and a hint of a smile plays at the corner of her mouth.

"I'd have to agree with option B." Her right hand slips behind my neck, tugging me close as she drops her head back against my arm.

I willingly comply, lowering my face close to hers. I pull her bottom lip between mine, sucking at the plump flesh before giving it a nip with my teeth. The tightening of her hand on my neck tells me she likes a little pain with her pleasure. Instead of taking her mouth, as she's expecting, I slide my lips down the exposed column of her neck, nibbling at the sensitive spot right by her shoulder. Pressing kisses all the way down to the swell of her breast, I use my free hand to pull the fabric of her dress and bra to the side, and lift her to me.

Her skin is delicate, almost translucent, and garnished with freckles. She smells fresh, light, something vaguely citrusy. Her pale pink nipple is tight and darkening with her arousal when I bend my head, taking her in my mouth. A deep moan rewards me when I pull hard, pressing the tip against the roof of my mouth with my tongue.

Her taste, soft skin, and open responsiveness has my cock straining in my jeans, weeping precum. I let her slip from between my lips and slide down the bench, kneeling in front of her, easing her legs apart as I push up her dress.

She looks fucking beautiful and wanton—one tit exposed, her white thighs splayed open, black underwear peeking from under the bunched up skirt—but most stunning is her face with the deep flush staining her cheeks and lips, and those shimmering green eyes burning into mine.

"I'm exposed," she says, although she doesn't seem in the least bothered with her partial nudity.

"I know," I mumble, my lips finding the tender flesh on the inside of her thigh. I inhale the scent of her arousal, and I feel it's warm evidence when I pull the gusset of her panties aside with my fingers, craving her taste.

"Keith..."

Spurred on by the plea in her voice, I press my face between her thighs, lapping at her slit with my tongue. Her legs spread even wider and her hands land on my head, holding me in place as she rolls her hips. *Christ,* this woman is going to make me blow. I slide first one, and then a second finger inside her, while my lips and teeth work her protruding clit. The moment I feel the ripple of her walls clamping on my fingers, I lift my head to watch her climax.

It's only then I notice the familiar pitch of sirens in the valley below.

Almost immediately my phone starts buzzing in my pocket.

* * *

Autumn

Fucking hell!

What was I thinking?

Slouched on that bench with my business hanging out everywhere—Keith's mouth and fingers making me forget my own damn name—anyone could've come by. *Jesus,* someone may have and I wouldn't even know.

I thought at forty-two I was pretty much in tune with my body. Knowing my own likes and dislikes and with a decent grasp of my sexuality, but tonight I surprised even myself. I would never have pegged myself as a closet exhibitionist, but shit...even though I hate to admit it, there's something to say for the added heat the possibility of discovery brings. I don't think I've ever come that quick or that hard before, and I haven't even seen his cock yet.

My body is still humming when Keith drops me off at my door, a quick hard kiss that still carries my own taste my only goodbye, as he runs back to his vehicle. With no small amount of regret, I watch his taillights disappear, only to admonish myself for being selfish. From what I could gather from his side of the few brief phone calls he made, there's another fire. One more in what apparently is a chain of them. Perhaps another person injured, losing their property, or God forbid, their life.

I can't imagine the pressure he must be under. The frustration he must feel.

Jack is meowing, getting my attention. He's standing by the small cat gate built into the back door off the kitchen. A small perk I didn't even see until I had moved in. The previous renters had a small pup, so it's technically a doggie door, but not in my household. I flip the small latch and Jack pushes outside, Panda close on his heels. I'm sure the others will follow. All my cats are free to go outside. They like to roam around, but they always come back for their meals. Back in San Antonio, they had that freedom day or night, but here I'm a little more cautious, locking them in overnight.

I find the other three on my bed. They barely lift an eyelid when I change into comfy clothes. I'm not ready for bed yet. Not when I know the darkness will only bring old painful memories tonight. I've got half a bottle of wine somewhere, and a Netflix subscription that will help me forget, but first I'm checking in with Sophie.

Me: Are you up?

I've barely installed myself on the couch when my phone rings.

"Hey, girl, how's San Antonio?"

"Booo, I don't want to go to work tomorrow," Sophie complains. "I'm going to m-miss Roman, he's already at the fire station. I liked s-spending all this time with him. And you of course," she adds quickly.

I chuckle. "Oh, please. I know which way is up. I'm just happy you got back home safe, but I miss you guys. It's empty here."

"Doesn't have to be. From what I could s-see a certain handsome police chief would only be too happy to fill your void." She snickers at her own joke.

"Well…actually…" I have to hold the phone away from my ear, Sophie is squealing so loud.

"S-shut the front door! Damn, that m-man m-moves fast."

"Not that fast," I correct her. "We had dinner tonight and that was nice, but he got called away." I'm not about to tell Sophie about that very memorable time between dinner and his call. That's something I want to keep for me.

"Any plans for a repeat?"

"I just told you he got called away on an emergency, there

was hardly time to consult our planners," I point out. "I'm sure he'll call."

"He'd better," she immediately fires off. "Or I'll have Roman—"

"Puleeze. Leave the poor man out of it. I can take care of myself." I hear the flap of the cat door in the background. "I should let you go, I've gotta make sure my cats are inside so I can lock up for the night."

"Fine, but promise you'll keep m-me updated?"

"I promise, if there's something notable to share I'll let you know."

After saying our goodbyes, I drop my phone on the couch and go in search of my kitties. The lazy three are still curled on my bed, and I find Jack in the kitchen crunching some kibble after his late night run. I can't see Panda anywhere though.

I get a whiff of wood burning. The neighbors, the next house over, occasionally light up their backyard firepit. I actually quite like the smell. It reminds me of bonfires and marshmallows. I walk to the back door to see if Panda is back yet, when I notice a weird glow inside the small shed against the back fence. I move to open the back door when my foot slips on something. On the floor, right below the cat door, is an envelope. I pick it up and find my name on the front in printed capitals. Chills run down my back, and just as I put my hand on the doorknob, I hear a crash of glass and flames come shooting from the shed's small window.

CHAPTER 9

Keith

"Tell me you've got some leads on this fucker."

I turn around to see Curtis Buxton approach.

"Working on it, Boss," Tony says beside me. "Trust me, we're hitting it as hard as we can, but we've got near nothing to go on."

"Goddammit! Find something," Curtis barks, running his hands through his gray hair.

I can't blame him. I feel the same frustration.

The house at the end of Delwood Avenue is nothing but a burned-out skeleton. The surrounding trees are scorched, and if not for the fast response from the fire department, we'd have had a wildfire on our hands. Two ambulances left already, one with the disabled resident, who'd been pulled from the house, and one for the firefighter who had part of the ceiling collapse on him during the rescue.

"Call in a few more patrol units," I tell Tony. "Canvass the neighborhood house by house. Any fucking thing they've seen today or in the past few days. Unusual activities, people who seem out of place, vehicles that don't belong. Anything. No personal judgment calls on what is pertinent information: I want officers to take down every single detail, and I expect reports on my desk tomorrow."

"You've got it."

I watch him walk toward his vehicle and get on the radio before turning to the fire chief. "Any first thoughts on the fire itself?"

"Fire inspection is already here waiting for the all clear before they go in."

"Fuck, Curtis. Don't you start hiding behind procedure. You've been on the goddamn job for thirty years, you've gotta have some idea."

"First guys on the scene said it looked like the fire was burning its way into the house. Like someone had doused the outside and lit a match to it. Definitely arson. It was fast though, faster than those trailer fires. Kerosene and methyl alcohol traces were found at those earlier sites, but I'm willing to bet they'll find gasoline in this mix."

"But wouldn't insulation have provided a firewall?"

"Slow it down, sure, but there are lots of pathways for fire to find its way in. Once inside, with temperatures already high, it would spread fast." With one last look at the remnants of the simple single-story house, Buxton walks off to join a group of his men by one of the engines. I watch as a couple of the guys follow him to his vehicle and climb in. I'm guessing they're off to see their brother in the hospital.

I'm left staring at the still smoking scene with mounting frustration. I know first thing tomorrow, I'll have the mayor on the phone, or God forbid, in my office, and I have nothing concrete on our arsonist. The fires themselves are the only source of information for now, but maybe they can provide me with a rough profile on the perp. Time to go through all the reports again and add what little I've learned tonight.

My phone starts buzzing in my pocket the moment I turn toward my Tahoe. It's Autumn.

"Hey, Red. Look, I'm sorry I had to cut the night—"

"Keith?" The pitch of her voice has the hackles stand up on my neck.

"What's wrong?"

"I may have a problem."

Under-fucking-statement of the year. By the time I get off the phone with her, I'm already coming down her street. The moment I step on the sidewalk I can smell the smoke. Instead of going to the front door, I head around the side of the house, and walk up to a group of people standing around the smoking remains of Autumn's shed. I'm surprised to find Evan Biel among them.

"How did you get here?" I ask him, after pulling him aside from what I now understand are some of Autumn's neighbors who came out to help.

He shrugs. "I caught the call on my way to the hospital. Most of our guys are either there, or still at the scene on Delwood. I had no idea this was Autumn's place. Surprised as hell to find out she was out here with a fucking garden hose and managed to put the damn thing out with the help of the neighbors."

"Were you off tonight?" I ask, noting the sharp look in Evan's eyes as he regards me.

"I was." He is very deliberate in his response. "I got a call at home that Beacham was taken to the hospital, got in my car, and listened in on the scanner on my way. That's how I found out about Delwood, and heard this call come in. I live on the north side of town, it was virtually on my way, and as I mentioned, seeing as a lot of our guys are busy, I thought I'd check to see what I could do. As I also just pointed out, the fire was out when I got here. I notified the station right away, so they don't have to send our already depleted numbers out for nothing."

It's clear he knows my question wasn't half as innocent as I'd hoped it would sound. His explanation sounds reasonable, and I would probably accept it at face value, if I didn't personally see him at the earlier fires as well. Still, I'm just on a fishing expedition, not looking to alienate the fire department without some concrete evidence. So I simply nod my understanding and change the subject. "Where is she?"

"She went to check on her neighbor."

"Okay, let me go check on her."

"Hang on, Blackfoot," he stops me. "Something you might want to see." He flicks on a small flashlight, and I follow him over to the burned-out shed, where he shines the light on something in the charred debris.

"Is that?"

"A cat. Yes. I can't be sure, but from what I can see, the fire started inside the shed." He points at the two walls still standing and I see what he means: the boards are charred on the inside, but are only barely touched on the outside. "Like I said, I can't be sure, but I've seen something similar before in fire insurance fraud."

"You mean someone lit the damn cat?" I'm not a cat fan, but even I can't stomach the thought of something so horrific. I can't even imagine what it would do to Autumn. I hope to God all five of her damn cats are safe in the house. "Does she know?"

"Dunno. She didn't say anything, just went inside to calm down her elderly neighbor.

"So the fire was set."

"Without a doubt. Nothing flammable was kept in there, just some gardening tools and empty pots, and as you can see, it started inside. I'll call the chief."

"Busy night."

"No shit."

As Evan pulls his phone from his pocket, I head back to the front of the house, and knock on Mr. Bartik's front door. Autumn opens almost immediately and forces a little smile when she sees me.

"Hey." I reach out and brush at a streak of soot along her jaw. "I hear you did pretty good out there." She shrugs, leaning into my touch, but clearly not in the mood for platitudes, so I move onto something concrete. "How's the old man?"

"He's okay. I just wanted to make sure. I was actually about to head back." She moves past me, pulling the door closed behind her, and slips into her own front door. I follow close behind.

Once inside, she stops in her tracks, but when I shut her door, she swings around and is suddenly in my arms.

"The bastard got Panda," she sobs in my shirt.

It doesn't take much to figure Panda is one of her cats. It's also clear she unfortunately wasn't spared the view of the poor thing's charred remains. I let her cry, but when I start rubbing my hand up and down her back, she stiffens and pulls back, grabbing the hem of her shirt to wipe at her wet face.

"I have to show you something." I follow her into the kitchen, where she grabs an envelope off the counter, and then opens a drawer and pulls out an identical one. She offers that one to me. "It was in my mail slot last Wednesday when I got home, along with a bunch of flyers."

"You take it out, your prints are already on there. I don't want to add mine."

She pulls out the sheet and puts it on the counter.

ENJOY!

It's written in black ink on notepaper. "Is there anything on the envelope?" She flips that over and places the second envelope next to it. Identical printing on both envelopes. "Did you open the other one?"

"I didn't want to."

"That's okay," I quickly reassure her. "Do you have tweezers and a couple of ziplock baggies?" She nods and opens another drawer, pointing at the box of freezer bags, before she disappears into the hallway.

The cop in me has taken over, but Autumn seems to have used my professional approach to regain her composure.

"Will this work?" She hands me a pair of tweezers, and I use it to handle the second envelope and pull out a similar piece of notepaper.

"Can you open up one of the freezer bags? That way we can handle the note without smudging any potential evidence."

When she holds the plastic bag open, I slide the note inside. I take it from her and lay it flat next to the first one. Same printing, same pen, and by the looks of it, the same notepaper.

The message gives me chills.

LIKE YOUR GIFT?

* * *

Autumn

"Fucker."

Keith is swearing up a storm as he whips out his phone and starts taking pictures.

I'm numb, staring at the words on the notes.

My gift? *My fucking gift?*

Suddenly I see red. I swing around and blindly knock the almost empty bottle of wine into the sink. It feels good. Gratifying. This morning's coffee cup is next. With a rewarding crash it flies apart in pieces on top of the broken bottle in the bottom of the sink.

"Whoa, tiger." Keith's arms come around me, pinning mine to my sides.

"Like my gift?" I grind out between clenched teeth. "That cock-sucking miserable piece of shit killed my cat, and he wants to know if I like my fucking gift?" I struggle against Keith's hold, but he's not letting go. Just as quickly as my rage flared up, it deflates. "Why would someone do that? What does any of this have to do with me?"

"We'll figure that out."

I lean back against him, finding a little comfort in the firm tone of his words. "I should check on the cats," I mumble, mostly to myself, but Keith loosens his arms and I step free.

"You do that." He turns me and drops a kiss on my forehead. "I'm going to make a few calls. It means you'll have a few more people roaming around your place, but what happened here may be part of a bigger investigation, and I don't want to miss anything."

"That's fine." I look out the window at the charred debris.

"Red?" My eyes track back to his. "We will figure this out."

I nod, pressing my lips together as I turn toward the stairs. Halfway up, I notice Jack sitting at the top, watching me as I take the last few steps. Normally not a particularly cuddly cat, he doesn't squirm when I pick him up and bury my face in his fur. Clutching him tightly, I walk into the bedroom, and set him down on the bed, where the other three are still huddled together. Jack saunters over and curls up right beside them, but his eyes stay on me.

Pulling open a drawer, I grab some clean clothes. The ones I have on are still damp, and I reek of smoke. A shower would help.

The cats are still where I left them when I step out of the bathroom ten minutes later, feeling moderately better after a thorough shampoo and a good cry. Grabbing my brush from the dresser, I quickly tug it through my hair before braiding it. A soft knock sounds at the door, before it opens a crack and Keith sticks his head in.

"Are you okay?"

"Better now," I admit, tying an elastic on the end of my braid and meeting him at the door. Instead of leading the way downstairs, as I expected him to, he slips inside the room. First closing the door behind him, he then cups my face in his hands and drops his head down, crushing my mouth with a bruising kiss. "What was that for?" I want to know when he finally lets me up for air.

"For an evening that should've ended right where we're standing."

"Agreed." A corner of his mouth tugs up at my response.

"Good." He lets go of my face and grabs one of my hands instead. "Ready to meet the second-best detective on the force?"

"Second-best? Why not the best?"

He grins and pulls me out the door behind him.

"You've already met him."

CHAPTER 10

Autumn

Tony Ramirez is the guy I first saw Keith with at The Irish.

It would appear a certain level of hotness is a prerequisite of Durango PD's finest. Like Keith, Tony is dark, with the shimmer of gray in his hair that only cranks up his appeal another notch.

"Sorry we kept you up so late," he says, handing me a card before he opens the front door. "If you think of anything, don't hesitate to give me a call. Any time, night or day."

A low growl sounds from behind me as Keith reaches around and snatches the card from my hand. "She can call me."

"Excuse me," I pipe up, twisting my head around to throw a scathing look at the big man. "*She* is standing right here, and *she* is old enough and wise enough to decide for herself who to call."

I perch a hand on my hip and hold the other out. Tony bursts out laughing behind me when Keith reluctantly returns the card to me.

"Didn't think I'd live to see the day," Tony taunts, grinning. "The most committed bachelor of La Plata County, brought to his knees by a ballsy redhead."

"And you," I turn on the detective, "are just as bad, using me to bait him. Now I've had a long fucking night and if you two want to compare dick size, go right ahead, but you'll have to do it without me. Lock up behind you." Without another glance at either of them, I walk out of the small hallway and head upstairs.

The low rumble of a muted conversation drifts up the stairs as I'm brushing my teeth, and by the time I flick off the light in the bathroom, I finally hear the front door close. The silence is a little unnerving, and I'm starting to wonder if kicking both of them out was such a stellar idea.

My bed looks inviting, even with my feline roomies taking up a lot of it. I'm exhausted. I just want to go to sleep and not think about my poor little Panda for a bit. My eyes are gritty from forcing back the tears that keep wanting to surface. Fishing my nightie from under the pillow, I whip off my shirt and drop it on the chair by the bed.

Two of the cats suddenly lift their heads, and I sense more than hear someone entering behind me, freezing me on the spot.

* * *

Keith

"She's a firecracker," Ramirez offers as we watch Autumn stomp off upstairs. "You lucky bastard."

"Asshole," I grumble handing him the ziplock bags with

the notes and envelopes. "And do your damn job instead of hitting on my girl."

"That's no girl. That, my man, is all woman. She's got balls too, tackling that fire by herself." My friend is clearly impressed, and it makes me even more irritable than I already was.

"Have all you need?"

"As much as I can get, anyway. A lot will depend on the fire inspector's report. Busy night for those guys."

"What does your gut tell you?" I ask him. I know what mine tells me, but I may be a little too close to this particular investigation.

"I'm sure you picked up on the fact our first arson occurred not long after she arrived in town." I feel myself start to bristle, but keep it in check. I asked him for his opinion; the least I can do is hear him out. "It's also highly coincidental that she works in the new burn center. However," he says, dragging the word out, and a little of the pressure releases from my chest. "My gut says she's got nothing to do with this, other than someone appears to be looking for her approval. You'd do well to keep an eye on her."

"Plan to." Apparently that strikes him as funny, because he chuckles as he pulls open the door.

"Right—good luck with that."

I close and lock the door behind him. No way I'm leaving her alone tonight. Kicking off my boots, I walk through the main floor, making sure all windows, the back door, and the cat gate are secure. I should probably crash on the couch, but I know she has a spare bedroom, and I'd prefer to be closer, just in case.

Autumn's door, the first one at the top of the stairs, stands open. I tell myself I just want to make sure she's okay when I head there, instead of down the short hallway to the spare room. I almost turn around when I see she's in the middle of changing, but the sight of her back has me walk straight up to her, my hand already reaching out.

I run my fingers over the thick ridges in her skin from base of her neck down to the middle of her back.

"I was fifteen," she says, her voice tight. "It was an accident. The fabric of my top melted into my skin." A shiver runs down her back.

Grabbing the nightgown I notice on the bed, I slip it over her head. I don't quite trust myself to speak for fear I say something wrong, and this most definitely is not the time to ask questions, she's dealt with enough of those tonight. Instead, I wait for her to put her arms through the capped sleeves and turn around. Her face is pale, dark circles stand out under eyes that look dry but red-rimmed. I flip the covers back and wait for her to step out of her pants and crawl in. Neither of us says anything. Tucking her in, I brush a strand of hair that's escaped her braid off her face, and lean over to brush my lips over hers.

"Are you leaving?" she asks softly when I head for the door.

"Only as far as your spare bedroom, sweetheart."

* * *

I didn't expect to fall asleep, but apparently I did.

I wake up to the smell of coffee and immediately check my phone for the time: six forty-five. Sitting up, I find three cats on the bed—all three staring at me. One of them—mostly white and brown with some back patches—seems to be the most curious when I hold my hand out. Not my pet of choice by any stretch of the word, but I have a good idea how attached Autumn is to them, so it's in my best interest to try and make friends. It lets me scratch its head, leaning it into my palm.

"She likes you." My eyes shoot up to find Autumn leaning against the doorpost. "I was coming to see why my brood hasn't come down for their breakfast. Usually they have me tripping over them until they get fed." I notice she's trying not to look at me, keeping her eyes mostly downcast.

"Red." Her eyes flit up. "Come here." I'm pretty sure part of her wants to tell me to shove it, but she pushes away from the post and slowly walks over to the bed. When she's within reach, I grab her by the hand and pull her down to sit on the edge of the mattress. "Did you sleep at all?"

"For the most part." Her eyes are focused on the movement of my thumb as I stroke the top of her hand.

"Why not try to get a couple more hours?"

"I have to be at work for eight anyway."

"You're going to work." It's more of a statement than a question, but Autumn picks up on my disbelief anyway.

"It's not like I got hurt or anything," she snaps, trying to pull her hand back.

"Don't get all riled up because I'm concerned. Yesterday was not a picnic."

"I'm well aware of that."

"Right, and you also realize that *I* know it was probably much more traumatic in your case."

"Why? Are you talking about my scars?"

I look at her with an eyebrow raised. "I'm not asking you to tell me about them, but you don't have to for me to know that those burns hurt a fuckofalot and for a long time. On a fifteen-year-old, those scars run much deeper than skin."

"I'm fine."

"Yes, you are," I soothe, pulling her against my chest. Not really my place to be picking at someone else's scab. We all have them, the things that never really heal, that we carefully tuck away. We all have our own way of covering up to the outside world.

Tangling my hand in her hair, I tilt her head and take her mouth. It only takes a little coaxing for her to soften her lips and let me inside. I kiss her deeply, but when her fingers start exploring my chest and concentrate on a nipple, I have to break away before I lose all control. Both of us are breathing hard.

"All that's keeping me from following through where our date left off last night, is the smell of your grade A coffee."

* * *

I stand by the door and wait for Autumn to stuff her phone in her purse and dig out a bunch of keys.

"Do you have a spare key?"

Autumn turns her head, looking at me with an eyebrow raised. "A bit fast, don't you think?"

"Smartass. No, it's always a good idea to leave an emergency key with a friend or a neighbor for eventualities. Just in case."

"And I'd give one to you because..." she teases.

"Who better than the interim chief of police, who also happens to be the guy you're dating."

"Is that what this is? I admit it's been a while, but from what I can recall, one date does not constitute *dating*."

I'm glad to see the tension around her mouth and eyes relax a little. I already put her through the paces this morning over coffee and toast. Made her go over most of the answers she'd given Ramirez last night, in hopes daylight may prompt something she hadn't thought of before. I've pushed enough for today.

"It does in my book," I counter, pulling her close and pressing a quick kiss on her mouth. "Come on. You're going to be late." And I need to make sure there are some security measures in place.

"Hang on." She walks off to the kitchen and returns right away, holding out a key in her hand. "For emergencies." I tuck it in my pocket as we head out the door.

"I'll check in with you later." I bend through the open window of her car for a quick kiss before I watch her drive off.

Fucking Stan Woodard is waiting in my office by the time I get to the station. Figured he'd come knocking sooner or later.

"How many does that make?" he asks, before I even have a chance to sit down.

"You know how many it makes, Stan. Probably one more than yesterday around this time." I'm not quite ready to include the shed fire until I get the report back from the inspector.

"I understand there were two."

"Can't confirm that yet. There are a few things that might suggest that, but I want to be sure first."

Stan tents his fingers, nodding like he's processing the information, but I already know what his next question is going to be. He does the same thing every time he's preparing to put the pressure on.

"How close are you to catching this guy?"

And there it is—the push—which means I have to be fucking diplomatic, not my best side.

"You know that's impossible to predict, Stan, but I'm hoping the fire inspector's report will help us get a step closer. All I can tell you is, we have some of our best men on this twenty-four seven."

"People are getting restless, Keith. They hear fire engines go out all the time—smell smoke in the air—it makes them jumpy. It's been dry since early May, they worry about wildfires. All it takes is one spark."

No shit, Sherlock. I fight not to roll my eyes. "Preaching to the choir, Mr. Mayor. Now if that was all, I should get back to my investigation."

Stan's no idiot, and he knows I'm not one either, so this whole dog and pony show of him dropping in to throw his weight around is a total waste of time. It's posturing. He's showing his constituents he has their best interests at heart. I wouldn't be surprised if the *Durango Herald* is outside waiting to capture him walking out of the station. The perfect picture of a conscientious mayor, whose first concern on a Monday morning is the well-being of his town. Something like that.

This is why I don't want this job. Stan wants an ally in the office, someone he'd like to be able to influence—who can make him look good—but I'm not that guy. I want to be out there in the trenches, where I can focus all my attention on the investigation. Especially now, when someone I have a personal connection with, might somehow be connected.

"Sleep well?" A smirking Ramirez comes walking into my office and drops into the chair the mayor just vacated.

"If you're here to bust my balls, you can turn the fuck around. I've used up all my patience for the day."

"Stan putting the thumbscrews on? I saw him talking to a reporter out there."

"Not surprised." I lean my elbows on my desk. "Give me some real news."

He flips open his notebook. "Forensics picked up the charred remains of the cat last night. They're supposed to be working on it first thing, so hopefully we'll have something soon. None of your girlfriend's neighbors recall seeing anything, but it wouldn't have been difficult to get into the backyard. There's no motion lighting so he'd have had the dark as cover."

I refrain from reacting to the label he slaps on Autumn—it's exactly what he's looking for. "I noticed the lack of lighting last night. Should be easy to fix."

"Is she at home?" Tony asks. "I'd be more than happy to swing by and—"

"Back off, Ramirez. She's at work and anything that needs taking care of, I'll handle."

"So noted, but seriously, you may want to consider, if our guy has a hard-on for her, lights may not be enough. You may want to try and convince her to relocate temporarily."

He points out what's been on my mind. The guy seems focused on Autumn, and I have no way of knowing what his endgame is. For all I know, he's one of her neighbors who's developed an unhealthy obsession. Whoever it is knows who she is and where she lives. My first instinct would be to move her somewhere else, but I already know that will not go over well. She's fiercely independent.

"I know," I tell Tony. "But as you've seen firsthand, she doesn't take well to being handled. Shit, we're just getting to know each other. I'm still feeling my way around here."

"Uncharted territory for you." He smirks, knowing me too well, and turns serious again. "You need me to back you up, you know where to find me."

"I hear you," I acknowledge before moving on. "What else have you got?"

"One of our guys did catch something interesting at the Delwood scene. One of the neighbors saw a guy walking along the ridge behind the houses." He consults his notes. "The woman thought it was a hiker, he had what looked like one of those big packs on his back. Not a lot of detail, so I'll head back there today to see if I can find out some more."

"Good. I have something for you to note down. You know

Evan Biel, right? Fire Department? He was on scene at the trailer fires. I ran into him again last night."

"At Delwood?"

"No, in Autumn's backyard."

At that Tony's eyes narrow. "You don't say."

CHAPTER 11

Autumn

"I keep bumping into you."

I catch Evan walking out of the burn unit just as I'm coming down the stairs.

"I could say the same." He smiles, but it's not convincing. He looks exhausted. "One of our guys got injured on a call last night. I went straight to the hospital after I left your place. I'm just heading home now to catch a few hours before my shift starts."

"I'm sorry." I put a hand on his arm. "I was told about two new patients, that's why I'm down here, but I had no idea one was a firefighter."

"Yeah. Part of the roof collapsed on him before they could get the victim out of there. His biggest problem is not burns, though. His protective gear minimized those, but his helmet got knocked off and he's got a closed head-injury. Hasn't woken up yet."

The strain is showing on his face, and I feel for the normally upbeat guy. This must weigh on him heavily.

"Knowing that, I appreciate you coming to my rescue last night even more."

His face transforms into a genuine grin. "Enough to stop seeing me as brother material?"

He's teasing, I know, and maybe it's just his fatigue coming through, but I wonder if there's not an undertone of regret in there somewhere. I don't want to inadvertently lead him on.

"I'm actually kinda seeing someone," I blurt out.

"Kinda? How do you kinda see someone? You either are or you're not."

"Fine. I guess I'm seeing someone," I correct myself and observe him for a reaction. "It's early days yet. I mean, I don't usually…date." I let a snort escape. "One might say I'm allergic to anything that reeks of long-term."

"But not this time?" he probes, looking just curious and nothing more.

"Like I said, it's early days, but…no. I don't really feel the urge to hoof it the other way the morning after," I admit.

Evan chuckles at that. "I don't think you'd get very far. Blackfoot seems a little territorial." My mouth falls open. As far as I know I've only once mentioned Keith's name and it was not in a particularly positive light.

"How—"

"Wasn't exactly hard to figure out. He not only gave me the stink-eye and the third-degree last night when he found me in your yard, but it took him only a couple of seconds to ask where you were. The Blackfoot I know would've been all about the investigation."

"I see." I smile to myself. It would appear, I'm not the only one in this budding relationship who is operating well out of their comfort zone. That makes me feel a little better. "You should get home," I nudge Evan, whose jaw almost unhinges with a massive yawn. "Get some rest."

"Yeah. I'll catch you later."

The strain back in the lines on his face, he walks toward the exit, and I aim for the patient rooms.

* * *

It's close to two when I finally have a chance to grab a bite. I pick up a coffee and some yogurt in the cafeteria and head outside to the small courtyard. It's a nice spot, enclosed by a rock garden with waterfall that provides a peaceful oasis from the busy hospital. Perfect to relax the body and brain for twenty minutes.

Busy day, but I'm grateful for it because I haven't really had a chance to think about last night—about Panda. Part of me wants to call Sophie, just to be able to talk to her, but I know she'll be upset for me and what is the use in that? Still, a friendly voice would be nice.

The door to the courtyard opens and Jen steps out with a coffee, spots me sitting on the bench, and walks over.

"Nice out here, right?" she asks, plopping down next to me. "I love coming out here on my last break, when my feet are sore and I'm about to forget my own name. It gives me enough of a boost to get me through those last couple of hours."

"Yeah, it's peaceful."

"You seem a little down today, everything okay?"

My normal response would probably have been something like *I'm fine*—partially because I don't like complaining and partially because I prefer keeping to myself—but I hesitate only for a minute. "It's been a shit twenty-four hours, to be honest."

"How come?"

I stick to the basics. "A fire broke out in the shed in my backyard, and one of my cats was trapped inside."

"Oh no, I'm so sorry." Jen immediately puts a comforting hand on my shoulder and that is enough for my emotions to form a ball in my throat. "Do you know how it happened?"

"The fire? I don't know."

"It's just weird, there seems to have been a wave of fires recently. I mean we've had four patients come into the unit, these past couple of weeks, who sustained their injuries in a house fire. I can't remember seeing that before. We get a lot more electrical or chemical burns usually."

I make a noncommittal sound, not quite sure what I should to say to that. I got the impression last night, the fact these fires appear to be connected is not common knowledge. Although, I'm sure Jen is not the only person wondering about this.

We sit quietly for a while, just listening to the sound of water falling and sipping our coffees when she suddenly asks, "What was your cat's name?"

"Panda. Black and white. She looked like one: had a white chest and face, with these black spots covering her eyes."

"Cute. Did you name her?"

"No, all my cats came from the shelter already named."

"All? How many do you have?"

"Five. Four now, I guess." Jen tries to hide the shock on her face, but I catch it and smile. "I'm the proverbial cat lady. I just can't say no."

"Oh, I'm not judging," she says quickly. "It's just I can't keep a plant alive. Heck, I can barely look after myself properly most days. I can't imagine taking on one pet, let alone five, but I guess they make for good companions."

I'm pretty sure the look she throws me is one of pity, and I can imagine what she sees. Lonely single woman, fast approaching middle age—who fills her life with animals—must strike a pathetic picture in her eyes. She can't be more than ten or twelve years younger, but sometimes that's light-years removed.

Funny, my girls in San Antonio are around her age, but they never make me feel old. Fuck, I wish they were here.

"I should head in. My last appointment for the day is probably waiting for me already." I get up and toss my now empty cup in the trash.

"Right behind you," Jen says, her cup following mine in the bin. "I should be good for those last couple of hours."

We part at the stairs, and I make my way over to the small cluster of offices and treatment rooms that make up the outpatient side of the new burn center. Aside from Sandy, the center's receptionist, I'm the only one who takes up permanent residence there. The other two offices are used on rotation by specialists.

"Your three o'clock cancelled," she calls out when I pass her desk. "Something about throwing his back out? Anyway, I slotted him in for next week. Poor guy seems to have the worst kind of luck." Jeff Youngman, the farmer who was caught in a barn fire, certainly seems to have a decent run of misfortune in the past six or so weeks.

"Sure sounds that way. Okay, it'll give me a chance to catch up on my admin. I'm a little behind entering data on the new patients we've added this past week."

I'm about to enter my office when Sandy calls out again. "Oh, before I forget: you left your phone in your office, it's been ringing."

The moment I slide behind my desk, it starts ringing again, right on cue.

* * *

Keith

"My screen still shows 'asshole.' Guess I should probably change that."

I blow out a big breath of relief when she picks up. I was about to drive out to the hospital. I've been trying to call for the past twenty minutes and started thinking the worst. In hindsight pretty dumb, since I'm sure there are times she's dealing with patients and can't answer.

"I might still live up to the title."

"Should I be worried?" I can hear the smile in her voice.

"Hardly." Phones should be used solely to relay messages, but I find myself leaning back in my chair, enjoying the sound of Autumn's sexy voice. "Where are you?"

"In my office. You?"

"Same. Is your door closed?"

"Nope."

"Would you consider closing it?"

"Nope," she says again, this time popping her P.

"Tease."

"How am I a tease?"

"Your voice is sexy."

"Bullshit, I sound like Dirty Harry after a heavy night on the town." She chuckles and the raspy sound goes straight to my cock.

"It works for me. Come to think of it, you've got his squint down too. Very hot."

She bursts out laughing, and I find myself grinning at the silly banter, when I hear a throat clear. My eyes shoot to the door. Tony's head is poking in, amusement on his face.

"Should I come back?" he asks sarcastically.

"Give me five." I'll never fucking hear the end of it.

"I should let you go," Autumn quickly suggests.

"No, it's just Tony. He can damn well wait." The idiot in

question is grinning in the doorway. I wave him off. "I was actually just calling to check how your day is going, and when you plan to head home."

"I had a patient cancel, but I've got some work I have to catch up on—why?"

"I just want to make sure everything's okay at your place. If you give me a heads-up when you leave, I'll just pop over, check things out."

"Do you think that's really necessary?"

Fuck, now I've worried her. "More for my own peace of mind than anything else. I'm up to my eyeballs and will likely be working late. Indulge me on this."

I can almost hear her thinking in the pregnant pause that follows. Finally she says, "Okay. I do have to grab a few groceries on the way home, but I'll just be in and out."

"Sounds good. I'll let you get back to work, and I've got Tony hanging around outside my door. Later, Red."

"Soon."

And damn if that word didn't sound just like a promise. At least to my libido it does.

"You can come in, asshole. I know you're out there lurking."

"You're cute," he ribs, as expected. "Already all domesticated and shit. Having an actual conversation on the phone. Next you'll be picking up milk on your way home."

"Fuck off, Ramirez."

"Yeah, no, I don't think so," he says, suddenly serious as he waves a report in my face. "Guess they were feeling the pressure too, reports on both scenes are back from the lab and the fire inspector, and I have a victim statement too."

Tony goes on to outline the findings. Despite a slightly different cocktail as accelerant, it looks like the work of the same guy. Christ, the thought of more than one arsonist at work is enough to give me sleepless nights. Just one is enough.

"Here's an interesting thought." Tony flips open the reports on both scenes side by side. "Based on the percentages of each accelerant in the cocktail—which match to the decimal—the Delwood house and the shed fire were set by the same individual. However, in the case of Autumn's shed, there was no trace of accelerant sprayed on the structure as at the other sites. Looks like he may have tied a soaked rag to the poor cat's tail, making it an effective incendiary device. He wanted her attention in a big way."

"Sure fucking looks like it. Anything on the notes?"

"Partial thumb print on the envelope of the second note. They're running it through AFIS. The envelopes didn't yield much otherwise. They are working on typing the ink and the stationery, but unless there's something to compare it to, it's not the kind of information that's going to help us find him."

"So what then? We already figured his victims were pretty random. There isn't really anything that connects them. We just found out the guy has a hard-on for Autumn, and she is clueless as to who might do something like that. She says she has no enemies." A mental image of her badly scarred back comes to mind, and I wonder if I'll need to press her on a little background after all. I'm not ready to share that bit of information with Ramirez until I find out if it may be connected to the case. Then I have no choice.

"Motive. We need to look closer at motive," Tony points out.

"Easier said than done. It would require getting into the mind of someone who is clearly off his fucking rocker."

"Why not get our friends on Rock Point Drive to have a look? They have access to the Behavioral Science Unit and may be able to get us a profile on the guy."

He's referring to our local La Plata County FBI field office, only a few years old. The SAC, Damian Gomez, is a good friend and will be open to lend a hand if he can. "I'll give him a call tonight," I consent. "Also—although I know it's not something any of us are comfortable considering—we have to look a little closer to home. You know the stats on repeat arsonists."

"You're talking about Biel?" He looks at me sharply. I knew he picked up on my comment earlier today.

"For one, but goddammit, it's going to be a minefield. I like the guy, and I'd like nothing more than to eliminate him right off the bat, but he's friendly with Autumn, and other than the Delwood fire, he was on scene at the others and just happened to show up at her house last night. We have to look into him very quietly. We should probably put together a list of other first responders who showed up at all the fires, except perhaps the one on Delwood. Whoever is responsible couldn't have been there and at Autumn's house at the same time."

I watch as Ramirez gathers his reports and gets up. I'm sure this weighs on him as much as it does on me, but we can't afford to leave a stone unturned. We have bitter few leads to go on as it is.

"I'll handle it myself," he says with a stiff nod, walking out of my office.

After a couple of hours of squinting at the puny font they use these days, my eyes are gritty. It's giving me a headache. The ping of an incoming text supplies a welcome distraction, as I pick up my phone.

***Red:* Leaving now. Gonna hit Nature's Oasis. Home in 20.**

***Me:* See you there**

I grab my phone and my keys. It'll only take me two minutes to get to her place, but I want to check in with Mr. Bartik first. The man was very friendly when I knocked on his door after Autumn left this morning. He was very concerned for her and didn't take any convincing at all to let me make a few minor security adjustments.

Both the back and the porch now sport a sensor light with camera. It's not much, but it sure as fuck makes me feel a little better. When it comes to her safety, I feel like I'm walking a tightrope. My choice would be to haul her out of there and hide her at my place, but that would require strong-arming her, and I'd like to avoid pissing her off too much at this stage of the game.

The lights will probably tick her off already. What is it they say? Easier to ask for forgiveness than for permission? We'll see.

I stop by the desk sergeant on my way out, and drop my reports on the reception counter.

"Can you get someone to copy these reports and enlarge the print? I don't understand why they have to make it impossible to read. Whatever happened to twelve point Times New Roman?"

Mike has about ten years seniority on me and doesn't think twice about bursting out laughing at my expense.

"Sorry to bust your bubble, Boss, but the font hasn't changed. Try these." He tries to hand me his reading glasses. "Time to join the rest of us old-timers and get a pair."

"Bullshit."

His deep belly laugh follows me out the door.

* * *

I step off the porch when she pulls in the driveway and have her door open before she has a chance.

"Hey."

She smiles getting out of the car and I lean down for a kiss. I would never have thought myself to be one for public displays of affection, but she makes it difficult to keep my hands—or lips—off her.

"Hey back," she says, looking a little startled. "I'm surprised you waited outside for me. I thought for sure you'd be using that key you finagled out of me this morning, and be on your knees checking under my bed for boogeymen by now."

"Are you nuts?" I open the back door and grab the two paper bags of groceries from the seat. "And risk getting attacked by your army of felines?"

"Chicken," she jokes back. "They only scratch a little."

I fake shiver and turn toward the house, Autumn following behind, chuckling softly.

"What the fuck is that?"

I stop on the top step and turn around. Figures she'd spot it right away. She seems less than pleased.

"That is a motion sensor light with camera, and before you ask: yes, there is one by the kitchen door out back too." With her lips pressed tight and a snap to her step, she whips by me, unlocks the door and stomps into the house.

That went well.

I follow and put the bags on the kitchen counter, watching her as she fills the cat bowls on the floor with kibble. Not speaking. I take in a deep breath. "I want you safe. Not just for you, but for me. I'm stuck between a rock and a hard place here, Red. My instincts would have you tucked away somewhere safe until I can figure this case out, but I already know that would go over like a lead balloon." The only reaction I get is a loud derisive snort as she starts unpacking the groceries, but I soldier on. "With this active case, on top of my already ridiculous workload, I can't be here all the time to keep an eye on you, like I want to. It would make focusing on my job even more difficult. This seemed like a good solution. There's an app we can download on your phone that allows you to check in, even when you're not home."

Her hands have stilled and her eyes scrutinize me closely. "You did that today."

"This morning, right after you left," I confess. When I see her eyes tighten, I quickly add. "But I checked with your neighbor first. He was on board right away."

A shadow of a smile appears at that but quickly evaporates when she focuses on me. Of course. "How much?" At the sight of my confusion she clarifies. "How much for the lights and the cameras?"

"Don't worry about that," I start, but I can already see by the stubborn set of her mouth that it's not going to fly, so I try a different tack. "How about we split the cost, since it's going to give us both peace of mind."

"Fine. And don't think I don't know I've been manipulated."

I bite the inside of my cheek not to chuckle out loud as I tag the back of her neck and pull her close, wrapping her in my hold. "Thank you for letting me off the hook."

She must be able to hear the smile in my voice because her sharp little fist punches me in the gut, right before she slips her arms around my back.

"The truth?" she mutters under my chin. "It does make me feel safer. Thank you for caring."

CHAPTER 12

Autumn

This week has just flown by.

I worked late most afternoons, trying to stay on top of the expanding workload, but today I'm heading out early. I need to stock up on groceries, and I promised my neighbor a homemade meal tonight.

He was chatting with Keith on the porch a couple of nights ago, just as I was coming home. I walked into a spirited discussion on Hungry Man frozen dinners. Apparently there's a difference between the Salisbury steak and pulled pork versions. I wouldn't know, I haven't had a frozen dinner since college, and even then they all tasted equally disgusting.

When Keith admitted to having been so swamped this week, he'd resorted to eating a couple of frozen dinners at his desk, Mr. Bartik mentioned existing on the stuff. It immediately made me feel guilty. I'd lived beside the man over two months, and other than a few polite hellos, hadn't made an effort to be a better neighbor. I immediately suggested he come over tonight for a home-cooked dinner, which seemed to be well received. I instantly decided I'd make that effort on a regular basis.

I invited Keith too, but he wasn't sure if he'd be able to make it.

Chicken potpie is on the menu, and I quickly grab some cheat ingredients that will have dinner on the table in less than an hour. The old man had told me he didn't eat 'rabbit food,' so salad is out of the question, but I figure I can sneak some steamed broccoli on his plate. I add some fresh berries to my cart—they would work with ice cream for dessert—snag a bottle of wine and head to the cash register.

"Need a hand?" I swing around at Evan's voice behind me and almost drop the groceries I was determined to carry to my car. "Here, give me those." He relieves me of some of my bags.

"Thanks. It's my own fault," I admit, digging through my purse for my keys. "I don't want to bother taking the cart so I try to carry everything. What are you doing here?" I glance at him as I unlock the car.

He grins. "Groceries for the firehouse." He loads the bags into the back seat before straightening.

"Again?"

"Boys eat a lot, what can I say."

"I bet. By the way, I'm sure you heard your friend was released yesterday?"

"Scott Beacham? Yeah, some of us dropped by last night. He seems to be doing much better."

"That's great. Well, I should head out; my dinner date is probably waiting at my door already. Thanks again." I throw him a smile and open the driver's side door.

"Guess Blackfoot's still hanging around?" There's something in the way he says that I don't particularly care for.

"As a matter-of-fact, yes, he is. I'm not sure what is going on with you and him, but do me a favor, keep me out of it.

Oh, and just for clarity's sake, it's my elderly neighbor I'm cooking for tonight, although I'm not quite sure why I'm even telling you."

I notice the instant look of regret on his face, but ignore it and slip behind the wheel. I know something is up between the two men, because I've had that same question from Keith as well, concerning Evan. If they have shit to sort, they can do it on their own time. I'll tell Keith the same thing next time he brings the other man up.

A quick peek in my rearview mirror as I drive out of the parking lot shows Evan, hands in his pockets, his eyes following my car.

As he has every day this week, Keith is waiting for me on the porch. Never more than to check my place, give me a kiss that curls my toes but doesn't go anywhere, and rush back out to whatever is growing on his plate that day. To say I'm frustrated is putting it mildly.

It was almost a week ago his mouth was between my legs, leaving me with a promise of things that remains unfulfilled. At this rate, I'll be back in San Antonio before I've even have a chance to test the waters with him. The moment the thought enters my head, I feel guilty. The man is here every day, showing his concern and care—instead of letting sexual frustration cloud the value of that—I should consider myself lucky. It is just so out of my frame of reference. I'm used to the instant sexual gratification, without the added complexities of building a real relationship.

"You know, I appreciate you doing this every day, right?" I start when he meets me at my car to help me unload. He looks up a bit confused.

"Yeah? Why do I get the feeling there's a 'but' coming?"

"Not really, just wanted you to know I'm grateful. I just don't want to take you away from important things, when you can also see me come home on the camera via that monitoring app I know you downloaded on your own phone as well."

He gives me a lopsided grin, knowing he's busted. I figured that out quickly when every morning I'd get a text, wishing me a good day, just as I sat my ass behind the wheel of my car. It probably should've creeped me out, and it would've from anyone else, but from Keith it seemed in character. Being protective without being too controlling. I'm sure it's a struggle, which makes me appreciate it even more.

"Caught on to that, did you?"

"Wasn't that hard. Your surveillance skills need a little polish," I tease him as we walk toward the house.

"Noted." He takes the keys from my hand and opens the door for me.

"So what I guess I'm saying is, you don't *have* to show up every day. Just check the camera feed."

Keith sets down the bags on the counter, does the same with the few I have in my hands, before pulling me flush against him, his arms banding tight around me. "You want me to give up the five-minute bright spot I look forward to every day? Because that's what this is. Five minutes out of another frustratingly busy day of me trying to crawl into the dark mind of a serial arsonist, while dealing with the daily grind of a job I don't particularly like."

"Oh." My eyes blink behind my glasses and my mouth falls open. It's all I can manage while my brain is knitting his words into a warm blanket I can wrap around on a cold, lonely night. The concept of being a positive light in someone's life is new to me.

"Yeah," he says, bending down to take advantage of my still-parted lips with a deep, hungry kiss. I play mindlessly with the elastic he occasionally ties his hair back with and pull it free, twisting the strands in my fingers. My tongue curls around his and I rise on tiptoes, eager to hang on to his mouth. "Babe," he groans, coming up for air. "You're killing me."

"Serves you right," I mumble, trying to get my bearings. "You've got me hanging on by a thread."

"I know." He lifts his head; heat and regret blend in his hazel eyes, burning into mine. "If it's not too late, I'd like to come by after my meeting."

"I'll set some dinner aside," I offer.

"Much appreciated, although you should know it's not your chicken potpie I'll be craving."

"Oh." Heat curls low in my belly and I inadvertently lick my parted lips. Keith seems mesmerized before he tears his gaze from my mouth.

"Yeah," he rumbles.

* * *

Keith

Sweet fucking torture.

It's that Tony and his buddy from Denver, Joe Benedetti, are waiting for me or I would've blown off work and stayed. It's been a buildup of anticipation with every stolen kiss this past week, and I've had blue balls since Saturday night.

I'm meeting the guys at a BBQ place on the north side of town to avoid too many familiar faces. The restaurant must be packed, judging by the parking lot, I barely manage to squeeze the Tahoe into the only available space.

I spot Ramirez sitting with an imposing silver-haired guy at a table on the patio outside. When I walk up, I notice the man is not nearly as old as his hair color implies. He has, at best, only a few years on me.

"Keith Blackfoot." I hold out my hand and the guy gets up to shake it. Fuck, I'm a solid six foot one, but this guy has to be at least six five, if not more. Built like a goddamn linebacker too.

"Joe Benedetti." He is surprisingly soft-spoken.

"I went ahead and ordered us an assorted platter off the grill for three," Tony announces, pouring me a beer from the pitcher on the table. "Saves time."

"Fine by me." I take a sip of my beer and focus on Joe. "So Tony tells me you might be up for a new challenge?"

"I might. He's told me a little background on what went down here last year, although most of the story filtered down the ranks in Denver as well."

"I bet."

"I also heard you were a shoo-in for chief."

I bark out a laugh. "I'm sure that's the story going around, being fed by our mayor who thinks manipulation is gonna work on me. It won't. This job's not for me, too much diplomacy required that I am short on." I lean forward on the table. "Which is why I'm not afraid to ask, why a guy with a solid track record at the Denver PD, would consider moving to our little town and run the police department here? Sure, the title of police chief sounds good, but I'm sure the pay rate won't be that much different from what you make in the big city. It just seems a bit sedentary from what you're used to." I ignore Ramirez, who is kicking me under the table. I don't mean to antagonize his friend, but I'm gonna be putting my neck out for this man, so I'd like all the cards on the table.

"Lost my wife to cancer six months ago. Kids are eight and twelve and see their mother everywhere they go. I'm all they've got. Sedentary sounds good to me." I'm sure the monotone delivery is meant to conceal emotion, but his loss is evident in the eyes he turns on me. "That explanation enough?"

"Fuck man, that's tough. I'm sorry for your loss." I chance a glance at Ramirez, who is shaking his head at me. I ignore that too. "Glad you told me, though. You may not like me saying this, but relatable motivation will go a long way to getting you this job. One of the reasons Stan Woodard has such a hard-on about me taking this job is I have lifelong roots in this community. He wants qualified, experienced, and reliable. The first two are easily marked off, and with what you just told me, the last one will be too."

We spend some time discussing the job until the server arrives with a large tray of assorted grilled meats and a bucket of fried potato skins, and we collectively dive in. All talk is suspended while we eat. When there's nothing but a pile of rib bones left on the platter, I toss my napkin on the table and turn to Joe.

"When do you have to be back?"

"The oldest has a soccer game at three on Sunday. I'd like to be there, depending on what the plan is."

"Free tomorrow?"

"Absolutely."

"Bring your paperwork? Resume, diplomas, certificates, latest performance reviews?"

"As instructed."

I pull my phone from my pocket and dial. "Yeah, Stan, it's Keith."

"Burning the midnight oil?"

"So to speak. Are you busy tomorrow afternoon, say around four?"

"I have a meeting in my office at two-fifteen. I should be done by four. Why?"

"I have some ideas I need to run by you, and I have a limited window to do that in. I'll be there at four." Before he has a chance to ask more questions, I hang up and turn back to the table. "You heard. We have a meeting in the mayor's office tomorrow at four. Dress nice, he's a sucker for a good suit."

"You say you don't like manipulation?" Joe observes, a sardonic smile on his face.

"I don't like it used on me. I never said I didn't like using it." That earns a chuckle.

"Touché. And for the record, I did bring a suit, just in case, but it's Brooks Brothers, not Armani."

"Won't matter. He won't know the difference," Tony, who's been quiet through most of dinner, pipes up. "So four tomorrow, I assume you don't need me there?"

"You'd be wrong. By the time we walk into that meeting, Joe should be well prepared in order to convince Stan he's the right man. It'll take you and me to make sure he is, and we should both be there for support. We have a busy day ahead."

"My turn," Ramirez says, snatching the bill up the moment the server brings it. He drops a few bills on the table and we make our way outside. "Want to grab a quick beer at The Irish?"

"Not me," I announce. "I've got some unfinished business to attend to."

Tony snorts. "That unfinished business wouldn't have a mass of red hair, now would it?"

"Kiss my ass," I grumble, which only makes him laugh harder.

"I'll pass, thanks, but maybe she can—"

I aim a fist at his shoulder before he can finish that sentence.

"Watch it." I warn him before turning to the other man. "Good meeting you. I hope we didn't scare you off."

"Not a chance." He gives my hand a firm shake.

"Good. In that case, roll call is at seven in the morning. See you then."

I climb behind the wheel and do a quick check of the camera feed on my phone, just in time to catch Mr. Bartik enter his own front door. Perfect timing.

With a grin on my face, and hunger already building, I head for Autumn's. I may be too full to sample her chicken potpie, but I'm pretty sure I can handle feasting on her.

CHAPTER 13

Autumn

"Let me pack you up some leftovers, Mr. Bartik."

I had surprisingly good time with my elderly neighbor, who regaled me with tales of his childhood in Poland, and his long boat trip to the United States in 1954 as a young teenager with his family. Apparently, his was one of the last landings of immigrants to be processed through Ellis Island, an interesting story all by itself.

His history is rich, from the bakery in New Jersey his parents established all the way to his move across the country to follow a girl he'd set his eyes on. Ana had been his wife for fifty years when she passed away in 2012, and he'd been alone ever since. She'd been the love of his life, but sadly they never had children.

I'd already resolved to pay more attention to my neighbor, but after tonight I wanted to adopt him. There was something so tragic about a kindhearted man who worked hard and loved hard his whole life, only to find himself alone at the end of it.

"Joseph, please, and you don't need to go through all that trouble," he says, ready to leave.

"No trouble at all. I made enough to feed an army."

"I'm sure your young man would have no problem finishing it." I almost snort at his description of Keith, but I guess in the eyes of an almost eighty-year-old man, we're all kids.

"Don't worry about him," I assure Joseph. "I've already put some aside."

Ignoring further protest, I pack up two containers he can freeze and eat whenever the mood strikes him. When I show him out and hand him the leftovers, he grabs my hand and in an old-fashioned gesture, kisses the back of it.

"I hope that boy is smart enough to hold on tight. You remind me of my Ana, she was a redhead like you and could cook like a saint, fight like the devil, and love like a sinner." His watery blue eyes sparkle.

Ten minutes later, when I'm putting away the last of the dishes, I'm still smiling at his words. To love like that, still so strong even after death rips you apart, is tragically beautiful. I'd grown cynical over the years, with too many negative experiences to taint any dreams I might've had of a happy ever after, but this old man made me a believer again.

Which is why, just moments later, when I hear a key turn the lock of my front door; I'm already on the move. Keith barely has a chance to step inside before I launch myself in his arms and pull him down for a kiss.

"Jesus, Red," he mumbles when I let him up for air. "Best fucking welcome ever, but what was that all about?"

I grin up in his face and shrug. "Oh, just feeling blessed today."

"Had a good dinner with the old man?" he asks when I pull him inside.

"Yes. You should try and be here next week; he's got some

interesting stories to tell. You'd get a kick out of it." I open the fridge and pull out the plate I put aside for him and go to pop it in the microwave.

"I would, would I?"

Keith takes the plate out of my hand and sets it on the counter before closing me in with his arms. I feel his breath against the shell of my ear and the result is a Pavlovian effect on my body. Heat floods low in my nether regions and my nipples pull tight as I almost inadvertently lean back against his broad chest. Instant turn-on.

One of his large hands slowly moves up from my stomach, and brushes over my breasts in a slow perusal. By the time it curves around the base of my throat, I'm panting. With one strong finger under my chin, he tilts my head sideways and his mouth slants over mine. The next moment he swings me around, leans his back against the counter, keeping me in front of him with one hand still at my throat. My knees almost give out when I feel the fingers of his other hand slip under my waistband and tuck between my legs, cupping me there.

"Your dinner," I mutter with my last thread of coherent thought when he catches a breath.

"Not hungry." He groans when he slips a digit between my folds, slick with my arousal. "For potpie," he adds. "Christ, Red. Tell me now if you don't want this ending up with me balls deep inside you, because I'm so damn ramped up, I don't think I could stop."

"I don't want you to stop." The low growl in response comes at the same time a second finger slips inside me.

"Take off your shirt."

His voice is gruff and his tone demanding, but I'm not even considering refusing his request. My top and bra land on the kitchen floor, and seconds later, my pants and underwear are pushed down my legs. He shifts us around so I'm once again facing the counter, the large uncovered window in front of me, open to anyone with an eye on the back of my house.

I don't ever turn my back on lovers. Never. Yet with Keith, I don't question the vulnerable position I put myself in. I'm not ready to examine why that might be, especially since his hand once more slips between my thighs as he encourages me to widen my stance. With his body he presses me forward, leaning over the counter.

"Don't move."

With my hands braced on the counter, I feel cool air hit my flushed skin when he backs away. I try to follow his blurred reflection in the window. Hearing the slide of a zipper and then the rustling of foil has a charge run down my spine in anticipation. I fully expect him to grab my hips and power inside me, but instead I feel his lips trace over my exposed back, mapping the outline of my scars. Despite the lack of sensation in that area, I feel the light brush like a trail of electricity on my skin.

"You are so fucking gorgeous, Red," he mumbles against my skin.

I can't completely hold back on the sob that surges up, and his fingers press into my hips; helping me stay grounded. The next moment I feel the blunt head of his cock probing and finding my entrance. He catches me by surprise again when he eases himself inside me with infinite gentleness, filling me slowly.

"Look up, Autumn," he mutters in my hair. "Look at us."

My eyes lift, and in the bright light of the kitchen against the dark of night outside, I see pale skin and the bright mane of my hair perfectly outlined against the dark looming figure surrounding me from behind.

"Keith..."

"That's right, baby. That's...Fucking...Right..."

Every word is in sync with a cadence of deep forceful thrusts, lifting me onto my toes. Each drive forcing a whimper from my lips as he touches places inside me that have my toes curl on the cool tiles of my kitchen floor. My head rolls back and forth against his shoulder as I feel a climax building out of control.

All it takes is the sharp firm pressure of his fingers on my erect nipples to propel me over the edge. I barely notice the increasing rhythm of his thrusts until he plants himself deep, my toes barely touching, and bellows out his release.

* * *

Keith

"Are you sleeping?"

I softly stroke the pads of my fingers over the curve of her hip. She's draped half over me: head on my shoulder, an arm slung across my stomach, and a leg entwined with mine.

"Mmmm," she hums, the vibrations skittering over my sensitized skin.

"Mind if I stay?"

At that she lifts her head, chin resting on a hand on my chest, those green eyes with almost unnaturally long lashes even more expressive without the red-framed glasses. Those were tossed carelessly onto the nightstand when we rolled into bed for rounds two and three. I'm getting old—feeling the burn in my muscles and raw chafe of my cock from the mind-blowing friction of her tight pussy—no longer used to the intense action. It's been well over a decade since I had my last all-nighter, but damn if I don't want her again.

"I don't mind," she says quietly appraising me. "I probably

have a spare toothbrush in one of the drawers in the bathroom vanity. Towels in the linen closet in the hallway."

"Gotcha." I bend my head to hers, kissing the tip of her nose.

"Are you hungry? I still have your dinner in the fridge."

"I'm good. Still full from my dinner meeting."

"That's right. I never got around to asking how that went."

I'd mentioned hoping this meeting might mean the end to my interim duties of COP. "We'll see tomorrow. I like the guy. He seems to know what he'd be getting into taking on this job, and he wants it. Single dad with two young ones and he wants to get out of the Denver rat race."

"I can't blame him. This would be a great place to raise kids."

I detect a wistful undertone and squint my eyes, but she immediately plasters a big smile to cover up. Whatever it is we've got going on here, it's much too soon to press her on a subject like kids. I'd fucking love to know what put that sad shadow in her eyes.

"It is a great place to raise a family, or at least it will be again, once we get this firebug off the streets."

"Any luck?" She wants to know and I hate that I can't give her any good news.

Ramirez and I have been spinning wheels all week, going over reports, picking them apart to look for a solid lead, but so far we have nothing to show for it. Nothing seems to connect the locations or the victims, other than they were easy targets. We've looked into any possible connections to Autumn, I even called Roman in San Antonio to find out whether he knew whatever happened to her idiot ex, or whether she left behind any enemies, but that didn't bring up any red flags either.

Ramirez requested reports on any random fires over the

past twelve months to see if he could find a pattern, but there wasn't a fire unexplained before a little less than two months ago.

The only bit of good news is that there have been no fires since last Saturday night. I'm not an idiot, though; I don't for one minute believe this temporary reprieve is the end of it.

"Still looking into a couple of things. Also, I talked to a friend of mine at the FBI field office; they are working on putting together a psychological profile. Once we have that, we'll have a better idea of who we're looking for."

"Hmmm. I've been trying to come with people I know, either through work or at the hospital." She snorts, laughing at herself. "I even considered my ex-husband for a moment, but with him living with his new wife up in Canada now, I doubt he has anything to do with it. Even if he wasn't two thousand miles away, he was worried about lighting candles at fucking Christmas. I'm pretty sure he's lacking the balls to do something like this."

I give her shoulder a squeeze. "Red, love talking through shit with you. I've never been in a place where I could do that, but we're in bed and you're talking about your ex," I point out. "I'll talk about anything, but let's keep that dipshit out?"

I feel more than I see her chuckle as she presses her face into my chest. "My bad." Her eyes sparkle when she looks up at me with a cheeky grin. "It'll never happen again, but just for the record, there isn't a man I know who measures up to you."

"Good to know, babe, but let's get some shuteye. I have to be up early and give Benedetti a taste of the Durango PD before I introduce him to our mayor. I can guarantee that will not be an easy meeting."

Her smile softens and she scoots a little up my body, pressing a sweet kiss on my mouth before settling back against my side. Her arm slides possessively across my stomach again, and a cute as fuck little sigh of contentment escapes her lips.

Two minutes later she's asleep, her breath feathering through my chest hair. I follow not too long after, my body relaxed and sated, and my last thought is how fucking amazing she feels in my arms.

CHAPTER 14

Keith

"Chief Blackfoot, good to see you."

I'm pretty sure he uses that title on purpose to annoy me. Or maybe he thinks if he does it often enough it'll stick, I don't know, but it grates on me.

"Mayor."

Stan Woodard gets up from behind his desk and claps me on the shoulder, he gazes curiously over my shoulder where Tony and Joe walk in behind me.

"Detective Ramirez," he acknowledges with a nod, before he stretches his hand to Benedetti. "Don't believe we've had the pleasure."

"Stan, I'd like you to meet Commander Joe Benedetti of the Denver PD Major Crimes Division."

One eyebrow shoots up, but the politician comes out just in time, as his mildly irritated look is quickly replaced with his camera-ready smile.

"Not sure what brings you here, Commander Benedetti, but it's a pleasure to meet you."

"It's Joe, Sir. I understand the office of Chief of Police is still open and would like to throw in my hat for consideration."

We went over the tactics for this meeting beforehand and Joe is playing his part perfectly.

"That's interesting." Stan throws me a sharp glance, before plastering on his diplomatic smile again and turning back to Benedetti. "I wasn't aware news had traveled as far as Denver. Please, have a seat." He waits for us all to comply before he continues, "I have to admit, I'm caught a bit off guard. The department has been operating quite well under the capable hand of Chief Blackfoot. I wonder where you heard we might be looking to replace him?"

"News travels, Sir. I came down to visit a friend and found out about the vacancy. I've been looking for a move to a smaller community than Denver to raise my family."

"A family man myself, I can certainly understand that. I'm sure your qualifications are beyond reproach, Commander Benedetti, but we were under the impression our temporary solution would turn into a more permanent one."

"I'm only bridging a gap, Stan, you know that," I interrupt. "I have no intention of taking the job on a permanent basis." The sharp glance flies my way again, his irritation palpable. "Joe Benedetti would be an absolute asset to the department."

"I see, and what makes you think—"

"Perhaps you should at least have a look at my credentials," Joe interrupts him, dropping the thick file he and Ramirez compiled today. "I've also included a proposal with some structural tweaks to the department that will not only improve interdepartmental communications, but will also save the town a healthy chunk on the budget."

Money talks, and it sure as fuck does with Stan, who pulls the paperwork toward him. For the next half hour, he flips through the pages, grilling Joe on details every so often. At the end of it he slaps the folder shut.

"Very well. Leave it with me, and I'll discuss this with council this coming week."

"Actually," I pipe up. "Since Benedetti has to return to Denver Monday morning at the latest, and this matter has been left unresolved for almost a year, it might be in everyone's best interests to call an emergency meeting sometime tomorrow?"

"I can't have council come in on a Sunday," Stan protests as expected.

"Sure you can, Stan," I correct him, handing him a list. "You've done so three times in the past twelve months alone and for matters less pressing than this one. Besides, I've already checked with the bulk of the council members, and all those I've spoken to are willing to get this matter taken care of as soon as possible."

"I don't see the urgency."

I lean forward in my chair, making sure his attention is focused on me. "Then you're not paying attention. We have an arsonist on the loose that everyone—including you, Mr. Mayor—are looking to see behind bars as soon as possible. Ramirez has put in eighty hours in the past five days alone, and I've not been able to pull my weight on the case because I get mired down in my goddamn interim obligations. This is not a tenable situation, Stan, and this is an opportunity for you to take positive action that will have an impact not only on this case, but the future stability of the department." With that last comment, he sits up a little straighter. Municipal elections are the first Tuesday of April every odd-numbered year, and every improvement he can add to his list of accomplishments before this term is up, he'll be able to use as part of his campaign. Stan's not a fool, but he is definitely pissed that he's been cornered.

"Commander Benedetti," he says, his eyes landing pointedly on Joe. "Provided I'm able to convene a meeting at such short notice, would you be ready and available for council questioning tomorrow?"

"Absolutely."

"You bet we will," I add in my two cents, and I swear Stan rolls his eyes.

It's already after six when we walk out of City Hall.

"That went well," Tony points out, grinning.

"Gotta strike the iron while it's hot, and we didn't give the man too much wiggle room. I'm sure I'll be on his shit list for a good while, but that'll only help our case. I'm pretty sure Joe here can head home on Monday and get his shit sorted on that end."

"Jesus, I came here just to explore options, and I may be leaving with a new job. I feel like I've been on a fucking roller-coaster ride. Good thing the kids' school is out for summer, it at least will give me time to get them settled in before the new school year. I'll also need to find a house."

"I know someone who can help with that," Tony offers. "If there's time tomorrow, I'll introduce you. She's a great real estate agent."

"Tomorrow. Shit. I'll miss my little guy's soccer."

I clap a hand on his shoulder. "Yeah, but think—by the end of this summer—you'll have a job that'll be close enough to the soccer fields you could easily pop out to watch his practice."

"Let's hit The Irish. That's one thing we left out of our tour today." Tony grins and starts walking.

"Not taking the car?" Joe asks him.

"That's another benefit of working in Durango: the pub is around the corner from the office."

"This just gets better and better," Joe mumbles under his breath.

Grinning, I pull my phone from my pocket. "You guys go ahead, I've got a quick call to make."

Today's is a fucking great day, there's no way I'm going to celebrate without Red.

* * *

Autumn

My neighbor is funny. I was on my way out the door when Mr. Bartik, or Joseph as he insists, stuck his head outside. He must've been listening for me. He wanted to thank me for dinner and the leftovers, mentioning he ate those for breakfast because he'd run out of oatmeal. Since I'm heading to the grocery store anyway, I offer to pick some up for him and the next thing I know, he produces a list.

"You think of anything else, you've got my number."

My body is a bit stiff today and it's tempting to grab the car, but I force myself to leave it in the driveway. The walk will do me good.

I remember waking up briefly this morning when Keith left, pressing a kiss to my forehead, but I must've fallen back asleep right away. Finally hauled my ass out of bed at eleven. I can't remember a time I slept in that late past my teenage years. I may not be the cheeriest in the morning, but I'm an early riser. Getting up that late threw me off my rhythm, and as a result, it was already two by the time I got my ass in gear.

It's only a quarter mile or so to the City Market, and the weather is great for a walk. I don't need a lot myself and from the quick glance I had at Joseph's grocery list, none of it is particularly heavy.

Every step I take, I'm reminded of the workout my body

was subjected to last night, under Keith's very skilled guidance. In all my years of occasional flings, and even my marriage before that, I've never been put through the paces quite like he did. I've also not actually slept with anyone since my divorce. Sex was more about filling a physical need, one that did not require batteries or my own hand. Once the need was filled, there was no other reason to stay or invite them to stick around.

That's not the case with Keith. He uses everything in his arsenal: his hands, mouth, cock, eyes, and that voice. Even after our bodies were sated, I didn't want him to leave. The man has me feeling weightless, with only him to anchor me. He doesn't just play my body like an instrument, he makes my soul sing.

Crossing Main Avenue, it occurs to me that people here are so friendly. Everyone I encounter seems to smile and nod, as if they know me. It's not until I catch my reflection in a store window, that I realize I've had a smile plastered on my face the entire time.

It doesn't take me long to grab the few things I need, plus whatever is on Joseph's list, but it is a tad heavier than I thought. By the time I'm halfway home, I'm cursing myself. With every step the damn bags feel heavier.

"Hey! Autumn?"

I swing around and see Jen jogging after me. Grateful for the momentary reprieve, I set my bags down and wait for her to catch up.

"What are you up to?" I ask her with a smile. She's dressed in flashy pink active wear, looking like she's heading for a workout, but that doesn't quite mesh with the shopping bags in her hand.

"Ugh." She wipes at her brow, trying to catch her breath. "I was bored, so I thought I'd go for a jog."

"A jog?" I look pointedly at the bags sporting the names of some of the high-end stores along Main Avenue.

"I said I was thinking about it," she deadpans, and I bust out laughing at the big-eyed innocent expression on her face. "I swear I had every intention, but then I spotted that Blu Boutique had a sale on. They have these fabulous kimonos that look to die for with a faded pair of jeans and a tank. Perfect shabby chic. I got two," she admits with a sheepish grin, opening the one bag so I can have a peek.

"Nice prints," I admire.

"Thanks. Anyway, so I obviously couldn't jog with a bag in my hand, so I kept shopping instead." She leans in and stage-whispers, "I've already spent half my paycheck—please rescue me from bankruptcy and come with me for a drink?"

I laugh at her antics. She's actually really nice, a little off her rocker, but sweet and funny too. I point at my own bags. "I have to get these groceries home, though. Otherwise I would've loved it."

"That's okay. Some other time." Her voice is perky but doesn't quite hide the flash of disappointment on her face, and I make an on the spot decision.

"You know what? If you really have nowhere to be, I'm just two blocks down, walk me home? I just need to give my neighbor his groceries and put my own things away, but I have a bottle of wine in that bag we can tackle."

"Sweet," she chirps, bending down to grab the heavy grocery bag I was indicating and starts walking. Bonus.

* * *

"...so anyway, I told the guy he could shove his come-on line where the sun don't shine and swivel."

I snicker at Jen's description.

We've been telling each other some of our worst encounters with the opposite sex, and I haven't laughed this much since my last girls' night out in San Antonio. It feels good just to chill, talk about silly stuff, and giggle like schoolgirls.

But I'm also coming to realize that underneath Jen's bubbly and youthful exterior, she hides a maturity I wouldn't have given her credit for, had I not seen it surface in her dealings with Joseph. He took to her like a moth to the flame when we dropped his groceries off. She gentled immediately, taking time to get to know him a little. By the time we left his place to go to mine, the two of them had made plans to play cards at the Legion next week. Apparently, Joseph used to go weekly, but hasn't been able to walk the few blocks to get there for months.

I have a whole new appreciation for Jen.

"What about those guys with their shirts open one button too far? Ever seen those? When their only claim to manhood is the healthy rug on their chest, and they use every opportunity to sometimes literally rub that in your face? Ewww. Also, nine out of ten wear a gold chain, or something equally atrocious, to draw attention to their number one attribute. It always reminds me of John Travolta in *Saturday Night Fever*. Of course it was hot in the late seventies, which is where they should've left it." Her full body shiver makes me laugh, and I remember one occasion where I had the same reaction.

"I dated a guy once who looked like a yeti. Not only were his pubes halfway to his knees, it took me ten minutes of digging to find his dick, only to discover it hadn't been worth the lengthy excavation." True story, I remember saying I needed a bathroom break and hightailed it out of his dinky apartment like the devil was on my heels.

"Oh good Lord, don't make me spit out my wine."

"Did you want some more?" I ask her, already getting to my feet to grab the bottle in the kitchen. My phone rings on the counter and I snatch it up, seeing Keith's name appear on the screen. "Hey, honey." The term of endearment slips quite naturally from my lips.

"Where are you?" he asks without a hello. Immediately my hackles go up.

"Home. Where are you?"

"Ditching Joe and Tony and on my way to your place. You sound fucking sexy calling me that."

I cast a quick glance at my living room, where Jen is snuggled in on my couch, two cats on her lap.

"Actually, I have company," I softly announce.

"*Fuck*. Who? Can you get rid of them?"

"Well..."

"Never mind, that was rude. Okay, back to plan A, which was to celebrate the fact we were able to corner Woodard into calling an emergency council meeting for immediate consideration of Benedetti for Chief of Police."

I can hear the relief in his voice.

"That's awesome news! Congrats—that deserves a celebration."

"There's a party?" Jen's attention seems immediately piqued.

"Who's that?" Keith asks in my other ear.

"Jen's here. You know Jen Raymond? I work with her at Mercy?"

"Bring her."

"Sorry?"

"I was calling to see if you'd come have a drink and maybe grab something to eat with us. Bring Jen along."

CHAPTER 15

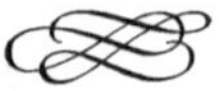

Keith

The place is packed. Not surprising on a Saturday night.

Ramirez already looks to have a table secured.

"She coming?" he asks when I sit down, a smirk on his face. He doesn't seem impressed with the glare I throw him, but instead pours me a beer from the pitcher he somehow managed to get on the table already. "Got her an extra glass. Or does she drink wine?"

"Guinness most likely. Keep the glass for her friend, she might drink beer."

"Friend? Only one?"

"Jesus, Ramirez, think maybe it's time to grow out of that?" I shake my head at him. Might be a little hypocritical, because a few years ago I wasn't much different. Take what you can when you can.

"Not both for me, dipshit, I thought maybe Joe—"

"Joe nothing," the large man grumbles, his face a blank mask as he stares Tony down.

"Christ, sorry man. I'm an idiot."

I reach over and slap him upside the head. "Yes, you are." I turn to Joe and radically change the subject. "You hungry? They have a pretty decent fish and chips here, and the burgers aren't too bad either."

Tony is just pouring my second beer—the first went down a little too easy—when he tilts his head to the bar. I look over to see Evan drinking with some of the guys from the firehouse.

Ramirez has looked into him, as inconspicuously as possible. Nothing showed up, other than he was at all but one of the fires. Unfortunately, it would've been better for him had he been at that last fire up on Delwood, it would've meant he couldn't have lit the shed in Autumn's backyard. Technically, it would be possible for him to have set both.

His is not the only name on that list of first responders, but after the shed fire, I'm starting to feel we might be barking up the wrong tree with that.

I see a flash of familiar red hair in my peripheral vision and turn my head, catching Autumn coming in with the girl from the hospital in tow. Her eyes scan the crowded pub. I'm about to stand up and call her over when I see her making a beeline for Evan. I catch the fucker throwing me a quick look —clearly aware of my presence—before bending down to kiss her cheek. Something tells me he hasn't been as oblivious to our investigation as we'd hoped.

"What's your girl doing over there?" Ramirez points out, with all the sensitivity of a bull in a china cabinet.

"Saying hello to a friend."

I keep a close eye as Evan greets the blonde friend much the same as he did Autumn, making me feel a little less homicidal. Finally he points out our table, and the girls make their way over, Evan mock saluting me from the bar when I stand up. I should probably clear the air with him sometime in the near future.

"Here you are."

Her smile is a little hesitant—even uncomfortable—as she approaches the table. I hook a hand behind her neck and pull her close enough to land a hard kiss on her lips. Her fingers curl into the front of my shirt and I almost forget where I am, when I notice a change and lift my head.

It's like a goddamn priest walked into the pub. Conversations are hushed and we seem to be the center of attention. *Fuck.* Everyone seems to have an unhealthy interest in my goddamn love life. With a sharp glare at the curious looks, I turn resolutely to the blonde behind Autumn.

"Jen, right? Come have a seat. I don't know if you've met Tony Ramirez?" She nods, giving him a little smile when he holds out a chair for her, but then her eyes take in the large, brooding, and mostly silent Benedetti. "And that is Joe Benedetti, a friend from out of town." She does the nodding thing again, and he glares at her from under his eyebrows.

"Autumn, you know Tony, but I'd like you to meet Joe."

Her offered hand and warm smile wipe the scowl off his face. "Nice to meet you, Joe. Hope you're having a good time, and Durango is all you expected."

"Likewise, and it sure looks to be."

I give Autumn a squeeze before pulling out a chair for her. Smart girl. Without letting the cat out of the bag, she manages to acknowledge Joe's purpose for being here.

Drinks are served, food ordered, and the noise level in the pub has returned to its former volume.

Autumn engages Joe in conversation, asking about his children—two boys—which seems to disarm him. It's clear the man dotes on his kids. Her friend, Jen, seems comfortable chatting with Tony or me, only casting an occasional glance in Joe's direction, who seems to be ignoring her.

Halfway through dinner, Joe gets a phone call and excuses himself from the table, disappearing into the small hallway by the restrooms. Two minutes later, he's back at the table, a pleased tilt to his mouth.

"One o'clock tomorrow," he announces, sitting down.

Tony claps him on the shoulder. "Right on."

"I'll be there," I put in, and Autumn smiles at Joe brightly. The only one looking confused is Jen. "Joe is considering moving here. He's visiting to check out his options," I explain, without going into too much detail, but it appears enough for her.

Evan stops by the table on his way back from the men's room, and the conversation drifts to best areas to look for housing.

"Would love living just outside of town somewhere, but I've got young kids, I don't want to isolate them. Besides, they need to be able to get to and from school."

"There's a reasonably new residential subdivision just up from the college," Jen offers. "Or on the west side of town, along Arroyo Drive. Both those areas have decent-sized family homes on large lots. Good views too."

"True. Arroyo Drive is just a bit up from where I am," Tony clarifies to Joe.

"Can I get anyone another drink?" The waitress sidles up to our table.

"Not for me," Jen says, throwing up her hands. "I have an early shift tomorrow."

"Your bags are still at my place," Autumn points out.

"Would you mind bringing them on your next shift? Not like I need that stuff right away. I'll be wearing scrubs for the next six days in a row." She gets up and pulls a few bills from her pocket, dropping them on the table.

"But you walked," Red persists shoving her chair back. "I'll just—"

"I was heading out too. Same reason, early start. I'll make sure she gets home," Evan offers, getting up himself. He doesn't waste time, blowing off any protests from Jen, and with a hand on her elbow steers her firmly out the door.

"Are they an item or something?" Surprisingly, the question comes from Joe.

"No," Autumn answers. "Evan's a firefighter, and Jen works in the burn unit at Mercy Hospital. They bump into each other."

I'm about to call the night short myself, hoping for some alone time with Red, when a call comes in on my phone. The name on the display brings a smile to my lips.

Luna Roosberg.

I quickly get up and with a mouthed, *"Be right back,"* already answering the call, I find a quiet area.

* * *

Autumn

"Hey, Sweetheart…"

I don't hear anything else when he walks out of hearing range.

Joe and Tony are oblivious, continuing their earlier discussion around housing. I, on the other hand, am very aware of the warm smile and soft voice whoever is calling Keith evokes from him. The hamburger I just ate suddenly feels like a rock at the bottom of my stomach. My mind is retracing conversations we had. I'm pretty sure he said he had no siblings. This is stupid. I'm a grown up, I can just ask him later.

For the next ten minutes I try to focus on the conversation, but I get more and more restless as time goes by. When he's not back after twenty, I pull some money from my purse, toss it on the table and get up. "Guys, I'm wiped. Joe," I turn to him with my hand held out. "Good meeting you and I'm keeping my fingers crossed we'll see you here permanently soon. Tony, nice to see you again, it was a pleasure."

"You should wait," Tony suggests. "I'm sure Keith will see you home."

"Oh, no need," I lie waving him off. "I drove, I'll be fine."

I can tell both guys are uncomfortable, but I don't want to sit here waiting any longer. Inviting me to join him and his friends, and then abandoning me at the table for whoever the hell this *sweetheart* may be, is definitely not cool. With a big fake smile on my face, I give them a little wave and head out the door.

It's not until I turn the corner that I hear the heavy tread of running footsteps behind me.

"Hold up," Keith calls out, but I don't slow my step, having worked up quite the snit. "Jesus, Red," he pants, grabbing my arm when he catches up. "What the fuck are you thinking, taking off like that?"

His attitude is fuel for my own and I rip my arm free. "I'm thinking I want to go home. Simple as that," I snap at him.

"You should've waited for me," he growls. "I would've walked you home."

"Really? You were gone for quite a while, Keith. For all I know you could've left out the back door." I don't turn to look at him but can feel the anger coming off him.

"That was a work call. A colleague. That's gonna happen, Autumn. I'll get called away from time to time. It's my job."

"Right," I fire back sarcastically. "Because you call all your colleagues *Sweetheart.*"

"Fucking hell, woman. Luna is a friend as well. We have a history."

I snort at that, the rock in my stomach turning into hot

churning lava. "I'm sure you do." I increase my pace and turn onto the path to my porch.

"*Jesus*, will you wait a goddamn minute?"

At the top of the steps I swing around, not willing to give in to the hot tears that burn my eyes. "I did that already. Twenty minutes is a fucking long time when the person you finally dare letting your guard down for walks off to talk to his *Sweetheart*. It feels like hours."

"I'm sorry, but I was waiting for her call. I wasn't gonna blow her off."

And so the knife drives home.

"Good to know. Thank you for seeing me to my door." I turn around and jam my key in the lock.

"And here I thought you were different," he mutters behind me, twisting it for good measure.

I slam the door behind me, and beeline it straight for my bedroom, where the smell of Keith lingering on my pillow finally triggers the tears.

* * *

Keith

Well, shit.

I'm not sure what the fuck just happened, but I don't have time to dwell on it. Joe and Tony are settling up the bill, and we're supposed to meet up with Luna at the FBI field office on Rock Point Drive.

Since I talked to her boss, Special Agent in Charge Damian Gomez—who also happens to be a friend—earlier in the week, Luna has been playing around with the few bits of evidence I shared with them. The FBI resources are vast in comparison to what the Durango PD has available to them. It's the reason I contacted them in the first place. She called to let me know they have a profile for the arsonist, and some possible leads to explore.

I asked Joe along, it's a great opportunity to introduce him, and besides that, the more sharp eyes on this case, the better.

"Did you clear things up with Autumn?" Tony asks when I catch up with them by my Tahoe, still parked outside the police station.

"What are you, my therapist?" I bite off, getting in behind the wheel.

"Nope. Just a good friend who'd like you to not fuck up a good thing." Ramirez climbs in the back seat, leaving the passenger side for Joe.

"How can I fuck anything up when I don't even know what the hell happened?"

"Not pretending to know anything about anything," Joe pipes up beside me. "But when you leave your woman's side to answer your phone with an endearment generally reserved for love interests, it usually doesn't end well." Tony snickers from the back seat.

"Fine, but I've known Luna since college. She's like a sister to me."

"Did you explain that?" Joe asks calmly.

"For fuck's sake, of course I did. I told her Luna and I have history."

This time it's not just fucking Ramirez losing his shit behind me. Joe's bellowed laugh joins in.

It takes me a minute to get a clue.

Fuck.

CHAPTER 16

Keith

"Yo, Keith, are you with us?"

Luna's voice pulls me from my thoughts. Those have doggedly circled around Autumn and her tear-filled eyes as she turned her back on me and disappeared inside. Not a good scene and it gnaws at me. Especially what I said when I lashed out at her.

"Sorry, what was that?" I try not to notice the amused smirk on Ramirez's face. He's having way too much fun at my expense.

"I said the ex-husband is out. He's currently on an Alaskan cruise with his new wife. Also, the hero complex theory doesn't really fly for a few reasons. First of all, the method of incineration is effective but rudimentary and brings the risk of discovery. The perp has to actually light the accelerant. Most first responders, and especially firefighters, would likely use a more sophisticated method of ignition. Which brings me to the next point: the different accelerants used point to someone who is still experimenting. Finding the right mix for his purposes."

"You keep saying *his*," Joe points out. "Do I take that to mean a woman is out of the question?"

"Not necessarily," Luna's boss, Damian Gomez, responds for her. "But a female arsonist is rare, especially a serial one. Also, there was the sighting by one of the Delwood neighbors, she clearly indicated a man."

"That is if we assume the guy with the backpack wasn't just a hiker going up the mountain," I point out.

"Actually, Luna has a theory on that."

I turn to Luna, who is putting an image on the screen. "I was studying the fire inspector's report, which kept talking about the even distribution of accelerant. It's the same at all the scenes except for the shed, but I'll get back to that one. He describes a wide burn pattern, which would suggest something that can spray a large area evenly. That, combined with the sighting on Delwood, made me think of a sprayer like they use for the application of pesticides or whatever. Like this one, they often come with shoulder straps."

"But wait a minute," Tony cuts in. "You were just pointing out even distribution, but these things operate with hand pump. That wouldn't—"

"Actually—this one is battery operated. A rechargeable lithium battery pack, much like a leaf blower or weed whacker. One hit of the button, and the spray would be continuous and even."

"So what does that mean?" Tony asks. "We look for someone who works in landscaping? Forestry?"

"Not necessarily. These things are readily available at any supply or home improvement store. Heck, you can even order them off Amazon these days."

"Not exactly a lead then," I point out, and Luna shrugs her shoulders.

"Maybe not, unless you know make and model, but it's one more item to check off suspects against. Although considering the types of accelerant used, combined with the sprayer, I would venture to say this individual does not live in downtown Durango. You can add that to the list."

The list she refers to is the one she handed me when we walked in: a profile sketch of our firebug. Call it a checklist of attributes and identifiers. According to the profile, the perp has probably been experimenting setting fires long before he hit our radar. It also details his need for attention, right now focused on Autumn, and the caution to watch for escalation. We've already seen that with her cat.

"You said you'd get back to the shed fire," I prompt Luna.

"Yes, that's the anomaly. I don't think that one was planned, or at least not planned well. Evidence indicates we're dealing with the same perp, given the identical composition of starter used, but the method screams impulse. What it indicates to me is not only his desperate need to get Autumn's attention, but he is watching her." She pauses a moment, giving me a hard look. "You're going to want to keep a close eye on her."

Tony barks out a laugh. "Maybe I should take over that task. Lover boy here is going to have to get back into her good graces first."

"You have a relationship with this woman?" The question comes from Damian, who's been mostly quiet, letting Luna take the lead.

"He did, until he fucked it up." I toss Ramirez a scathing look, my hands clenched to white-knuckled fists on the table in front of me. Something that doesn't go unnoticed by Luna.

"You do?" she prompts me, and reads the expression on my face, because she continues without waiting for my confirmation. "If he's been watching her, he'd be aware. It's going to piss him off."

I think back to the first time I kissed Autumn. It was on her porch, the Friday night I walked her home after darts at The Irish with Chief and Sophie. Christ, the Delwood fire was the next night. The night I had my head between her legs on the outlook point by the college. In fucking plain view. I kissed her again on the porch when I dropped her off, and barely an hour later her shed was on fire.

Last night, Jesus. This guy was watching and I fucked her against the kitchen counter in front of the goddamn window.

A feeling of dread freezes the blood in my veins and I pull out my phone, checking the monitor feed from the security cameras. The house is quiet, looks like she left a light on in the kitchen, but other than that it's dark. She must be in bed. A surge of guilt hits me, and I get to my feet, feeling the sudden need to get over there. "We should go," I announce and the other two follow suit. "Thanks. This helps—a lot." I lift the paperwork Luna handed me when we came in.

"Keep us in the loop, and if there's anything else," Damian offers, shaking my hand.

"And keep her safe," Luna adds, a smile forming. "Even if it means groveling."

Oh, I'll be groveling all right. Red will make sure of it.

"What's the sudden rush?" Tony wants to know when I pull out of the parking lot.

"Kissed her on her porch Friday night. Next night I got called out to Delwood. Kissed her again on the porch and half an hour later her shed was on fire. Haven't seen her all week until last night..." I let that thought trail, waiting for them to clue in.

"You kissed her on the porch again?"

"Not exactly. It was in the kitchen."

"Why do I get the feeling we're not talking about kissing anymore?" Joe weighs in, hitting the nail on the head.

"Let's just say if what Luna says is true, and our guy is

watching, he would've gotten an eyeful last night. Enough to send him into a rage."

I stop at a red light at Camino Del Rio, and pull out my phone again. This time when I check the monitor at the back of the house, I see a faint orange glow at the bottom of the screen.

"Shit!" I toss my phone at Joe and peel through the red light heading north, narrowly avoiding a pickup truck going in the other direction.

"Jesus, are you trying to kill us?" Tony yells from the back seat, but I ignore him.

"Address," Joe says beside me, already dialing 911.

"945 East 3rd Avenue," I bite off.

The car is silent as he rattles off the address to the dispatcher. No sooner has he hung up, when I hear Ramirez behind me on the phone. "Send all you've got to 945 East 3rd. Right fucking behind the station. Duplex fire. Single woman on the left, old man on the right. Fire is en route."

"Red on speed dial," I tell Joe, as I do my best to stay focused on the road.

I'm blowing through backstreets to try and avoid the Saturday night crowds, going as fast as I can get away with.

"No answer," he reports.

"Keep trying."

I hit 3rd Avenue from the south, just as a patrol car with flashing lights stops in front of Autumn's place, two blocks away. The orange glow of fire is visible from here, and smoke billows from the house. I run the Tahoe over the median and half up the sidewalk on the other side.

"Go!" Joe yells, shoving the gear in park as I propel myself from the car.

Jesus. It's like the house is surround by a ring of fire, eating its way up the walls. Most of the porch is already engulfed in flames, and Officer Conley is hesitating at the base of the steps. "Get the old man!" I yell at him while barreling past, throwing myself full force against Autumn's front door. The heat of the flames feels like it's blistering my skin as I retreat and hit it again, this time managing to break the lock from the post.

"Autumn!"

Flames are shooting from the kitchen, the sudden airflow providing fuel for the fire. The house is hot and thick with smoke, as I blindly find my way to the stairs up to her bedroom. I hope to fucking God that's where she is.

* * *

Autumn

I wake up to the sound of my phone ringing somewhere in the house and immediately burst out coughing at the smoke in my room. Panicked, I blindly feel around the bed for my cats. My fingers graze fur before the air becomes so thick, I'm forced to roll out of bed on the ground, grabbing hold of the small warm body and tucking it under my arm. Crawling as low to the ground as I can with only one useable arm, I make my way into the hall and over to where I'm guessing the stairs are.

The smoke is blinding and I'm forced to press my face into the carpet to try and get a clean breath in my burning lungs.

"We've gotta get out of here." Keith's voice suddenly sounds at my ear.

"...get others," I cough, batting off his hands.

"No time. Let's go!" he yells, plucking the cat from my

arm and half pulling me down the stairs. There he barks at someone, "Her cats. There's three more."

He half carries me out onto the porch, where cool air hits me and I inhale as deep as I can, resulting in a painful hacking cough. Tears stream down my face and darkness creeps in as I gasp for breath.

Next thing I know, I'm on my back in the grass, blinking up at the leaves of the large maple in my front yard. The instant I feel the pressure over my nose and mouth, I wrestle to get away, but two strong hands hold me down.

"Easy, Red. It's just oxygen. They're taking you to Mercy for smoke inhalation." My watery eyes find his hazel ones, and he must read the question on my face. "We've got two. The multi-colored one and the gray tabby. Joe's got them safely locked in my truck. The cat door was unlatched though. The others may have escaped out the back."

I manage to wrestle one hand free and push away the mask. "Mr. Bartik?" I manage before the mask is firmly returned over my mouth. My heart sinks when I notice his eyes flit away for a second.

"Already en route to the hospital. Not gonna lie, honey. He doesn't look good. They were working on him as they loaded him up."

Fresh tears fill my eyes as I nod my understanding. Poor Joseph.

My head starts to swim and I feel darkness creeping in again as I'm being rolled onto a board.

* * *

When I open my eyes again, I'm in a bed and I can't breathe.

"Don't fight it. You've been intubated; it's doing all the breathing for you. Your airway became compromised on the way to the hospital." Jen leans into my view, smiling. "Good to see you awake though. I'll let Dr. Landis know, maybe we can get that tube out."

She starts to move away, but I manage to grab her arm, hoping to be able to convey my question with my eyes. She seems to understand when I let my eyes roam around the room before landing on her again.

"He was here all night. Mostly sleeping in that chair over there." She indicates a recliner in the corner of the room. "I just sent him out to grab a coffee. He should be back shortly."

As if by design, a very tired-looking Keith walks into the room, a carryout cup in his hand.

"I'll leave you to it then," Jen says, giving me a pat on the shoulder and stepping away from the bed.

Keith immediately takes her place, grabbing my hand in his. "Glad to see those green eyes, honey. I know you'll want to know about the cats," he says, sitting down on a stool, not letting go of my hand. "The good news is, there's no evidence either one of your missing cats died in the fire. Ramirez contacted the humane society and they'll be on the lookout. The other two are staying at his place until I have a chance to take them to my house." At this my eyes grow big. "The back of both units is burned badly, Red. Not to mention the smoke and water damage in the rest of the house. There's no way you can live there for the foreseeable future. We'll find a solution, but for now you and the cats are moving in with me."

Dirty bastard. He knows I can't say anything, but that doesn't mean I can't show my displeasure in other ways.

"Ouch!" he yelps when I twist the fingers of his hand backward. "Shit, woman. You almost snapped my fingers off." My single raised eyebrow sends the message home firmly. "I'm not handling you," he says softly, leaning in and brushing a stray lock of smoky hair from my face. "I'm keeping you safe. I didn't follow my instincts last week, when that son of a bitch paid you a visit, and look what happened. I can't make that mistake again, Red. No matter how pissed it gets you, I need to do what I can to make sure he can't hurt you again."

His eyes show me the truth of his words. I show my understanding by finding his hand. He lifts mine, kissing my palm before he laces our fingers.

"You should probably also know I talked to Chief and Sophie. She was ready to hop on a plane, and I suspect he probably had to tie her up to stop her. I promised them an update today."

"Well, Ms. McCoy, I hear you are with us again." Dr. Landis' booming voice sounds from the doorway. "If your young man wouldn't mind stepping out of the way, I'd like to have a look at you."

A giggle gets stuck behind the damn tube at his description of Keith as my young man. Of course not that surprising, since at almost seventy-two, Dr. Landis is one of the oldest physicians at Mercy.

Keith steps aside and shows me his phone, gesturing to the hallway with a wink.

It's not until he walks out of the room that I realize he hasn't mentioned Mr. Bartik at all.

CHAPTER 17

Keith

"Congratulations again."

I shake Benedetti's hand. We just got here in time for him to hop on the last flight to Denver, but we had to race from City Hall the second our business there ended.

In a little less than four weeks, he should be back, ready to take on his new office as Chief of Police. Needless to say, the emergency council meeting had the outcome we'd hoped for. The choice really wasn't that difficult, Benedetti comes highly qualified and motivated. Clearly a much better option than my reluctant, unhappy, and burned-out ass offers.

The prospect of being able to put all my energy in one case at a time again soon, lifts a weight off my shoulders.

"Thanks. Tell Tony thanks for the hospitality and good luck with your arson case."

"Now a murder case," I correct, thinking of poor Mr. Bartik.

The EMTs worked hard to get him back, but he was called DOA when they arrived at Mercy. His autopsy is scheduled for first thing tomorrow and I haven't told Autumn yet. In fact, I've threatened the hospital staff with bodily harm if they even dropped a hint. Luckily she was out like a light when I left, still under the influence of sedatives. She still has the tube; her throat apparently remains too swollen to risk removing it.

"Right. Wish Autumn all the best for me, and give her my sincere condolences. I'll be in touch when I have definite dates, but in the meantime, if there's anything I can do, you've got my number."

The last boarding call for the flight to Denver comes over the crackling sound system, and with a lift of his chin, he rushes through security.

Moments later, I'm on my way back to Mercy, which is only a ten-minute drive from the airport.

"Ramirez." Tony answers at the first ring.

"He's off and I'm heading back to the hospital. Anything on next of kin?"

"Nothing. Bartik's wife died in 2012 and she had a brother who passed away two years ago. Guess he was the last one standing."

"Christ."

"Sobering, isn't it?"

"Sure fucking is. I'll check in later."

Jesus. The man was eighty years old, and from what Autumn mentioned, had a rich history, a long marriage, but all of that died when he did. Sad. I can't help but compare my own situation: my mother was the only family I knew until she passed away five years ago. I never knew my father. Sure I have friends, but no family, no real legacy to leave when I die.

I'm forty-four years old and other than my work, my years have little meaning. I've never given it any, but that has to change. I don't want to die alone and simply disappear.

Morbid thoughts I try to shake off when I step into the hospital. I stop by the nurses' station to check on any developments. Jen isn't there, but another nurse tells me Autumn's still resting and Dr. Larkin will be in to check on her. See if perhaps the tube can't come out tonight.

Just as I turn for Autumn's room, I see Evan come out and intercept him in the hallway.

"Where did you go last night?"

He looks shocked by my question, but then anger sets in. "Are you for fucking real? You're asking me that?"

"Just doing my job. It's not a difficult question. You left The Irish around eight thirty? Nine? Where did you go after that?" I persist.

"Home. I fucking went home. Brought Jen to her door and then walked home. Why this fixation on me? You think I could do something like this?" The kicker is, I believe every word he says. The hurt in his eyes is real. "I'd never do anything to hurt her. Or anyone for that matter. Jesus Christ, I can't believe you'd even consider that."

Suddenly tired, I run my hands over my face. "I don't. I mean, I did, I fucking looked into my own men to see if anyone stood out. If anyone paid specific interest to Autumn. You're one of the few people she actually knows. I just want to get her safe."

"Yeah, well let me tell you, you're barking up the wrong tree. Wasting time focusing on me is not going to get her any safer." He gives me a hard stare before stepping around me. I hear his footsteps fade as he walks away.

Autumn's eyes are closed when I walk in, the sound of the machine still helping her breathe a steady rhythm in the room. Her hair, still dull with soot, is spread out over her pillow. Her glasses are sitting on the nightstand, my guess is someone found them at the scene and Evan brought them over. They hadn't been there before.

Nor had the envelope they were sitting on.

The hair on my neck stands straight up and I pull my phone from my pocket.

"Ramirez? Get your ass over here and bring a fingerprint kit and evidence bags. We've got a situation."

Using my phone, I snag a few pictures, before grabbing a pair of medical gloves from a box hanging on the wall and snapping them on. The night table is on wheels, and I carefully roll it to the far side of the room, pulling the recliner in front to block it. I don't want anyone touching it—even accidentally—until we've gone over it with a fine-tooth comb. I just hope the hospital is as clean as it proclaims to be, and that nightstand was wiped clean after the last patient, or the thing could be covered in prints.

Next my eye falls on the door handles. Another place anyone coming into the room would have to have touched. A long shot, granted, but you never know. I pull off my gloves, leave them inside out and slide them over the handles, propping the door open.

It's all I can do for now until Ramirez gets here, and I can leave her side to get a clear account of who all visited her room during my absence.

Taking a seat on the stool next to her bed, I rest my head in my hands, wondering if I have lost my touch. Not only had I left her room earlier, under the assumption she'd be safe in the hospital, I'd also just basically dismissed Evan from my list of possible suspects not ten minutes ago, and here he is, back at the fucking top. My judgment is off.

A tug on my shirt has me turn to find Autumn's worried green eyes blink up at me.

"Hey." I reach out and stroke my hand over her hair. She scans the room and turns back to me with a questioning look. I consider lying to her, but just for a minute. "Someone left another note. Here. In your room."

* * *

Autumn

My hands get cold and clammy at his words.

With my mind still sluggish, it takes me a moment to reach a full understanding of the implication. Whoever almost burned my house down, had the balls to come into this room.

And I was too fucking drugged to even notice.

No more sedatives.

"Let's see if we can get that tube out, shall we?" A smiling —and clearly oblivious—Dr. Landis walks into the room, one of the nurses behind him, pushing a cart.

Instead of leaving the room, Keith merely rounds my bed and stands guard on the other side, giving the doctor space to examine me.

"Your blood work came back much better and your throat looks less irritated. We'll give this a shot." He dons gloves and carefully peels the tape used to anchor the tube, away from my cheeks. It stings, pulling the fine hair up by the roots. Guess it saves me a wax job. "Now, this part won't be pleasant. You'll want to cough, but it's important you keep that to a minimum so as not to aggravate your airway any more."

Unpleasant is an understatement. It feels like my lungs are coming out along with the tube. My throat spasms and I fight to keep from coughing. The nurse offers a drink of water from the straw she aims at my mouth. It helps a little.

"Give it a few minutes before you even try to talk," Dr. Landis says, patting my shoulder. "We'll keep you on an IV for a little longer, just in case. Everything goes well, that can come out at the next shift change, and you'll be heading home tomorrow morning."

I wince at his words. Ironic, isn't it? Just a few weeks ago, I still had most of my belongings packed up in boxes. My place was just a temporary roof over my head, but in the short time since, it has become a home. Catalyst was Sophie and Roman's visit, but getting a sense of belonging through the friends I was making contributed greatly.

The nurse hands the cup to Keith, telling him I can take only little sips, before she follows the doc out of the room with her cart. As soon as they've gone, he moves back to the stool on the other side, forming a barrier between me and the door.

"Where is it..." I croak out, the effort resulting in a coughing spell that feels like I'm swallowing razorblades.

"Goddammit, Red. You were told no talking two freaking minutes ago." He shoves a straw in my mouth, scowling as I take a few sips. "Ramirez will be here any minute to collect the evidence. It's still on the nightstand, I haven't had a look at it yet."

* * *

Keith

Not even a minute later he walks in, evidence collection case in his hand. I point him to the bedside table, and leave a still slightly drowsy Autumn in his care, as I go to get some answers.

The same nurse, who was in the room earlier, is working on the computer behind the counter.

"Excuse me..." I take a quick peek at her name tag. "Lisa, were you on all afternoon?"

"Along with Marjory and Faiza."

"I need to know who all visited Ms. McCoy's room between noon and now."

"We're not required to keep track of that," she says, a little defensively.

"I get that, but you would notice, wouldn't you?" I prompt.

"Well, I did see the red-haired guy go in. The one you were arguing with earlier? He was barely in there. I didn't see anyone else."

"How about your colleagues? Would they have seen anything?"

"Possibly. I can ask them when they get back from break," she says with a shrug.

"That would be great. In the meantime, are there any other rooms empty? I'd like to have Ms. McCoy moved."

The woman's eyebrow shoots up. "We can't just move people around."

I lean over the counter, handing her my badge. "The name is Blackfoot, Durango PD. We can if the room they're in becomes evidence in an investigation." That seems to impress her enough, and she points to the door at the end of the hall. "That one is free. I'll switch her name tag to the other door."

"Please don't. I'd prefer to keep a low profile for now."

It takes only a couple of minutes to move Autumn's bed into the other room.

"I'll have to notify the next shift," Lisa points out. We're standing in the hallway just as her colleagues walk up. "Did either of you guys see someone go into room 310?"

"Haven't paid attention," the older of the two, a heavy-set woman with graying hair admits.

"Yeah, I saw that cute guy," the young woman wearing a hijab says. "The one who was in here on the weekend when that injured firefighter was brought in. I figured he was part of Mr. Beacham's crew. I saw him go into 310."

"He is. Part of his crew, I mean," I clarify when the woman throws me a curious look. "They're both from Fire Station 2. Did you see anyone else?"

"He's a police detective," Lisa explains, addressing her colleagues in an almost whisper. "Investigating a case."

I turn to the younger woman. "Any chance you saw anyone else go in? Hanging around her room, maybe?"

She shakes her head. "No. I mean we had a bit of a rush after lunch, it's possible someone went in, but I didn't see it."

I thank them and head back inside the new room. Autumn's eyes are on me the moment I walk in.

"Mr. Bartik?" she finally asks—her voice still raw—when I take a seat next to her bed. I knew the question was coming, and judging by the look on her face, she's expecting the answer I have to give her.

"I'm sorry," I tell her, taking her hand between mine as her eyes close. "They got him out at the same time we got to you, and worked on him all the way to the hospital. He didn't make it. They suspect the smoke inhalation was too much for his body to take. An autopsy is scheduled for tomorrow, we'll hopefully know more then."

She nods, a few tears slipping from under her closed eyelids.

It's quiet in the room; the only sound the ticking of the plain clock hanging over the door, marking minutes going by. I think she's fallen asleep again when her eyes suddenly open.

"He has nobody."

"I know."

"He wants to be buried next to his wife. He told me he

misses her every day—misses waking up to her in the mornings. She's buried at Greenmount Cemetery. I told him I'd take him to see her, but I never got the chance."

"You still can," I tell her softly. "You can make sure he gets to rest right by her side."

CHAPTER 18

Autumn

"I'm fine, Sophie."

I roll my eyes at Keith, who is grinning behind the wheel when I repeat myself again.

I was just released and he's driving by my place to pick up a few things I might need on the way to his house. I have no idea where he lives, the only thing he told me is his place is secure, so I'm going willingly. My first reaction when he reiterated I was coming with him, had been to dig my heels in, but frankly the thought of staying at some hotel by myself makes me uncomfortable. I don't generally scare easily, but I am now.

Stupid hospital rules had me wheeled out in a damn wheelchair—despite my assurances there's nothing wrong with my legs—and Keith insisted on helping me into the passenger seat. I was about to tear into him for treating me like an invalid when Sophie's call came in on his phone. Mine had been on the counter in the kitchen and apparently didn't survive the fire.

"Are you s-sure you don't want m-me to come until you're back on your feet?" The hands-free setting projects Sophie's sniffly voice through the car's sound system.

"Positive," I say as firmly as I can with my raspy voice. I know I sound horrible, which is probably why Sophie keeps persisting, but aside from that I'm fine. "Chief is right, honey, I may not be the safest person to be around. Don't blame him for looking out for you."

"But who'll be looking out for you?"

"I will," Keith's deep rumble cuts in, spreading a warm feeling from the pit of my stomach.

It's a strange sensation, to be at the receiving end of things. I'm usually the one to do the caring for. I've done that since I was ten years old and my father walked out the door, leaving my mother a mess.

"Keep her s-safe," Sophie says softly after a pause.

"My house has a top-of-the-line security system, and we'll pick up a new phone for her today. She'll be able to stay in touch with you," he assures her, and I throw him a grateful smile.

He pulls up along the curb in front of my place, and my heart sinks at the sight of the caution tape still surrounding the mostly burned porch and the blackened house behind it.

"We can't go in the back—it's been boarded up—and the porch is unstable but a stepladder has been rigged up to get in the front. It's still considered a crime scene. My guys are patrolling regularly, to make sure some idiot doesn't decide to ransack the place. At least until we have a chance to clear out your belongings."

"And Joseph's," I add wistfully, a sharp stab of sadness hitting me square in the chest.

"And Joseph's," he echoes. "But first let's get you a few things to tide you over, and we'll brainstorm how to take care of the rest. I've already been in touch with a storage facility not far from the hospital, which has a large unit available. Temporarily," he adds quickly. "Until you can figure out what's next."

"Shit. I haven't even contacted the landlord yet," I point out, looking sideways at Keith's profile, who seems to be clenching his jaw.

"Be hard. Bartik *was* your landlord."

"What? I never knew that, I've always dealt with the real estate office and my rent was made out to Barnes and Finley, the law office on East 12th. I was under the impression the owners were out-of-towners."

"Guess he preferred it that way. I imagine living next door to your tenants can be difficult at times. Especially at his advanced age. Easier to let an agency take care of it and avoid knocks on your door every time a tap leaks."

"I suppose."

"Come, let's grab your things and get out of here."

I'm grateful he doesn't even question me climbing the ladder to get inside, but he does stay right behind me, making sure he can catch me if I fall. Something I'm very grateful for the moment we step inside. Already lightheaded from the small amount of exertion getting up the ladder—the wrecked state of my house has me sway on my legs—and Keith's arms instantly brace me.

"The upstairs is much better," he whispers in my ear, as my eyes take in the devastation.

The kitchen is unrecognizable, and in what was my living room, the furniture—blackened and still soggy—is shoved out of the way in a pile against the far wall. Nothing salvageable there. The pictures I'd so painstakingly hung just a couple of weeks ago hang dirty and lopsided on the wall.

Stepping out of Keith's hold, they're the first thing I salvage. The sum of my life represented in a handful of snapshots. He silently takes the stack of frames out of my hands and puts them on the floor by the door.

I'm doing my best not to mentally inventory all that might be lost, or I might lose it on the spot. Instead I head up the stairs, trying not to touch the layer of soot coating the walls. The smell inside the house has my throat spasm, and I launch into a coughing fit.

"You okay?" Keith asks, concerned. "Let me know if you want to go sit in the car. I can grab what you need."

"I'll be fine," I manage, forcing myself to breathe slowly in and out through the nose. It helps a bit.

My bedroom looks no different than normal. Nothing appears out of place, but here too everything is dirty and wet. I walk over to my nightstand and pick up my Kindle, still lying there. The screen is blank, and stubbornly stays that way, even after I try turning it on. I discard it on the bed. I can't deal with this right now.

"I brought a garbage bag," Keith says behind me. "We'll toss everything you need in there. It's all going to smell like smoke, but we'll wash it at my place. Don't think too hard right now."

Squeezing my eyes shut, I let his words bolster me before walking determinedly to my closet. Ignoring the fact even my clothes haven't escaped both water and soot, I grab a few random things and shove them in the bag Keith holds open. Shoes are next, a lot of them ruined beyond salvation, but I manage to secure a few pairs. I can't wait to get out of these borrowed hospital scrubs and lost-and-found sneakers. At least the stuff in my dresser drawers isn't in such bad shape. Underwear, T-shirts, shorts, and yoga pants all get dumped in the bag.

The bathroom is next. Much the same as the rest of the house, so I ignore anything that was out in the open. Toothbrush, razor, hair stuff—it can all be replaced. I pull open the top drawer, holding my jewelry, and clear it out. Second drawer nets me a few toiletries that are still packaged and unopened; I promptly toss those in the bag as well. And the third drawer…*oh shit*.

Keith—who's leaning in the doorway—chuckles as I quickly slam that drawer shut.

Ignoring him—and the hot blush on my cheeks—I do a quick scan of the cupboard before straightening up. Instead of stepping aside to let me by, Keith moves farther into the bathroom, forcing me back before determinedly reaching for the bottom drawer.

"We'll bring this too," he says in a low voice as he pulls out Old Faithful: my purple, ten-speed, waterproof, full girth, G-spot tickler. "I'm sure we can find some use for it."

He tosses it in the bag and puts a hand on my elbow, steering me into the hallway. His deceptively innocent touch sends heat pooling between my legs.

"Anything you want to pick up on the way?" he asks when we get back into his SUV. "Or we can go home, get cleaned up first."

"Your place first," I manage, wheezing by the time I'm buckled in. Perhaps coming here hadn't been such a great idea. It's like sucking in air through a thin straw.

Keith takes one look at me and reaches in the back seat where he tossed the medication I was sent home with. "You're pale. Take a hit of this." He hands me an inhaler I was told to use as needed. "Two puffs," he orders, scanning the sheet of home care instructions they handed him.

Doing as he says, I can feel my airway relaxing within seconds and I send him a little smile of assurance. Only then does he start up his SUV and pull away from the curb. I have to admit, I'm curious to see where he lives. I just know it's somewhere off the beaten path.

That's confirmed when he takes a road leading out of town and into the mountains behind the college.

"It's not far," he assures me, and a few turns later, we end up on a quiet road with only a few houses nestled in the tree line on either side. Keith pulls into a long driveway going up to a good-sized, gorgeous, one-level log home with a green roof, peaked over the center of the house. Thick full logs support an open porch along the front, and I spot a couple of rocking chairs and a small table on one side. Perfect spot for morning coffee.

"Wow, this is beautiful."

"It's a nice spot. Just fifteen minutes from downtown but you wouldn't know it up here. It's quiet, just the way I like it."

He's right; I can't hear anything but the peaceful sounds of nature when I get out of his SUV. I never considered myself an outdoorsy person per se, but the beautiful setting and clean air may have just turned me into one.

Curious, I walk up to the house, the sound of a car door slamming behind me. The porch is a mere step up and I run my hand along one of the rough-hewn logs holding up its roof.

"Let me show you around," Keith offers, unlocking the rustic front door and carrying my stuff inside.

I follow him into a large main room that looks like it was taken straight from *Architectural Digest*. Exposed logs span the cathedral ceiling and line the walls. Either side of the spacious room has a hallway leading to the rest of the house. A large stone fireplace sits slightly off-center on the far wall, a worn tan leather couch and a couple of lazy chairs facing it. To the left of the entry is a dining area: a beautiful large harvest table, surrounded by six sturdy-looking dining chairs. The table is empty except for a pile of newspapers and a discarded coffee cup on the far end. I'm guessing that's where Keith has his morning coffee. Very little adorns the walls, other than a well-stocked bookcase and a few impressive racks of antlers. The only reminder of the twenty-first century is the large screen TV mounted over the fireplace, and the modern open kitchen, extending from the dining area toward the back, where stainless steel appliances gleam. I'm officially jealous.

"Let's get your stuff in the laundry and then I'll show you the rest."

I follow him down the hallway on the right, where he opens the first door to a small laundry room. I decline his offer to wash my stuff for me, already mortified enough without having him sort through my undies. He doesn't push it, just quickly explains the settings on the washer, before discreetly leaving me to do my own sorting.

The first load running, I go in search of Keith. Sticking my head into the next door, I find a full bathroom with a nice sized tub. Immediately across from it, facing the front of the house, is what looks to be a spare bedroom. A simple twin bed and nightstand the only furniture in the room.

"I'm in here," Keith's voice calls out from the end of the hallway where a door stands open.

He's perched on the edge of a desk, in what is clearly an office space, an impressive collection of monitors and assorted electronics behind him, and bookshelves lining the rest of available wall space. A club chair with footstool sits next to the front window, and on the other side of the room, French doors open to the outside where I can just see a little of an amazing view beyond. "You're welcome to use this space. There's enough to read, and I have Wi-Fi so feel free to use my computer." He indicates a notepad next to the large iMac on his desk. "I wrote down the password."

"Thank you," I mutter, wincing at the reminder my laptop didn't survive the fire.

My shoulders slump, thinking about the vast number of details comprising my life that will need to be restored somehow. I don't even know where to start. At least I was given a week's leave, hopefully enough to get a decent start on that.

"Not today," Keith mumbles, walking up to fold me in his arms, apparently able to read my body language. "Today you take a breath, tomorrow you make a list."

I nod my head against the comfort of his shoulder, taking a moment before I lift my head, finding his bent down already.

"Thank you," I repeat, after rising on my toes and brushing his lips lightly. "Now show me the rest of your dream home."

The other wing of the house is laid out much the same as this one, except the larger bathroom is on the front of the house, with a big walk-in shower and separate toilet. On the opposite side of the house is a room full of exercise equipment, and a large picture window facing the stunning view behind the house. The master bedroom is at the end of the hall, running the full depth of the house. The space is sparse, with a closet, a dresser, and a large bed matching the rustic features of the house. It faces the rear, where another set of French doors leads to a deck spanning the entire back. A second discarded coffee cup sits on the small table just outside, wedged between two rustic wooden chairs, showing it as another favored spot. I can see why.

What wasn't apparent, coming in the front, is the property sits right at the edge of a canyon; giving the impression you're sitting on top of the world.

"Can't imagine what it's like, waking up to this every morning," I say, half to myself, as I open the door and walk outside.

Resting my hands on the railing, I take in the view, when the heat of Keith's body braces me from behind.

"You don't have to imagine." His warm breath strokes the shell of my ear. "You're welcome in my bed."

CHAPTER 19

Keith

"What was on the note?"

I look up to where Autumn is curled up on my couch with a John Grisham book she found in my office. She's been quiet the last couple of hours. Withdrawn. I barely managed to get any lunch into her.

One moment she was warm in my arms, the next she disappeared to the other side of the house, when I took a call. After, when I went to look for her, I could hear water splashing in the guest bathroom and I assumed she was taking a bath. When I knocked on the door to check on her, she assured me she was fine.

I used the time to make a few more calls. I checked in with the station to see if there was any news from either the fire inspection or this morning's autopsy—there wasn't—and among other things, caught Ramirez up on my earlier conversation with Luna. She'd offered to have the far more advanced FBI lab take a closer look the evidence collected so far, including the latest note. I'm not about to turn down the offer of additional assistance, especially since we don't have a hell of a lot to go on.

I heard the tub drain and Autumn moving around—going in and out of the laundry room—and then the pad of her bare feet as she retreated into my office. At some point, while I was outside grabbing my laptop from the Tahoe, she'd come out and was sitting on the couch.

Other than her, "No thank you," to my offer of a drink or something to eat, she'd been silent, even when I put a sandwich and a bottle of water in front of her anyway. Figuring she needed a little time to adjust, I let her be, so her sudden question catches me off guard. It's the first time she's brought up the note.

She twists around, staring at me over the back of couch. Her intense gaze has me ignore my plan to blow her off and I answer truthfully instead.

"*You should've been grateful.*" I watch shock register on her face and walk over to sit beside her on the couch. I put my hand on her knee, but she scoots into the corner, pulling her knees to her chest defensively.

"For what?"

"Who knows?" I shrug, turning my body to face her, but leaving her some space. Time for full disclosure. "What we do know is that whoever it is knows you—or thinks he does—and we're pretty sure he's been watching."

"Watching?"

"His notes suggest his purpose shifted from a twisted need to please you, to anger directed at you. But even before the last note, his focus and methods changed with the first fire at your place."

"I don't get it, why?"

"The fire in your backyard? That was an impulse. Unplanned. It was also the night you and I went out for dinner, and ended up at the lookout point." I note the sudden blush on her cheeks at the reference with some satisfaction. "I got the call on the Delwood fire, dropped you off at home, and kissed you on the porch. Not even an hour later, your shed went up in flames. Luna suggested the two things might well be related."

I can feel the shift in the air the moment I mention her name. *Fuck*. In the past few days, the reason for Autumn's abrupt departure from the Irish that Saturday night had all but been forgotten. We'd had other things on our mind. Now I get why she booted it when I answered Luna's call earlier, although for the life of me I can't recall if I'd called her 'sweetheart' again. It's entirely possible.

Looks like some explanation is necessary, although I won't be able to fully explain my relationship with Luna. Some things are not mine to share.

"I've never exactly been a choir boy," I start, trying to get her to look at me. "But I've also never been a cheat, Red." Her eyes narrow on mine before they slide off into the distance again. "Luna is a friend. More of a sister, actually. When I said she and I have a history, I meant I met her back in college. When I was in my final year and she was a freshman, we bumped into each other at a party. I hadn't seen her in about eighteen years when she surfaced here in Durango, and despite the fact she's a kick-ass FBI agent now, and not a timid first-year student, I feel protective of her." From the look on her face I can tell she remains dubious, but that's as much detail as I'm able to give her. She'll have to trust me. "You'll meet her soon enough," I add. "Her office is helping out with the investigation. We often pool resources on serious cases."

Autumn looks about as eager at the prospect as she might if facing a root canal. Next thing I know, she tosses me a big, fake-ass smile. "Look, I appreciate the explanation, but you really didn't need to. Not like we're in a serious relationship or anything." I almost feel the walls coming up as she tries to bluff her way out.

"I call bullshit." She seems shocked at my calling her out. "What's happening here may not constitute a serious relationship yet, but I, for one, hope that's the direction we're moving in." I lean forward, into her space. "And don't try to deny you don't feel the same: you're the one who took off twice while I was on the phone with her, and all but froze when I mentioned her name just now." I reach out and hook my hand behind her neck, pulling her close enough so our noses almost touch. "Any feelings I have for her are purely platonic."

She twists from my hold and gets to her feet. "Right. Again, good talk, but not necessary. I'm going to check on my laundry." With that she disappears down the hall, and I throw myself back on the couch, running a frustrated hand through my hair. Figures, she wouldn't be easy to convince.

Guess this is what they call karma: after a lifetime of avoiding relationships, falling for the one woman who does some serious dodging of her own.

* * *

Autumn

Just a friend.

I almost snort out loud. Last time I heard those words, my father was comforting Mom in the kitchen, after coming home in the early hours of the morning again. He claimed—like I'd heard him do a few times before—he was helping *a friend,* who happened to be a woman living just down the block. I'd seen her before at church, sitting just a few pews ahead of us. She was pretty, and I'd catch her tossing little smiles over her shoulder at my father. He told my mother it was the Christian thing to do, helping a neighbor in need, and Mom swallowed it down like she had every other time. He managed her well.

I didn't understand at the time what that 'need' exactly entailed, but I learned quickly when my father up and disappeared one night and never returned. The woman down the street disappeared right along with him, and I was left with a broken-hearted alcoholic, who had no one but her much too young daughter to listen to her woes.

Maybe that's why I ended up marrying a man who could barely order his own dinner at a restaurant without my input. His passive nature seemed like a safe option at the time.

Keith is not like that. At all.

He seems to know his own mind pretty well. He also leaves room for me to know my own. Most of the time anyway. To be honest, he's not really given me any indication I'm being manipulated. It's just my own ingrained lack of trust, which has me automatically disbelieve what could be a very valid explanation. My need for self-protection is so strong I'd rather risk being wrong than being hurt.

For all my external bluster, pretending to be all adult; I'm still that fucked-up, insecure adolescent inside.

Folding the last of my shirts, I take the stack of clean laundry into the spare bedroom, closing the door behind me. The small built-in closet is mostly empty—aside from some old sports paraphernalia—and I easily fit my things on the shelves. I quickly replace the scrubs I'd been forced to put on again after having my shower, with a pair of yoga pants and a shirt. Both are blissfully free of any lingering smoke smell, and for the first time in days, I'm feeling a little more like myself, albeit dead on my feet.

Stepping out of the bedroom, I hear voices and to my surprise, Jack—my tabby—comes sauntering into the hallway, as if he's lived here for donkey's years. Still, when I scoop him up, he curls right into me, breaking into a satisfied purr right away.

"Hey, buddy. How'd you get here? Is your sister here too? Where's Gizmo? She hiding somewhere? I bet she is, always a bit of a chicken, right, big boy?"

I'm rambling senselessly—as I often do to my cats—when I walk into the living room, where both Keith and Detective Ramirez gawk at me with amused grins. Whatever. I talk to my cats, I'm not gonna apologize for it.

"Thank you so much." I reach out a hand to the detective.

"Most welcome. The little girl scooted down the other hallway," he says, pointing toward Keith's bedroom.

"She's shy," I tell him by way of explanation.

"Wasn't so shy this morning when I woke up with her ass in my face," he says with a wink. "I picked up a couple of things for them over the weekend, I'll just go grab those from the car. You'll need them." He's back quickly, carrying a couple of large Walmart bags. "Here's their food, litter box, a couple of toys, and some bowls," he says, handing Keith one of the bags, before shoving the other one at me. "And this is the shit your boyfriend told me to pick you up. Hope it's the right stuff."

I take a peek inside, and the first thing I spot lying on top is a bulk pack of double-A batteries. Feeling a blush creep up, I mumble, "I'll just put this stuff away. Thank you so much." But before I can make my escape, Tony's voice holds me back.

"Oh, almost forgot about this." He pulls my purse from his shoulder and hands it to me, a little the worse for wear, but a welcome sight nonetheless. "I salvaged it from the house after the fire inspector went through. I wiped the outside, but restrained myself and didn't peek inside." I smile at his teasing, dropping the Walmart bag on the table so I have both my hands free.

"You rock," I tell him, digging through the contents to find my handy metal card case. It holds all my important cards: driver's license, bank and credit cards, and especially the various insurance cards. Those will save me a lot of grief. I triumphantly pull it out and flip it open, showing Keith what's inside.

"That'll help." He nods with only half of a smile, before turning to Tony. "Did you get the other stuff?"

"It's all in there." He points at the bag I dumped on the table and Keith immediately starts rummaging through it, surfacing with a familiar white Apple box. "You should be able to call your provider and have them transfer your account over right away."

"Thank you."

I give first Tony a quick hug, who smiles smugly at a scowling Keith, and holds on a little too long. The scowl disappears when I step into his arms and slide mine around his waist, tucking my head under his chin. I don't move, not even when Tony bids his goodbyes, citing, "Shit to do," before he walks out the door.

Keith's large hand in the middle of my back slides up under my hair and curves around my neck. "You okay?" I feel the reverberation of his deep rumble in his chest.

"I will be. I'll be even better if Boots and Ziggy show up."

"*When*," he corrects me. "When they show up. They're probably still freaked out and hiding, but they'll be scrounging for food soon, I'm sure."

"That reminds me." I try to step back, but Keith holds me firmly in place. "I should check on Gizmo. Feed them"

"You can check on Gizmo after you kiss me," he says, already lowering his head. "I've been starving for days."

His kiss is hungry but not rough. Fingers twisted in my

hair, his tongue strokes firmly, turning my mind a delicious blank—with every fiber completely focused on the sensation of his body surrounding me—consuming me.

When I feel my feet are no longer touching the floor, he lifts his head, looking at me from under his heavy brow.

"I don't think I'll ever get enough of your taste." Not sure what to say to that, I smile instead. "Go," he urges, releasing me suddenly. "Check on your critters before I forget you were just released from the hospital."

* * *

That night, after a simple dinner of sandwiches and soup Keith threw together while I was having a nap, I'm working on my to-do list. Both cats are curled up on the couch beside me, when I notice Keith talking on the phone in his office.

"I'll swing by to pick them up," I hear him say, followed by an already familiar creak of his office chair, and then footsteps coming down the hall.

I tilt my head back when he leans over the couch, his hair hanging down like a curtain tickling my chin as he bends to brush my lips.

"I have to head into the office for a bit. A few reports came in, and I want to look them over before tomorrow," he explains, and a feeling of panic claws up my throat.

"Can't someone bring them?" My voice sounds a little too high-pitched.

"You're safe here, Red. I swear. Very few people know where I live, and I'd like to keep it that way—especially now—which is why I'm going to pick them up. Tony would, but he's already home and I don't want ask him again. Look," he says, coming around the couch and perching on the coffee table in front of me.

Already I'm feeling stupid, but even more so at seeing the

guilty look on Keith's face. Seriously, for a woman so proudly independent, I'm acting ridiculously needy.

"It's fine. Never mind me," I wave him off, embarrassed, but he continues anyway.

"There are twelve cameras in total, covering the front of the house, the driveway and the back. There is a floodlight at the base of the driveway on a motion sensor, and two more—"

"Keith," I stop him, my hand to his mouth. "It's fine, really. I'm just a little skittish. Ignore me. My phone is all set up, if there's anything, I can always call. Please, just go, I feel bad enough keeping you from your work."

"Fair enough," he concedes, kissing my fingers before he gets up. "I shouldn't be more than an hour. Want me to pick you up anything from town?"

"I'm fine, thanks, but, Keith? Do you think I could pick up my car tomorrow?"

"Sure thing," he promises, "lock the door behind me, will you?"

I lock the door, grab the remote, snuggle with my guys on the couch, and find something mindless to watch on TV.

I must've been exhausted, because it doesn't take long for me to drift off. I don't even notice when some time later, Keith's strong arms pick me up from the couch, carry me into his bedroom, and tuck me into bed.

CHAPTER 20

Keith

"Meow..."

I blink my eyes open to find one the cats—I think her name was Gizmo—sitting on my chest, staring at me intently.

"Meow."

Autumn snuggles into my side, muttering something unintelligible.

Early morning light streams in the doors to the deck, and a peek at my clock lets me know it's probably time to get up. Not that I want to get out of bed.

When I got back last night, I found Red curled up on the couch with her cats, fast asleep. I was well aware she'd put her stuff in the spare bedroom, which is all hers to use, but there wasn't really a question when I picked her up that I would carry her to my bed. Of course the cats followed her there, and by the time I put my work aside and headed to bed myself, I had to battle two territorial cats to claim a spot next to her.

And one of them is currently sharpening its nails on my chest, determined to get someone's attention.

"All right," I whisper, snatching the thing up as I roll out of bed, trying not to wake Autumn. Tucking Gizmo under my arm, I pad down the hall to the kitchen, where cat number two, Jack, is sitting patiently by the food bowls. "Not sure how much you guys eat," I mumble as I set the girl down and grab the kibble from the cupboard. Both cats make it impossible to move, weaving between my legs, rubbing their bodies against me. "Guys, I'm gonna step on you if you don't knock that off. Do you wanna eat or not?"

"*Meow...*" This from a very impatient Gizmo. Jack is quiet, appearing to me more the strong silent type, but the moment I put the bowls down, both cats attack like they haven't been fed in weeks.

"Jesus, you guys almost took my fingers off."

"They're passionate about their food."

My head shoots up to find Autumn leaning against the doorway—no glasses, wearing just the shirt she'd been wearing yesterday, minus the pants I pulled off her before tucking her in—a grin on her face.

"Shit, I thought I was being quiet. Hoped to let you sleep a bit longer."

"And miss you bonding with my cats?" Her teasing smile has me stalk up and pull her in my arms.

"Are you making fun of me?" I rumble, reveling in the feel of her body against my now fully awake one.

"I wouldn't dare. Besides, you were pretty adorable." I respond with a growl as I walk her backward down the hall and into the bedroom. "What are you doing?" she asks, but the gleam in her eyes as she blinks up tells me she knows.

"I was going to make coffee." I back her up all the way to the edge of the bed and topple her onto the mattress, landing on top of her. "But I think I'll make you come first."

"I haven't brushed my teeth," she mumbles when my eyes zoom in on her sleep-swollen lips.

"I don't care."

"You haven't brushed yours," she tries again when I lean in.

"You don't care either."

She doesn't. The moment my mouth touches hers; she parts her lips and invites me in.

Kissing Autumn is better than any sexual experience I can recall. She gives all of herself in the way she eagerly responds to my touch, and in that moment, makes me feel like the center of her universe. The way her nails scrape my scalp when she tangles her fingers in my hair has every receptor sparking an electrical charge I can feel under my skin. The arch of her body as it looks for contact, has my blood roaring through my veins and flooding my cock.

A rush of emotions scrambles my brain. Hungry. Raw. *Primal.*

In an unorganized tangle of hands and limbs, the few scant pieces of fabric separating us are discarded. Skin to skin. Her legs restlessly rub along mine, as my hips almost involuntary buck, needing inside her. In an attempt to slow down the frantic pace, I break the kiss and trail lips and tongue along her jaw, down her neck, and over her chest. One hand lifts a breast, soft and pliable in my palm, and my mouth closes over the tight nipple, sucking deep. Her soft cry encourages me to give equal attention to the other.

Sliding off the bed to my knees, I lift her legs, bracing her feet against my shoulders as I pull her ass to the edge. Her relaxed body is spread wide open for me, showing a greater trust than I perhaps deserve.

There are no words, just sounds of two people lost to sensation.

I take my time exploring the slick, deep pink labia with

my fingers, using the pad of a finger to uncover the smooth little nub from under its hood. When her hips come off the bed helplessly, I shove a hand under her ass and lift her to my mouth. With my lips and tongue working her clit, I slide a thumb inside her, rubbing hard against the back wall of her pussy. The moment I feel her fingers tighten in my hair, and the flutter of her muscles around me, I replace it with my tongue, stabbing deep as I drive her to the edge. Exploring with the slick digit, I find her small puckered hole, and penetrate the tight muscle.

Almost instantly she ignites, crying out as her thighs trap my head. She rides my mouth on her pussy and my thumb up her ass hard, until nothing but shakes and shivers remain. It's then I notice the labored rasp of her breath.

Fuck. I'm an idiot. I'd almost forgotten.

Grabbing her inhaler from the nightstand, I climb back on the bed, pull her in my arms, and hold her until the hit of medication relaxes her airways.

"As much as I'd love to stay just like this, I have to go into the office. I'm going to hop in the shower."

I swing my legs over the side, bend down to kiss her lips, and pad over to the bathroom. The sight of her, naked and languid, with her red hair spread out on my pillow when I look back at her, I almost cave. However, I have a serial arsonist, and now murderer—with a hard-on for my Red—to catch. I can't afford to slack off. Determined, I go into the bathroom, turn on the water, and step under the shower. My cock still painfully hard, I lean a hand against the wall and with the other try to relieve some pressure.

"Shhhh," she says, as she steps under the spray behind me. She presses her front against my back and reaches around, palming my erection. "Let me."

Her grip is firm and her strokes are strong. It doesn't take long before I feel my balls pull up tight and a tingle shoot from my asshole up my back. Mouth open and my head thrown back, I cover her hand with mine and in a punishing rhythm, until I find relief, long strands of cum mixing with the water and pooling down the drain.

I'm instantly cold when Autumn's touch disappears, but she's back right away, her hands washing me with soap. With my hands braced on the wall in front of me I let her tend to me.

"Don't let me wake up from this dream," I say under my breath.

Warm lips press a kiss between my shoulder blades.

"Not a dream, honey," she murmurs, again with the endearment.

"This is too good to be anything else."

* * *

Autumn

"Let me give you Detective Ramirez's number. He's in charge of the investigation and will be able to tell you when you can access the site."

I rattle the number off the card I have for Tony to the claims adjuster, who promises to be in touch once he's completed his damage assessment. Then I scratch one more thing off my list.

I feel like I've been on the phone and computer all morning, talking to utilities to cancel services, setting up a temporary new forwarding address with USPS to have my mail delivered here for the time being, and talking to my boss at Mercy. The latter insisted I do not show my face until I'm completely cleared by Dr. Landis. Poor Sandy will have to cover for me. I also made a call to Sophie, who again offered to come. She was only partly assured I was well looked after, but her mood improved greatly when I confessed I'd slept in Keith's bed last night. She seemed resigned when I promised to come visit her as soon as I could, and in the meantime would keep in touch.

The only thing I haven't tackled is poor Mr. Bartik. I frankly don't know where to start. When I mentioned it this morning, Keith said he wanted to help with the arrangements, but first he needed to go over the coroner's report with his guys, to make sure nothing was missed. After that he'd talk to the coroner about releasing the body.

A piece of toast is all I had for breakfast, and I'm getting hungry. It's already almost two o'clock. Keith's fridge yields a decent selection and I fill a plate with some roasted chicken, a few slices of old cheddar, and a couple of cherry tomatoes. I refill my coffee cup and carry it down the hallway, and through the bedroom where I open the French doors to the deck. It's gorgeous. Not too warm with a nice breeze coming up from the canyon below.

Yeah, I could easily become an outdoorsy person from this vantage point. Looking out over unspoiled nature with the comforts of a beautiful, fully outfitted home behind me.

The cats have joined me out on the deck, sniffing around and exploring. There's nowhere for them to go, and they curiously stick their heads through the railing. I wonder if I'll ever find Boots and Ziggy. Both are chipped, but that only helps if they are found. Overcome with fatigue and my head filling with sad thoughts, I lean it back against the side of the house.

"There you are."

I startle awake at the sound of Keith's soft voice, right next to my ear, and straighten in my chair. Stiff muscles have my face twist in a wince and he immediately crouches down in front.

"Are you okay?" He reaches out and puts a hand along my jaw.

Grateful for the comfort, I close my eyes and press my cheek to his palm. "I'm fine."

"Every time I hear you say that I believe you less," he mumbles, leaning in to kiss my forehead.

"What are you doing home? I didn't expect you 'til later." From the tightening of his observant eyes, I gather my radical change of subject does not go unnoticed. Undoubtedly he'll get back to it later. If I've learned one thing about Keith, in the short time I've known him, the man has dogged tenacity.

"It's almost five. I tried calling a few times to see if you wanted me to pick up some dinner, but when you didn't answer, I got worried and came straight home instead."

"No wonder I'm stiff," I conclude, as Keith gets out of the way so I can get up and stretch. "I slept a good two hours sitting in that chair."

"You probably needed it."

"I'm sorry I worried you. I was talking to the insurance company and must've left my phone in your office when I went to grab some lunch. Are you done working?"

I watch him grab Jack—who somehow got on top of the railing and was teetering precariously—and tuck him under his arm. "Never quite done, but I'm not going back to the office tonight. There's a few things we need to go over, but let's see what we can come up with for dinner first." He leads the way inside, and carrying my plate and mug, I round up Gizmo and follow him.

Ten minutes later, I'm sitting on a stool at the kitchen island, where I was relegated by Keith, watching in amazement as he drops another round of Navajo fry bread in the cast iron pan with hot oil. As it cooks, he continues to chop jalapeños that he adds to the bowl of shredded chicken. Next are some shallots, a chopped green pepper, and a decent amount of salsa from the monster jar I'd spotted in his fridge. I wince when he uses his fingers to flip the fry bread over in the pan, but it doesn't seem to bother him.

"My mouth is watering already," I inform him, the smell of the fried dough waking up my stomach.

"Not much longer. I just need to grate some cheese, throw it all under the broiler for a minute or two and we can eat."

Fishing the last one from the pan, I watch him deftly fill the breads with the chicken mixture, top them with cheese, and arrange them folded into a baking dish he shoves into the oven.

"Oh. My. God. I love this," I announce around a mouthful the delicious flavors. Messy as all get out, but definitely worth the sauce running down my chin.

"I can see that," Keith deadpans, biting into his own with similar results.

I love this. Amid the chaos of my life, spending time here with him—relaxed and laid back, sharing an honest, uncomplicated meal—feels like an oasis. His calm presence seems to dull the protective barbs I usually surround myself with, and I find myself changing—opening up.

"Did you know the old man had severe asthma?" he asks suddenly, stopping me from voicing my thoughts aloud.

"Joseph? No. He didn't mention it."

"Yes, the guys found a corticosteroid inhaler on the floor by his bedside table and another one in the medicine cabinet in his bathroom. The coroner suspects the smoke may have triggered a massive asthma attack. I'm thinking he may have been disoriented and accidentally knocked his inhaler on the floor and out of reach."

I wipe my mouth to hide my sadness, before asking, "Does that make it not murder?"

"Oh, it's murder, whatever way you look at it. Premeditation makes the difference."

"Good. I want him to go away for a very long time for what he did."

"Working on that, Red. Which is what I need to talk to you about. Tony collected prints from your original room in the hospital, and there is one palm print on the door we cannot trace back to anyone who we know entered your room after you were admitted."

"So you think that's his? When he dropped off the envelope?"

"It's possible. We confirmed with the cleaning crew that the handles on every door in the hospital are cleaned every morning and every night. Part of their routine to ensure as sterile as possible an environment."

"That's good, right?"

"It is, but those prints only help if we have something to compare it to. At this point, it could be anyone walking in off the street. We need to narrow it down." He reaches over the table and grabs my hands. "We think this person is somehow connected to the hospital. He seems to have information that wasn't exactly public record. Like where you live and what hospital room he could find you in after he set your house on fire. I want to send a few of our guys to check your offices for prints. It's the only area that is relatively contained in terms of who comes in. It's possible he's been in there at some point."

CHAPTER 21

Keith

"Did you get the storage units sorted out?"

I'm standing in the open door, waiting for Autumn to grab her bag.

We have an appointment with the funeral home in twenty minutes, and she's annoyed I insisted on picking her up. Tony helped me get her car up here yesterday—mostly so she doesn't feel so locked away—but I much prefer driving her myself. Now that she's starting to feel a little better—and therefore is getting restless—her barbs are starting to show again.

Not that I mind, her feisty spirit is one of the things that attracted me to her to begin with. It's an intrinsic part of who she is.

"Yes, of course I sorted them out," she grumbles, following me to the SUV. "I just don't know why the hell we need to empty out the entire house over the weekend."

"First of all, *we* doesn't apply. You don't see the doc until Monday, and you're not going back in that house without an all clear," I remind her, which earns me an eye roll. "The old man's asshole lawyer has made it clear he wants repairs to start next week, so he can get the house on the market as soon as possible. If we don't clear it out, it could all end up in a dumpster. Besides, I've got a couple of friends who are available this weekend and offered to lend a hand for beer and pizza."

She doesn't say anything else, just buckles in and stares out the window as I drive down to the road. She hasn't really been out of the house since I brought her home on Monday.

The Barnes of Barnes and Finley was a real piece of work. He'd shown up at the police station this week, demanding the house be released immediately. He'd waved around a copy of the old man's will that stipulated him as executor. One look at the document clarified his need for urgency: aside from the single listing of the Make-A-Wish Foundation as beneficiary of the will, twenty-five percent of the proceeds of the sale of the house were destined for his own pocket. *Bloodsucker*. Joseph Bartik's body was barely cold.

The one bit of good news the guy brought was Bartik had been smart enough to prepay into a funeral package offered by Hood Mortuary, a local, reputable funeral home. Seeing as Barnes showed no interest whatsoever in that part of his obligation, I was able to use the release of an empty house on Monday as leverage to allow Autumn to make the final arrangements.

I still wasn't going to let her go alone.

"Will he be there?" she asks when we turn into the parking lot.

"Who, Barnes?"

"No. Joseph."

"He's been here since yesterday," I inform her, pulling into an empty space. "Why?"

"Do you think I could see him?"

I turn to her and see she's struggling to keep her composure. "We could ask if that's possible, if that's what you really want."

"It's not so much about what I want, but about what he deserves."

I'm not entirely clear what that means, but she obviously does and that's enough for me.

The woman who walks us through the funeral arrangements for next Tuesday, does not seem surprised by the request. She simply makes a phone call, asking someone to have Mr. Bartik prepared for a visit, and directs us to a small room down the hall.

"Take as much time as you need," the somber-looking gentleman wheeling the casket in announces. He lifts the lid and backs out of the room.

I hear Autumn take in a deep breath before approaching. I keep a step behind, just in case.

"I wish I could've made you more dinners, and you could've told me more stories, but I'm grateful having known you at all." Her whispered words soften even further. *"I'm so sorry."*

Breaks my heart when I see her lean in and kiss the old man's cold cheek. It bothers me she feels any responsibility at all. I follow her determined steps out and find her already waiting by the passenger side of the Tahoe after thanking the funeral director, who popped her head out of her office when I passed. I purposely wait to unlock the door until I can open it for her. She gets in and stares straight forward; her hands clasped in her lap.

"This is not on you." There is no response except for the small muscle twitch along her jaw. Leaning in, I reach for her, curving my hand around her face and turning her to me. "You don't carry any responsibility here."

"I know," she says sadly, covering my hand with her own. "But that doesn't make him any less dead."

I can't argue that.

Kissing her lightly on the lips, I make sure she's buckled in before I round the car and get behind the wheel. "Anywhere else you'd like to go?"

"Can we stop at a drug store? There's a few things I'm running out of."

"Sure, but did you check the bathroom cupboard? I have a few things stockpiled." A tiny smile plays on her lips as she turns to me.

"I did, and I'm thrilled to report that your supplies don't include tampons and pads. That would've been of concern, to be honest."

"Is that why you insisted on sleeping in the other room last night? You got your period?" I press her. I have to admit, when she announced after dinner last night she wanted a good night's rest and would sleep in the guest room, I wasn't too pleased. I didn't see the point since she slept beside me the past couple of nights, but I didn't want to argue with her —she didn't seem to be feeling well—so I let it be. It all makes a little more sense now.

"Yup. Fun times."

"Why didn't you just say so?" I point out, steering the car toward Walgreens.

"It's not really the kind of stuff you advertise."

"Why not?" I persist. "It happens. No reason to go hide in another room. For fuck's sake, I thought I'd done something to piss you off."

"Sorry, I'm just not used to it—this," she says, waving her hand between us.

"New for me too, but I always figured that kind of basic stuff is part and parcel of sharing space with someone. Like me warning you this morning to steer clear of the master bathroom for half an hour so the air could clear. Just a heads-up." I glance over to see her grin. "What?"

"It was pretty bad," she admits, chuckling.

"You were warned." I grin back.

"I needed my toothbrush."

By the time we get to Walgreens, she doesn't even argue when I go inside with her. While she hits the aisle with feminine products, I grab a bonus pack of condoms and some air freshener. We meet at the checkout and burst out laughing when the cashier does a double take at our collection of purchases.

* * *

Autumn

"Whatcha cookin'?"

I swing around at the sound of Tony's voice stopping me mid-chorus. Singing along to Aretha Franklin is my secret pleasure. Except I don't think it's a secret anymore; Tony is right behind me, peeking into the pan of meat sauce I'm cooking for tonight's lasagna. Keith is not far behind and rudely shoves the other man to the side, only to bend down and give my neck a little love bite. Possessive. Barely shy of thumping his chest. Still, it makes me smile.

"Making lasagna," I announce, leaning back against Keith when he slips his arms around me.

"Enough for one more?"

"Absolutely."

I grin at Tony, who seems at home enough to dive in the fridge and fish out a couple of beers.

"Want one?" He holds up a bottle, but I pass.

I normally would have at least one or two drinks a night, but I haven't had anything since the hospital. Don't really miss it either. I haven't really seen Keith drink anything either, until now. Probably more of a social thing for him. For some reason that pleases me. I know I already walk a fine line being a regular lone drinker, since my mother was a raging alcoholic. They say it can be a familial affliction, and I really don't want to go down that road.

"How long before dinner?" Keith asks, his chin on my shoulder, and his easy affection in front of his friend and colleague warms me from the toes up.

"Forty-five minutes or so?"

"Great. Gives us some time to work on my truck." He hooks a finger under my chin and twists my head back to plant a hard kiss on my lips, before letting me go.

"What's wrong with your truck?" I ask when he's already on his way out of the kitchen.

"Not the Tahoe. I picked up an old 1949 Chevy truck a while ago we're working on. We'll be in the garage, just holler when you want us in."

The garage is separate from the house, set back under the trees off to the side. I'd never really ventured out there, but I sure as hell will when dinner is ready. Keith never struck me as a man with hobbies, but finding out he has one only piques my interest.

It takes me a few minutes to assemble the lasagna. I slide it in the oven and am about to start on a salad when a ping on my phone alerts me to a text message. Assuming it's Sophie or one of the other girls, I wash my hands before swiping the screen, planning to give them a call back, but the message is not from them.

***Unknown number:* Hope you don't mind Jen gave me your number. You disappeared off the face of the earth. Wonder where you went. How are you?**

I'm puzzled and immediately call Jen's number. She answers on the second ring.

"Geeze, way to disappear," are the first words she says.

"Sorry about that. I should've stayed in touch. It took me a couple of days to get set up with a new phone."

"Where are you?" she asks, and I open my mouth to answer before I reconsider. If she's given out my phone number, how easy would it be to give out my location? Probably smarter to play it safe.

"Hey, I was wondering, did you share my number with anyone?" I answer her question with one of my own.

"Uhh. I may have. Why? Was I not supposed to? I thought you guys were friendly, so I didn't really think twice. He was looking for you. Wanted to know if I knew how you were."

"Who was it?"

"Evan, of course," she responds, as if that is a foregone conclusion.

"I see. All right, I guess that's okay, but next time please just let me know if someone is looking for me? I'd really appreciate it."

"Sure thing." I can hear in her voice she's a bit miffed, but that can't be helped. I get it, from what I've seen she's more than a little infatuated with the guy, and she probably didn't want to turn him down, but that doesn't make it okay.

"And for the record, I'm doing much better, thanks for your concern. I really didn't mean to keep you in the dark."

"It's those fires, isn't it? I remember thinking what a coincidence it is those started just as you moved here. Then your house with you in it. Someone is seriously pissed off at you."

I'm a little taken aback by her words, but she's not lying. Someone is pissed at me, and I'd do well to remember that. I've been lulled into a false sense of security here, but that text I assume is from Evan, illustrates how feeble that security really is.

"So it seems, and it cost a kind, innocent old man his life," I remind her.

"I'm sorry," she says sounding a little more contrite. "I'm sorry for handing out your number too. I really didn't think it would be a problem. I didn't think, period."

"It's okay. Things are just a little surreal now. Anyway, I should be there to see Dr. Landis for a follow-up on Monday, are you working?"

"Eleven to three."

"I'll try to pop down to see you then."

When I hang up, I text a quick response.

***Me*: I'm getting better. Thanks.**

There is no reply.

Salad made, I turn off the oven, and head over to the garage, where two grimy, half-naked men are bent over an engine that looks cleaner than the rest of the run-down truck, classic rock playing on an old radio.

Both guys are drool-worthy: Keith is bigger, wider in the shoulders and chest, but Tony is ripped, not an ounce of fat on him.

I clear my throat and get two sets of eyes, one a playful brown, and the other a vibrant hazel that gives me butterflies.

"Dinner is ready."

It's not until the guys sit down after washing up, and I set the lasagna on the table, that I mention the text message.

"Can I have your phone?" Keith grinds out, holding up his hand, but before I can hand it to him, Tony snatches it from the table.

"Leave it to me." He gets up from the table and starts

pacing as he stabs at the screen and puts the phone to his ear. "No, this is not her! Tony Ramirez, you numbnuts. What the fuck do you think you're doing? What do you mean you don't know what I'm talking about? I know you're not an idiot, Biel. I have a man sitting here who would easily rip your head off if you were standing in front of him. I took you for a smarter man. You fucking know there's more than a passing interest in you, this is not the way to get that spotlight off your back, you moron."

He doesn't seem to give Evan a chance to answer before ending the call. It's the first clear indication I have of Evan being a suspect. I want to object, but I can see how they might think that. Especially after he was apparently in my hospital room, right before that envelope was found.

Sitting back down, Tony gives Keith a sideways look. "Good enough for ya?"

"It'll do," is the growled response.

CHAPTER 22

Keith

"Ramirez!"

His head pops around the doorpost. "You bellowed?"

I ignore his quip and wave him in.

"Give me some news. Any fucking thing'll do."

We've been hitting nothing but dead ends and despite the quiet week, I can't shake the feeling—somewhere behind the scenes—tension is ratcheting up. My gut says he's going to make a move, and we're not even one step closer to finding him. The only thing we've had any success with is ruling out possibilities and eliminating names, leaving us next to nothing to work with.

Don't get me wrong, this week has been pretty spectacular in other ways, my house becoming a universe all its own with Autumn in it. Yet last night when she mentioned that text coming in on her phone, I realized the building tension is as real for her as it is for me.

She's getting restless. I can sense it. For someone who is

passionate about her work and always on the go, just putzing around the house, waiting for me to come home must get old fast. Come Monday, I fully expect the doc to give her an all clear, and after the old man's funeral on Tuesday, I have no doubt she'll be back at the hospital. There'll be only so much I can do to keep her safe. Except catch the fucker before he has a chance to try again, because there isn't a doubt in my mind he will.

"Sorry, Boss. We didn't find much in the burn center offices, since cleaning crews had just been through there on Sunday. I talked to the receptionist, Sandy, who was able to give me a detailed account of who'd been in and out of the offices, but nothing jumped out. She seemed surprised, though; apparently oblivious the fire might have been anything more than accidental. Spoke to the physical therapist, who occasionally sees patients there, she doesn't raise any flags. The only one I haven't been able to pin down because apparently he's on a golfing trip with his buddies this week, is the plastic surgeon who also uses the office from time to time for consultations."

"When is he expected back?"

"Monday. And yes," he says immediately, a hand raised to ward me off. "I'll be on his doorstep first thing."

"Good. What else do we have? This is not done, Tony. You know it isn't."

"I know. Treading water here, Boss. Have you checked in with Luna? She was going to try and trace down some of those battery driven sprayers sold in the area. I imagine that might be quite a list."

"Left her a message earlier." I sigh, running a hand over my face. "Although I'm sure she would've called if she found something. Fucking killing me to sit here with our thumbs up our asses, waiting to see what this bastard is going to do next, hoping he'll slip and give us something to work with.

Feels like we've been led around by our dicks. What are we missing?"

"If I knew that..." He lets his words trail off, his frustration as palpable as mine. "Instead of focusing on what we don't know, why don't we focus on what we *do* know?"

For the next twenty minutes, we make a list of knowns and safe assumptions based on evidence. The list is disturbingly short and raises more questions than it provides answers. One thing seems clear though, he is focused on Autumn. All we need is a viable suspect to check the list off against.

"Biel?" I throw out there, him being the only person of interest we've been able to consider, but Tony shakes his head.

"I don't think so. He checks a bunch of boxes when it comes to Autumn, but doesn't really meet the profile anywhere else. I've been digging deep, and it hasn't gone unnoticed, but my gut says we're barking up the wrong tree with him."

Hate to admit it—since the guy has been seriously pissing me off—but he doesn't really feel right for me either. *Goddammit.*

When Ramirez takes his leave, promising to meet up at eight the next morning, I check my watch. I should be getting home, or Autumn's surprise will be there before me. Stopped twice on my way out, I'm already running late by the time I get to the Tahoe and am in a rush to get out of there. That's why I don't see it until I'm already behind the wheel, about to back out of my spot. A note.

I slam the gear back in park, turn off the engine, and slowly get out of the car, while pulling my phone from my pocket. My eyes never leave the envelope stuck under the windshield wiper. "Ramirez still there?" I snap when Bolter answers.

"Left right before you."

"Get someone to cover the desk and meet me in the parking lot. Bring an evidence kit."

Shoving the phone back in my pocket, I lean over the hood, trying to get a look at the writing on the front without touching anything. This is new, and more than a bit unsettling. I recognize the printing, except it's my name instead of Autumn's.

Odd that Tony didn't see it. He usually parks in the spot next to me and would've walked past to get to his car. For the briefest moment, my thoughts go there, but I rein them in just as fast. No way in hell that's even a possibility. I'm clearly hard up enough for answers; I start questioning one of the few people I'd trust with my life. Besides, I didn't spot the damn thing either until I was about to drive off.

"What've we got, Boss?" Mike Bolter wants to know, walking up.

"That." I point at the envelope.

"No shit," is his dry comment as he dons a pair of gloves from the kit.

"Careful leaning on the hood. We should probably see if any prints were left before even going for the note."

Knowing I'll be stuck here for a while, I make a couple of calls while Bolter starts scanning the driver side fender and hood for evidence. The first I'm forced to leave a message, but Ramirez picks up on the second ring.

"You home yet?"

"About. Stopped for some gas. Why?"

"Where you parked beside me?"

"Aren't I always? Why are you asking?"

"You didn't notice anything on my windshield?"

"Hell no. What's going on?"

"Looks like our perp just made a move."

"The *fuck* you say. Be right there."

Part of me is excited at the prospect of new evidence to examine. The other part is pissed that I'm going to miss the look of surprise on Autumn's face.

I watch for a few minutes as Mike dusts a few spots on the hood, and I point out what looks like a print on the windshield. Leaving him to it, I scan my surroundings, my eyes catching on the lamppost at the far end of the parking lot. *Fucking hell.*

"Mike. Tell me that camera is working."

* * *

Autumn

"I know, just give me a minute."

Gizmo keeps butting her head against my hand, making it impossible to finish the report that is due by Monday. I didn't mention this to Keith—I can tell he's stressed enough already and doesn't need me to add to it—but I contacted Sandy at the office yesterday and asked her to upload the collected data to the drop box so I could analyze it from here. I was going nuts sitting on my hands, and the only alternative was to take up online shopping, which is an addiction my credit card does not need.

I make sure to save and upload my report, leaving it for the weekend to give it one last run-through with fresh eyes before I send it. Turning the computer off, I follow a prancing Gizmo, her tail high in the air, to the kitchen where, as usual, Jack is quietly waiting by his bowl. Both cats charge at the food the moment it's set in front of them. You'd think I was starving them.

I glance and the clock and am surprised to find it already past six, I haven't even been outside today.

No sign of Keith yet, although he messaged around

lunchtime to let me know he wasn't sure exactly what time he'd be home, but not to worry about dinner, he'd pick something up.

Feeling a little better about myself after a productive day, I grab a beer from the fridge, nab my phone, and take it out on the front porch to wait for him. I barely sit down when a message comes in.

***Asshole:* Sorry, something came up. Home by seven. With dinner.**

***Me:* Sounds good.**

I really should change that screen name.

Still smiling to myself, I drop my phone on the small table, and step off the porch. Looking to kill some time, I wander over to the garage to have a closer look at Keith's project. I'm not sure why—it's not like I have any particular interest in cars or engines—except maybe to get a clearer picture of the man. He's still so much of an enigma to me. Driven, professional, and a bit of a workaholic like myself, he can also be incredibly insightful, protective, and caring. I can see the man, but it's like I'm missing some pieces to fill out the picture.

I'm halfway there when I freeze in my tracks at the sound of gravel crunching under the tires of a car coming up the drive.

Instantly the hair on my neck stands on end. I know it can't be Keith and he would've warned me if he were expecting anyone else. Before I even finish that thought, my feet are moving full tilt toward the garage. I dart out of sight from the driveway, and keep my fingers crossed the side door is not locked. The knob turns easily in my hand and I disappear into the dark interior, pulling the door shut behind me and leaning my back against it, trying to listen over the thundering beat of my heart. More crunching and then silence.

I slip a hand in my pocket. *Fuck.* Left the beer and my phone on the porch. Whoever it is will see and know someone's home. I should've run back to the house and locked myself inside.

Frozen with indecision, I wait and listen.

Finally I hear a car door slam shut. And then a second one.

The sound, sharp in the mostly quiet surroundings has the effect of a starter pistol, propelling me into motion. There is one prevailing thought like a neon signal in my mind. *Hide.*

My eyes, a bit more adjusted to the lack of light, focus on the old truck cast in shadows in the middle of the garage. There is nothing in the bed but tools. Nothing to cover myself with. I slip around the other side, my hand fumbling for the door handle. It takes me precious seconds to discover it's actually a lever to open the door with and I carefully press it down. Someone must have recently oiled the hinges because it opens blissfully silent and I crawl inside, closing it just as carefully and sliding down on the floorboards, clutching a wrench I found lying on the seat.

I'm not sure how long I've been curled up in a ball—my stomach rolling and my bladder about to spring a leak—when I hear the crunch of approaching footsteps. One set. A loud metal screech and the sudden flood of outside light tells me whoever is out there pulled up the overhead door, and I grab my makeshift weapon even tighter.

I don't know why I expect him to come in through the

driver's side door, but my entire body is poised in that direction. So when the door behind my head is suddenly yanked open, I vault up, hitting my head hard against the molded metal dashboard.

"Jesus, woman. What the hell do you think you're doing?"

* * *

Keith

"What the hell happened to you?"

The words just fly out when I walk into the house to find Autumn sitting at the dining room table, a large icepack pressed against her head. Her eyes are shooting fire.

"Your surprise arrived," she says in an even voice.

I now notice a grinning Chief getting up from the couch, just as Sophie pokes her head out of the hallway.

"So I see." Ignoring them and stalking toward Red. "That doesn't answer what happened to your head?" I peel away the bag of frozen corn to uncover a bump the size of a baseball.

"She had a heart-to-heart with the dashboard in your Chevy," Chief contributes. "This was as she attempted to attack me with a wrench."

"I wasn't attacking you, dumbass," Autumn spits out. "I was defending myself."

Every word only adds more to my confusion. "Will someone please tell me what the fuck happened?"

"I will," Sophie volunteers, walking up. "When we got here there was a cell phone and a beer on the porch but no one in s-sight. The door was open but the house empty, s-so Roman went to check in the garage, and found Autumn hiding in your truck."

"I clearly wasn't aware anyone was coming," Red fills in, shooting me a pointed look, "so it seemed like the best idea under the circumstances."

"I see," I mumble, leaning down to gently kiss her forehead. "Can I just say in my defense, this was meant to be a surprise? And it would've been, if this idiot here," I point at a still snickering Chief, "had bothered to check his messages when he landed."

"My phone ran out of juice. I just plugged it in a minute ago," he says, walking to the kitchen counter when he picks up his charging phone. "Shit. I see what you mean. My bad, man."

"What was the m-message?" Sophie wants to know when a sheepish Chief shrugs at Autumn.

"I'm delayed. Wait for me at The Irish. Don't want you to freak Red out."

I look down to find Autumn's eyes warm on me. Much better than the ice-cold reception a few minutes ago. She reaches up to pull my head down and kisses me hard.

"The thought was sweet," she mumbles, fighting a grin.

CHAPTER 23

Keith

It's almost midday when I hear Autumn trying to muffle a coughing bout for the third time.

I didn't want her to come, afraid she'd only aggravate her throat, but she insisted, and to be honest, I did feel better having her close. Especially after that note last night.

"We should break for lunch," I suggest. The only person close enough to hear is Roman. The other three—Autumn, Sophie, and Ramirez—are upstairs, packing up what is salvageable from there. Chief and I are tossing anything that is not too damaged, in terms of furniture, in the back of the U-Haul cube van we picked up this morning. Anything that's solid wood or metal is coming, but any upholstered furniture is pretty much toast. If not from the fire itself, then from the smoke that will be impossible to get out. It'll only keep this nightmare alive for Red if she has to smell that every time she sits down on the couch for instance. Throw pillows, curtains, anything that can't really be washed goes into the dumpster that weasel lawyer had delivered earlier. He can take care of clean up.

"I could eat," Chief admits. "Maybe the girls want to head back to your place. Autumn doesn't sound too hot."

"I know."

"By the way, you never got around to telling me what the delay was last night."

I walk over to the stairs and peek up to make sure Autumn isn't within hearing range. "Found a note on my car. Stuck under the wiper," I explain, keeping my voice low. "Don't want to spring it on Autumn if I can help it. She's got enough on her plate cleaning this shit out."

"Good point, but you do know she'll be pissed when she finds out, right?" He smirks at me, one eyebrow up.

"Yeah. I know. Doesn't bother me." I shrug, hiding a grin of my own.

"What did it say?"

Instead of answering I pull out my phone and find the picture I took, holding it up for him to see.

MINE!! IT'S JUST A MATTER OF TIME.

"Poetic," Chief deadpans.

"Isn't it? And it gets better." I flip through the pictures to the grainy shot I took off the camera feed.

"That him?"

"Yup. Doesn't give us a really good look at his face with that ball cap pulled down low, but at least we have a physical description now."

"You gonna show her?"

"That's the plan, but not now."

"I see why you didn't object too hard to her coming. I was wondering about that."

"I'm just wondering now if that was a good idea. She's hoping to get cleared by the doc on Monday. She should probably get out of here."

"Sophie!" Chief yells up the stairs. "You getting hungry yet?" To me he says, "I'll see if I can get Sophie to convince her to let one of us take them home after lunch."

Lunch ends up being a couple of large pizzas. I make a quick call before joining the rest on the grass in the front yard, where the air is reasonably clean. Something tells me Autumn won't be too hard to convince to call it a day. I notice she's eating little, trying to breathe in deeply, and looking a little pale.

"What was it you wanted from your neighbor's place, Autumn?" Sophie asks after Chief spent some time whispering in her ear.

* * *

Autumn

"Any paperwork and maybe some photos. I don't want his entire life to be tossed into a dumpster. Maybe he had friends who would like to come to his funeral, I won't know until I have a look."

I was thinking about this yesterday. It seems so disrespectful, like tossing Joseph out with yesterday's trash. Out of sight out of mind. I didn't really know him, but from what little I do, he deserves better than that. At the very least, I want to honor him by learning what I can about his history, and maybe keep a little of his memory alive.

The thought of spending hours more in that house is overwhelming though. I didn't want to say anything, because everyone is here helping me, but I almost wish we could leave the rest for someone else to throw out. Every item disappearing into the dumpster holds some kind of memory for me, and it's making the sense of loss weigh heavier on my chest.

"Why don't we box up what you want from there, and take it home, s-sort through it there? S-since the upstairs is basically packed up; we can leave the guys to haul it out. I could do with a s-shower too."

As soon as Sophie mentions a shower, I realize this can't be easy for her either. Just the lingering smell of smoke can trigger bad memories, and my friend has her own traumatic fire experience.

Feeling guilty, I easily agree.

We head into my neighbor's side of the house—all taking a room each—and within twenty minutes we have four large file boxes filled with albums, random papers, loose photos, and stacks of letters. Utility bills and bank statements we leave behind. That's for Barnes to sort through. The rest the guys load up in Keith's SUV.

"I can drive," I offer, when it looks like Keith is getting behind the wheel. "Unless you don't want me to?"

"I'll just run you home," he says. "I want to make sure you get in safely and grab a couple of beers for the guys."

"Okay."

I don't bother arguing. I know something's been on his mind since last night. He's normally all about the close contact in bed, but last night he wrapped himself around me, his arms banding me tightly, and I was still anchored to him when I woke up this morning. Something happened to put those shadows in his eyes, and as much as I want to drag it out of him, I suspect Sophie and Roman being here is the reason he's keeping it to himself. For now. Because come Sunday night, after our friends fly back home, I intend to get answers.

When Keith parks the SUV next to Chief's rental, it occurs to me how much of a home this place has become in this short time. It also reminds me that I should probably start looking for another place to rent for the remainder of my contract with Mercy.

I'm hit with a stab of sadness at the thought of leaving this place—leaving Durango altogether—and wonder what it would look like if I were to decide to make a life in this town. A mental image forms, but right in the center of it is Keith.

"I'll get the boxes," he says, breaking through my thoughts. "You guys, go ahead inside."

Gizmo greets us at the door, happy when Sophie scoops her up for snuggles.

"Want me to put on a pot of coffee? Or would you rather have tea?" I ask, heading straight for the kitchen.

"Coffee. I need the caffeine boost."

I put on a pot and quickly put the remaining breakfast dishes in the dishwasher when Sophie calls out.

"Whose car is that?"

"What?"

"S-someone just pulled up."

I wipe my hands and join Sophie at the dining room window, just in time to see a petite blonde step from the vehicle and get folded into Keith's arms for a hug.

A sour burn starts churning in my stomach as I feel Sophie's hand squeeze my arm. *Jesus,* jealousy is an ugly thing, I'm not used to it. Instinctively I know who this is—I don't even need an introduction—but I'm not sure what she's doing here.

As I watch them walk up to the porch—Keith's arm slung casually over the smaller woman's shoulder—I mentally brace myself, putting on what I hope to God is a welcoming smile. Determined, I shake off Sophie's hand and reach for the door, opening it wide.

Keith takes one look at my face and I know, when he drops his arm from her shoulders, I haven't been successful in masking my confused feelings. "I'd like you to meet—"

"You must be—"

"Luna," we say simultaneously, making for an even more awkward moment.

The composed woman, who by Keith's description is a kick-ass FBI agent, nevertheless seems a little timid as she takes my proffered hand. "Nice to meet you, Autumn."

"Yes, of course. Me too. Nice to meet you as well, I mean." Her contained words and carefully measured movements make me feel like an ungainly buffoon as I almost stumble over my words, and my feet, when I try to step out of her way.

"I'm S-Sophie." Poor Sophie is left to make her own introductions as I try to restore my composure. Keith watches me closely.

"Luna was going to come help out at your place this afternoon, but since there's not much left to be done there, I asked if she wouldn't mind coming here instead."

"Awesome," Sophie pipes up. "Autumn just m-made coffee, want to come grab a cup?" Without waiting for Luna's answer, Sophie takes her arm and steers her into the kitchen, clearly giving Keith and me some space.

Before I can open my mouth to ask why he invited her here, I find myself pressed against his chest, his mouth whispering in my hair. "Like a sister," he mumbles, repeating what he told me before about his connection with the woman. "It would make me feel better to have her here while we finish up at the house. Please," he adds when I don't answer.

"Something's happened." I'm not a fool. I already knew

something was up, but the fact he doesn't want to leave me unprotected only confirms it. "Another fire?"

"No." He pulls back and takes my face in his hands, leaning down so our noses touch. "Red, do you trust me?" I don't even have to think; I just nod. When it comes to my safety, he may be the only person I trust. "Then hold off and know you've got nothing to worry about with Luna here until I get back. Focus on sorting through Mr. Bartik's stuff, let me take care of your house for you, and tonight—when all that is done—I promise I'll explain."

"I'm not a wilting flower, you know," I bristle, feeling more than a little managed.

"Well aware, Red, but this is not about you not being strong—it's about me only able to handle so much at a time." I look in his eyes and see a man weighed down by his responsibilities.

I immediately feel guilty, not having considered the stress he is under, and lift my hands to his face. "Of course," I agree easily, brushing my thumb over his tight lips, which immediately relax under my touch. "I can wait."

"Thank you, my love," he murmurs, already lowering his mouth to mine. "We won't be too long, and I'll pick up some more beer and Chinese on the way."

"Okay."

"I put the boxes on the porch just outside the door, do you want me to bring them in?"

"No, leave them out there. I don't want to stink up the whole house."

With a last peck on my lips he's off, closing the door behind him. I walk over to the window, watching him get into his SUV, trying to slow my heart down, which is still beating a staccato from the unexpected endearment that slipped from his lips.

It sounded really good.

* * *

"Guys, I know I'll probably need another one later, but I have to grab a quick s-shower. Wash this s-stink off m-me. I'll be right back," Sophie announces after we've collectively sorted through the first box.

It's been an interesting discovery so far, and I feel better having the beginnings of a timeline of Joseph's life laid out in order on the dining table. I'm not exactly sure why this is so important to me. Perhaps because I could see myself end up like him: with no family, no kids, and no legacy to leave behind. Maybe a tad premature to be thinking like that, but the reality is, until a few weeks ago, I never expected more out of my life than what I had at the moment.

My life has not nearly been as interesting as the old man's, but I have the benefit of having half of it left to live. And I want to do just that—live it fully instead of safely coasting to the end.

"About Keith and me—" Luna suddenly says when Sophie's gone for her shower, catching me by surprise.

"No need to explain," I cut her off, not really wanting to address the elephant in the room, but she seems determined.

"I think I do," she gently insists. "I'd like to clear the air, since we're bound to spend time around each other through him." I'm not so sure how I feel about that comment, so I try not to examine it too closely. "It took me a long time to warm up to him when I was assigned to the La Plata office. You see, I met him once before, under rather traumatic circumstances, and along with bad memories, I had shoved him to the very recesses of my mind. Not that he was in any way the cause, in fact, he was more like my knight in shining armor, but I couldn't help associating the trauma with him." She shakes her head and stares off in the distance. Surprisingly I find myself drawn into the—albeit vague—picture she paints, so I patiently wait. Eventually she speaks again. “I was an absolute pain in the ass at first. Angry at him for reminding me of things I’d successfully buried over the years, angry at him for knowing. But you know what they say: once the seal is off… Anyway, I got some help processing the shit that bubbled up, and my relationship with Keith benefited.”

“He says he’ll always be your protector,” I provide softly, internally trying hard not to imagine what exactly those benefits were.

“I believe that,” she says, grabbing my hand unexpectedly. “But I want to assure you it’s purely platonic. He’s part of my family. The man is like a big brother to me.”

“I realize he is now.”

“No.” She shakes her head and averts her eyes. “That’s what he always was, and will always be. We’ve never had…I mean, I’ve never been…”

“Intimate with him?” I probe carefully.

“Not ever.”

CHAPTER 24

Autumn

Dinner is a loud and rambunctious affair, and for the second time today, my thoughts drift to the possibility of making my stay in Durango permanent.

It's easy, when you're surrounded by friends, who all seem to be having a good time, but things may look a bit different if I take Keith out of the equation. For one thing, I'd be sharing this meal with just Sophie, maybe Chief. What if I made the decision to stay, only to wake up one day to an empty bed and a single setting at my dining table?

Durango is a fairly small place—contained, anyway—and everyone seems to know Keith. It would be difficult to sustain myself if things went south.

"You're thinking too hard," the subject of my thoughts whispers in my ear.

"There's a lot to think about," I fire back under my breath.

"I should be heading out," Luna announces, as she stands up from the table, looking back and forth between Keith and me. "I'm sure you guys are tired after today."

"Right," Tony mumbles, tossing back the remainder of his beer, and collecting the empty plates from the table. "Give me a sec and I'll walk out with you." He disappears into the kitchen.

Luna shakes her head. "He doesn't give up," she mumbles.

"Barking up the wrong tree is a concept he hasn't mastered yet," Keith adds, grinning. "It's that hot Latin blood."

"Well, he'd better learn fast, or that blood of his will be flowing," she bites off, just as Tony walks back into the dining room.

"Whose blood are we talking about?"

The table collectively busts out laughing.

* * *

Keith

"There's another note."

As soon as Ramirez chases after Luna out the door, we clear the rest of the table, but the women chase us out of the kitchen, clearly wanting a chance to chat by themselves. Keeping my voice down, I've been bringing Chief up-to-date on the case in the living room, when they walk in and sit down.

With a nod from Chief, I drop that bomb.

Autumn almost shoots out of the seat she just took beside me and I barely manage to pull her back down.

"Where is it?"

"At the lab. That's why I was late last night."

"It was sent to you?"

"Delivered to me is more like it."

"At the police station," she concludes, incredulously.

"The parking lot anyway. Ballsy, but stupid." I pull out my phone and show her the first picture, and she squints to read it.

"Are you kidding me?" she blurts out, sitting up straight. "Is he threatening you?" I almost chuckle at the indignant tone in her voice, but manage to rein it in.

"What does it s-say?" Sophie wants to know and listens as I read the message out loud for her. "In his dreams," she snaps, before turning to her husband. "We're s-staying."

"We're not," he replies calmly. "Keith has it covered. Besides, we both have to work on Monday."

Yeah, thanks. I needed that pressure. The truth is, I have painfully little covered.

"I can't believe you!" Apparently Sophie isn't going down easy, and it sounds like we're on the verge of a domestic blowup in my living room. "That's m-my best friend you're talking about."

"Listen, you know I love Autumn like—"

"No, I'm done listening. I listened to you last week and wasn't there for her when s-she was in the hospital. I worried m-myself s-sick, and now you want m-me to leave when s-she has a crazy person after her?"

"You should." The gentle suggestion comes from Autumn, who has been very quiet after her own initial outburst, and instantly quiets Sophie.

"But—" Her barely there protest goes unheard.

"Do you think," Autumn grabs Sophie's arm none too gently, "that after already carrying the weight of a kind old man dying, because he happened to be my neighbor, I want to take the risk of anything happening to either of you? It's bad enough I seem to have put Keith square in his sights, I'll be damned if I drag you into it too."

Her face flushed, she gets up off the couch.

"Wait," Sophie calls out. "I didn't m-mean—"

But Autumn is already on the move. She's not mad, she's about to cry and probably doesn't want anyone to see. Her friend is out of her seat, ready to go after her, but her husband holds her back. "Keith's got this honey," he repeats before giving me a nod.

Taking the younger man's sign—he is after all the more experienced one in love matters—I scoop up Jack from the back of the couch, and follow Autumn into the bedroom.

She's fully clothed, rolled up on her side, with her back toward the door. I carefully lean over the bed and set Jack on the mattress in front of her. Then I go into the bathroom, grab the box of tissues and wet a washcloth with cold water, and set them on the nightstand before crawling into bed behind her.

I loosely drape my arm around her waist so she knows I'm there, and wait for her to come to me. I hate I was the one to rip that last thread of resolve she was holding onto all day with my announcement. But I'd promised her—asked her to trust me—there wasn't a choice. Besides, I remember my mother telling me once when I'd found her in tears, crying wasn't a sign of weakness, but simply a much-needed release when the pressure gets too high.

I hope letting her cry without interruption helps her, because every sob from her body is like a hot dagger in mine.

Finally, I feel her hand find mine, and she pulls my arm tighter around her as she scoots her body back, looking for mine.

"I hate this," she says, sounding congested.

"I'm sorry."

"Don't you be sorry, that should be my line," she says, suddenly rolling over. "I don't want anyone else getting hurt. Especially not you. What if he—"

"He won't." I tuck her into my body. "I told you, he was

ballsy but stupid. One of our parking lot cameras picked him up sticking the note on my car. I have a still. It's not a great quality, but at least I have a better idea who to look for."

"Can I see?"

"Like I said, it's pretty grainy." I pull my phone from my pocket and find the image. Autumn takes it from my hand and looks at it.

"I don't recognize him." With her fingers sliding on the screen, she zooms in on the picture.

"His face is mostly obscured by the ball cap."

"That's not a ball cap. That's a trucker hat."

"Is there a difference?"

"Sure is," she says pointing at the screen. "Trucker hats are mostly mesh with a single fabric panel on the front. Usually with some kind of logo. They look almost boxy compared to ball caps." She squints and peers closer. "This one has a logo, I just can't make out what."

"Let me see?" I take the phone from her hand and try to decipher the blur myself, without success. "I should send this to Luna. She works with a guy who's a tech wiz. Maybe he can do something about the quality."

A knock sounds at the door and Chief pokes his head in.

"Sorry to bug you. Just wanted to know if you need me to lock up. We're calling it a night, Sophie's half asleep."

I sit up and swing my legs over the side. "No, that's okay. I'll take care of it. I have a couple of calls to make anyway."

"Sure thing. Night y'all."

Autumn's head pops up from the bed. "Night, Roman. Tell your wife I'm planning a big breakfast before you guys head back tomorrow."

"Will do."

As Chief backs out of the room, Red presses her body against my back, hooks an arm around my neck, and props her chin on my shoulder. "You know, if not for the fact that most of my belongings—alongside my dead neighbor's—are now at the bottom of a dumpster, and the obsessive lunatic who is responsible is still out there, this could have been a great weekend."

I put a hand on her forearm. "We'll have more," I tell her.

"You seem sure."

Her voice is tentative, which I don't particularly like. I turn and roll her on her back, closing my mouth over hers and kissing her deeply. When I feel her hands come up and tangle in my hair, I lift my head and hold her eyes.

"I *am* sure, and once we have this guy safely behind bars, I'm gonna enjoy proving it to you."

* * *

Autumn

"Everything looks fine. Any shortness of breath? Excessive coughing?"

Dr. Landis flips through his papers, reading glasses perched on his nose, before he glances up when I keep him waiting for an answer.

"Well, there have been moments," I finally confess, feeling Keith's strict eyes on me. If it had been just me in here, I might've lied. I'm sick and tired of hiding out. Don't get me wrong, I love being at Keith's place, but I don't look forward to spending another week twiddling my thumbs. "But as long as I stay away from irritants and don't overdo it physically, I'm good to go."

"That's what I think too," he says, slapping the file shut. "But I'm trusting you to take it slow, pace yourself, and I'll want your blood again a week from today. I'll call if something is off, and you'll knock on my door if you experience any issues. Agreed?"

"Absolutely."

Keith slings his arm around my shoulders when we walk down the hallway. I'm tempted to go upstairs and check in with Sandy, but I suspect he might have something to say about that. I can wait, now that I know I'm basically cleared for work on the provision I take it easy.

"Need to stop in anywhere while we're here?"

I look up; surprised he seems able to tap into my thoughts. "Nah. I'm good." Slipping my arm around his middle, I tuck into his side a little more as we head for the exit—just as Evan Biel pushes through the door.

I feel Keith's entire body grow taut with tension, and he stops in his tracks when Evan spots us and turns our way.

"Is he insane?" he growls, under his breath.

I tighten my hold around his waist, as if I could hold him back should he go charging. To my surprise, the closer Evan gets, the more Keith relaxes.

Evan looks straight at me, pointedly ignoring Keith. The guy must have a death wish.

"How are you feeling?" he asks with what feels like genuine concern.

"A lot better, thanks." I'm still clutching Keith's shirt at the waist, despite the fact I no longer feel anger radiating from him. Curious. "I just received the all clear from the doctor."

"That's good." He nods and looks down at his boots before lifting his eyes, first tentatively to Keith and then back to me. "I should probably apologize for pressing Jen for your number the other day. I didn't realize until after—well, after I was put in my place—that was probably not a good idea under the circumstances."

"Damn right," Keith growls beside me.

"Right. Anyway, I was worried. Still am."

"She's looked after," Keith speaks for me, and I pinch his side. He barely seems to register, still staring the other man down.

"So I discovered," is Evan's dry response.

"I appreciate it," I quickly say, before the two of them get into it in the hospital lobby.

Evan just nods. "I hear the old man's funeral is tomorrow. Me and a couple of the guys would like to come pay our respects, if that's okay with you?"

I take a deep breath, unsure how to respond. Under any other circumstances it would be a kind gesture, but I just don't know how I should take it. Keith surprises me when he answers curtly. "That's appreciated. Greenmount Cemetery at eleven."

"We'll be there."

My mouth is still hanging open in shock when Evan throws me a lopsided smile and walks off. Keith steers me out the doors, and it isn't until we get to the Tahoe that I find my words.

"What the hell? One minute you're ready to rip his head off, and the next you invite him for tea and crumpets?" He barks out a laugh, but I'm on a roll. "What's gotten into you? I thought he was top of your suspect list?"

The grin on his face is starting to piss me off, but just as I'm about to say something, he leans in and kisses my tightly pressed lips. "It's not him."

I'm pretty sure I heard that wrong. "What?"

"It isn't him. He doesn't walk right."

"Look, I'm not sure what—" He silences me with a forefinger on my lips.

"Red, I watched the camera feed probably twenty times. He's the right height, same approximate build, but he doesn't walk right. The guy in the video walks with slumped shoulders and a heavy tread. Biel's back is straight as a pin and he has a little lift on every step he takes. He doesn't walk right."

"No shit?" I mumble behind his finger, before opening my mouth and biting down on it.

"Ouch."

"Serves you right."

He's still chuckling when he climbs behind the wheel.

CHAPTER 25

Keith

"Wowza."

Most of Sunday and a few hours last night, Autumn disappeared into my office. She just walked out in a little black dress, I didn't even know she owned, looking like a million bucks. The woman has good legs and a spectacular rack. Not that it's news to me, I take every opportunity I can get to see her naked, but she never puts those attributes on display when she's dressed.

The little smirk and faint blush look good on her, but my attention is drawn to the two large pieces of poster board she's carrying. She just mentioned working on a little project when she asked to stop at Walmart for a few supplies yesterday, on our way home from the hospital.

"What's that?"

Instead of answering, she sets both on the couch, leaning them against the back. It looks like a collage of some sort, with photos and newspaper clippings, some official looking forms and a little Polish flag. I fish the new, and rarely used, pair of readers from my suit pocket and slip them on.

Along the top in tidy bold print is written: *The Life Of Joseph Aleksander Bartik.* Right underneath, next to the little Polish flag, is a document in a language I assume is Polish and looks like a birth certificate. There are a few pictures of a young boy, smiling gap-toothed at the camera. Then comes a travel document, listing all three in the Bartik family, and a picture of a teenager flanked by smiling parents in front of a ship. There are landing documents, a newspaper clipping with an image of the family standing in front of their newly opened bakery in Newark, New Jersey. There are dates, train tickets, a map, a dried boutonniere, and a wedding picture. Both boards are filled with little vignettes of the old man's life, and I have to swallow hard at the unexpected emotion washing over me.

She did this. She took all of the memorabilia she wanted from his house, and managed to put it all in a concise, exhibition-style chronicle of Joseph Bartik's life.

"That's beautiful," I croak, looking up at her with a lump in my throat.

"I don't want him to be forgotten." For a brief moment I wonder if it's healthy for her to take on such a heavy responsibility, but before I can comment she continues. "My mother was an alcoholic. After my father left, she destroyed any memory of him in her alcohol-induced rages. Three of those pictures I salvaged from the other house are all I have left of my childhood. Nothing else to pass on." She sniffs and magically pulls a tissue from her sleeve to wipe her nose. "This man kept a detailed written and illustrated history of his life, but sadly had no one to pass it on to. It makes me feel good to do this for him. For me."

"He would be pleased."

"Yes, he would," she says with a watery smile, and I take her in my arms for a quick hug.

"We should go," I remind her gently. "It'll take us close to twenty minutes to get there."

* * *

To my surprise, there's a quite a little group gathered at the open grave.

Biel, I knew was going to be there, but I didn't expect Fire Chief Curtis Buxton to be one of the guys he mentioned. I suspected Tony might come and show his face, but Luna was there as well, as was Jen Raymond, the nurse from the burn unit. At some point, Autumn must've called the funeral home, because at the edge of the grave, two easels were set up to hold her boards.

The result was a rather unconventional affair, with a brief reading by the funeral director, a blessing of the casket, but when the official part was done, the whole group stood around the boards, talking, and getting to know Joseph Bartik.

Autumn steps free from the group and walks up to me, a smile on her face.

"Is this weird?" she wants to know, looking up at me.

"No," I shake my head. "This is perfect."

* * *

"I feel bad not having any coffee and sandwiches to offer anyone."

Autumn is fidgeting beside me, so I reach over and still her hands, keeping my other one on the wheel.

"No one was expecting to be catered to, Red. Let it go."

She's silent for the next few minutes and I feel her restless energy fill the car. She's been a little on edge ever since we left the doctor's office on Monday. I thought it had to do with the funeral, but now I'm thinking that may not have been it. It wouldn't have been the encounter with Evan, now that I've been able to scratch him off the list of suspects. It doesn't take long for her to answer the question for me.

"I found a place I'd like to check out."

"A place?"

"Yeah, an apartment. Luna mentioned the other day that somebody at her work has a place for rent. It's actually not far from where I was, just on the other side of Main. The Jarvis building?"

"I know the place."

I don't say anything more, because I'm not sure how I feel about this development, which is probably why it made her nervous in the first place. Truth is, I've avoided thinking about this exact thing. I like sharing my space with Red, and maybe part of me was hoping she wouldn't want to leave.

"Right. Well, Luna mentioned today she could get me the key so I could have a look. Apparently it's empty."

"What—now?"

"No, and you don't have to come—I can go by myself—I just wanted to ask," she snaps and I realize I may have been curt.

I lift a hand from her lap and press my lips to the pulse point in her wrist. "I'll come. I'd like to come. I know the building, I probably even know the apartment, and you could do a whole lot worse."

"That's what Luna said. Especially for a short-term rental."

My eyes have been on something in the rearview mirror that has me a little distracted.

"Short-term?" I ask, trying not to let on my attention is focused on the old, burgundy Jimmy I spotted up at the cemetery, and is apparently still with me after making some random turns and twists through downtown.

"Where are you going?"

I make another left off Main and end up in the same subdivision of the Delwood fire. A fairly quiet residential area, where a tail would stand out like a sore thumb.

"Just taking you on a tour of Durango." I want to lie, but I promised her honesty in return for her trust, and convinced the truck is following us, it's probably time to let her know. "Actually, don't look, but we have a tail." Of course she immediately starts turning in her seat, but I give her hand a firm squeeze in warning. "Can you fish my phone from my pocket and turn it on?" I hadn't switched it on again after turning it off for the funeral. She does as I ask, holding it out to me. "Would you mind hitting two on speed dial?"

"Miss me already?" Ramirez voice echoes from the speakers.

"What's your twenty?"

"Pulling into the station's parking lot, why?" He's on alert right away.

"I'm looping around the Arroyo Drive neighborhood with a mid-nineties, burgundy Jimmy on my ass. I don't think he knows I spotted him, but I saw him parked near the entrance at Greenmount."

"License plate?"

"Can't tell, he's leaving too much distance for me to see. I'm gonna see if I can draw him toward the college. See if you can pick us up on East 8th." Leaving the line open, I make my way back to Main and turn south. I see the Jimmy turn onto the much busier thoroughfare two cars behind me. "Heading south on Main. He's still there."

By the time I turn left onto 8th, I notice Autumn is clutching the console with one hand, and the door with the other. "Relax," I reassure her, prying her clawed fingers loose and weaving them with mine. Her hold is almost painful. "It's the middle of the day. Unlikely he'll try anything. He's probably just on a fishing expedition."

"Is that him?"

"You have anyone else after you, sugar?" Tony quips, still listening in, before he turns serious. "Have a visual. Pulling behind him, can you see me?"

"I see you," I confirm, watching his unmarked Charger come into view.

"John Deere sticker on the gate. License…G…A…A… 6…7…7."

I turn left onto Rim Road, which curves around the college. I look over at Autumn when we near the lookout point. Clearly recognizing it, a deep red flushes her face. "Remember this place?"

"What are you on about?" Tony's irritated voice comes over the sound system.

"Wasn't talking to you, moron."

"Never mind, guess I don't wanna know. Hey, heads-up. I think I've been made, he's turning into the parking lot."

"Stay on him. I'm calling in the digits. Keep him busy while I get Autumn out of here."

"Will do."

* * *

Autumn

That was not what I'd consider fun.

Not exactly a high-speed chase by any stretch of the imagination, but my hands are clammy and my heart is still racing, even after Keith turns the Tahoe onto the drive.

He hits the button on his steering wheel when a call comes in, just as we pull up to the house. "Talk to me."

"Lost him. *Sonofabitch.*"

"How?"

"He was jerking me around the student resident buildings when he suddenly darted back out on Rim Road, cutting off a damn bus. By the time I was able to get around it, he was long gone. Did you call through the license plate?"

"Waiting for a call back."

"Did you put out a BOLO?"

"No grounds for it. For all we know he was sightseeing and happened to be going in the same direction. You know it requires more than that."

"*Fuck.*"

"If you don't have anything pressing back at the station, head up here. I won't be coming into the office after all."

"Ten-four."

"What does BOLO mean?" I ask, when he opens the door for me.

"Be on the lookout. If we know a specific vehicle—or driver—has been involved in a crime, we put a general call out for patrol to keep an eye out."

He takes my hand as if it's the most natural thing in the world. With the other he opens the door where both Gizmo and Jack are waiting.

"You're not going to the office?"

"I can work from here."

He doesn't say more, gives me a peck on my lips, and disappears down the hall to his office. I go the opposite way and slip out of my black dress, and into my favored yoga pants and oversized shirt. Doesn't look like we'll be going anywhere else today.

I've barely started washing up our breakfast dishes—

seems a waste to stick them in the dishwasher—when Keith comes stalking in.

"Short-term?" he repeats his question from earlier. The one I was happy to avoid answering after realizing what I'd given away. This is a subject I would've liked to avoid a little longer. At least until I had a semblance of control over my life again. I've been so preoccupied with getting my feet back under me, I haven't felt confident enough to make any long-lasting decisions. Of course, that means I haven't been entirely aboveboard with Keith about my temporary status here.

It's funny, because part of me was expecting something to come up while Sophie and Roman were staying here, but they never let anything slip. Given the fact I've all but moved in with Keith, they drew what would conceivably be a foregone conclusion—I'm here to stay.

I dry my hands and slowly turn to face him.

"Nine months and change," I answer, gauging him for a reaction. It's hard to tell, because his jaw is already clenched and his look impassive. "That's when my contract is up. I probably should've told you before."

"What exactly should you have told me?" he bites off, and I cross my arms defensively at the cold anger radiating from him. "Maybe that you're only here for a limited time? That you never looked for anything more in me than a temporary distraction, and will be gone the moment your time is up?"

"That's not—"

"Your words nagged at me. Fuck, this whole apartment business felt wrong. I was going to let it go, but you know how bad feelings have a tendency to eat at you? Well, this bad feeling was like acid burning a hole in my stomach. Turns out my gut instinct is alive and well."

"Keith." I put my hand on his arm in an attempt to calm him, but that only seems to aggravate him.

"I knew I was stepping into dangerous territory when I invited you into my house—into my life. I knew it, but thought maybe you could be my future. I shared things with you I've never shared with another woman. I let you in deep. Fuck, I let you in my *heart,* and all this time you had your foot already out the door."

"Please, Keith, listen to me. I haven't had—"

"Save it." He cuts me off again and turns on his heel, walking out of the kitchen without letting me explain.

I'm about to go after him when there's a knock at the front door, and Tony walks in. He stops in his tracks when he sees me.

"Are you okay?"

Immediately I plaster a smile on my face that feels almost painful. "I'm fine. Keith is in his office."

"Are you sure?"

"Yup." I nod my head, and even though I can tell he doesn't buy into it for a second, he has no choice when I turn my back and turn the tap back on.

I listen as his footsteps go down the hall, and I hear the door slamming shut.

My knees feel weak and I lean over the sink to stay upright.

You know that sensation when the bottom drops from your life, leaving a large gaping hole, and all you can feel is it swallowing you whole?

CHAPTER 26

Keith

She's beautiful.

Even with red blotches marring her skin and swollen eyes, the tears still clinging to her eyelashes. Even with the dull throb of betrayal still fresh in the middle of my chest.

She takes my breath away.

It takes every ounce of restraint not to crawl under the covers with her, but I can't resist stroking the back of my fingers over her soft cheek.

I never came to bed, never actually left my office, other than to take a piss and pay for the pizza we had delivered around eight o'clock. There had been no sign of Autumn, and the bedroom door was closed. With a pang of guilt I remember glaring, still angry, at the door, but I didn't bother to check on her even once. Yet after spending the night sitting out on my deck, staring into the dark canyon, a lot of the anger has dissipated, leaving a heavy ache behind. Seeing the evidence she must've had a rough night herself, fills me with regret.

I know I should've given her a chance to explain. Tony gave me shit about it last night when he came marching into my office and read me the riot act. I wasn't ready to hear it then, and this morning I just want to get this crazy bastard caught, get this looming threat taken care of, so we can maybe focus on what is—or is not—going on with us.

The license plate came back to a seventy-nine-year-old woman by the name of Amabel Jones. Her address is in a rural area just outside of Hesperus, which falls under Durango PD jurisdiction. It's where Tony and I are heading first thing this morning.

We did talk to Luna last night, who was able to send us an enhanced image of the ball cap—or trucker hat, whatever it's called—and despite the still less than ideal resolution, the green and yellow John Deere logo stood out clear against the white cap. The same logo Tony saw on the back of the Jimmy.

It could well be coincidence—I imagine there are lots of people with either a sticker or a hat—but I don't put much stock in coincidences. Still, it wasn't enough to justify getting warrants of any kind. It'll take more than that to convince a judge a little old lady may have something to do with the wave of arsons.

Luna volunteered to keep an eye on Autumn while Ramirez and I go check out Ms. Jones and got here five minutes ago.

I slip the note I wrote her under her glasses—so she'll see it first thing when she wakes up—and sneak out of the bedroom.

"Appreciate you doing this," I tell Luna, who is leaning against the counter with a cup of coffee in her hands.

"She knows I'm here, right?"

"I left her a note." Luna frowns, so I quickly add, defensively. "She was sleeping last night so I didn't have a chance to talk to her, and I don't want to wake her up. Yesterday was a tough day and she planned to work half a day this morning, she needs all the rest she can get."

"Do you think work is a good idea?"

I shrug. "The hospital is as safe a place as any. It's public, crowded, and has security monitoring the cameras twenty-four seven. Besides, you'll be there and depending on what we find in Hesperus, I'm hoping I can pick her up around noon to bring her home."

Of course, I don't even know at this point whether she'll want to come home with me. I behaved like an ass, butthurt and lashing out before I shut her down. If Ramirez weren't waiting for me at the station, I'd head right back into that bedroom, and hash this out.

"I have to go," I announce. "Call me if anything comes up."

"I've got her." Luna waves me off before turning back to the coffeepot for a refill.

When I walk into the station fifteen minutes later, Ramirez is talking to the desk sergeant.

"Boss," Mike greets me, but Tony just lifts his chin. "We had a bit of excitement early this morning."

"How so?"

"Conley was on a traffic stop. Pulled over a cube van with a taillight out, and the moment he walked up to the driver's side door, the thing beelined it. He went off in pursuit, up Junction Creek, and the idiot took the turn onto the 205 too sharp. Ended upside down in the creek on the opposite side of the road. He's in the hospital with a broken clavicle and a possible concussion."

"Fucking hell."

"Yup," Mike confirms. "We're gonna have to reshuffle the schedule. I've got Grand at the hospital with Conley. Jellicek and Boulton on patrol, and Maisano and Howell coming in to cover, but it fucks up the afternoon shift. We're already thin because of vacations, so gonna have to do a bit of juggling."

I spend the next hour or so trying to sort that goddamn mess out. By the time I walk out of my office, the schedule for the next seven days is covered, to the great chagrin of some of my officers. They can damn well suck it up like the rest of us. Jesus, I'll be glad when I can hand this shit over to Benedetti. About three more weeks, and I can pass it all on to him. I'm celebrating and getting hammered that day. I'm due.

Ramirez follows me out and gets into the passenger seat without a word. He stays quiet until I've hit the McDonald's drive-thru for a couple of coffees, but I know it's coming.

"Sleep well?" he asks, after taking a sip. *Asshole.*

"Peachy," I grumble, causing him to chuckle.

"I'm guessing from your sunny disposition this morning, you didn't fix it."

"Butt out, Ramirez," I warn him, not in the mood for another lecture.

"Figured you for a smarter guy, Blackfoot. Letting circumstances fuck up what may well be the best thing that ever happened to you."

"I said butt out."

"Fine," he says, way too cheerfully as he sits back, planting a dirty boot on my dashboard. "Guess I'm free to offer that pretty redhead temporary refuge in my spare bedroom. Maybe a shoulder to cry on, she'll need a friend. One man's loss is another's gain, right?"

I know he's egging me on, but still, my fingers clutch the steering wheel so hard to keep from planting a fist in his smug face. I'm afraid it'll snap in my grip.

"Off-limits," I growl. He blissfully shuts up the rest of the way to Hesperus.

It's already nine thirty when we pull into the long drive of a farmhouse, set back a ways from the road.

"Are those the remains of a burned down barn?"

"Looks like," Tony answers, sitting up in his seat to get a better look as we pass it.

The house is in some disrepair, shingles missing from the roof, the porch listing slightly and weeds growing tall along the stone path leading to it.

Its rough condition a perfect match for the burgundy Jimmy parked out in front.

* * *

Autumn

Light is streaming into the bedroom when I peel my gritty eyes open.

Falling asleep while crying is not recommended, and I almost start again when the full impact of what transpired last night hits me. Determined not to go down that path, I swing my legs over the side of bed and grab for my glasses. There's a piece of paper tucked underneath so I pick it up and fold it open.

Morning,
I'm running down a good lead this morning. Cats are fed.
Asked Luna to keep an eye out. Catch up with you later.
K.

ps. We need to talk.

Crumpling up the note in my hand, I pelt it at the wall with minimal impact, and therefore highly unsatisfactory. I'm tempted to pick up the alarm clock and haul it after, but I'm afraid once I start, I won't be able to stop. Shaking it off, I pad out of the bedroom, aiming for the kitchen where I hope to find some leftover coffee.

What I did not expect was Luna, at the stove, frying eggs.

"Morning. Hope you don't mind I started on breakfast. I'm starving and you'll need to eat something before heading to work."

"Uh...sure," I mumble, trying not to feel self-conscious as I shuffle to the coffeepot.

"Made fresh."

"Thanks."

It's crazy how territorial I feel having Luna in my kitchen. *Keith's* kitchen. Fuck, I can feel the waterworks threatening and I quickly pour myself a cup.

"Need a quick shower."

"I'll keep yours warm," Luna says, throwing me a smile, one I can't quite bring myself to return.

Why does she have to be so goddamn nice? Makes me feel like a grumpy ogre.

When I resurface twenty minutes later, moderately refreshed, and dressed for work, Luna is sitting at the dining room table, working on a laptop with an empty plate beside it.

"Yours is in the oven," she indicates without turning around.

I eat breakfast and drink a second cup of coffee, sitting across from her at the table. She seems deeply engrossed in whatever it is she's doing on the computer, so I let my eyes travel around the house. I'll miss this place. Jack saunters over and I lift him on my lap for some TLC. Gizmo is nowhere to be seen, but I'm sure she's sleeping somewhere.

"I should head out," I announce, not quite sure what the protocol is, but Luna clears that up right away.

"Sure thing. We should probably take my vehicle." She shuts her laptop, gets up, and shoves it into a worn leather backpack.

I drop the dishes in the sink, those are for later worry, snag my purse, make sure my phone is in there, and follow her outside. Once in the car, I steel a sideways peek at the other woman.

"Yours is an unusual name."

She glances over before refocusing on the road. "It's Dutch. Well, at least the Roosberg part is. Luna was just my mom and her fascination with astrology. She was planning to name me Cassiopeia, but my dad put a nix on that."

"Were you born there?"

"I was, actually. I came to the U.S. on a student visa when I was eighteen."

"That was adventurous," I note. "So your parents still live there?"

"My father, yes. Mom died the year before I left. My father remarried shortly thereafter."

I get the sense from her curt tone there is a lot more to that story, but I don't know her well enough to pry, so I let it be. The rest of the drive is quiet.

The hospital parking lot is already pretty full, the closest parking spot at the back, near the rear entrance by the waterfall garden. The smell of fresh-brewed coffee from the cafeteria hits right away when we walk through the doors.

"Do you need anything?" she asks, tilting her head in that direction.

"No thanks. I'll grab some water in a bit. You go ahead."

"Won't be long. Wait for me here where I can see you?"

"Sure."

I lean my back against the wall and take in the sounds and

smells of the hospital. Remarkable how quickly new surroundings become as familiar as a comfy slipper. Similar to Keith's home.

Before my thoughts have a chance to slide in that direction, Luna walks up carrying a large coffee cup.

"I just want to check in at the burn unit before we head up," I tell her. I never really had a chance to thank Jen yesterday for being at the cemetery. Never thanked Luna properly either, come to think of it. I put a hand on her arm as we head up to the next floor. "Thanks, by the way. For coming to the cemetery yesterday," I clarify when she looks at me puzzled.

"No worries." She brushes me off with a wave of her hand.

The burn unit is quiet. I've only seen the woman at the nurses' station a couple of times, but she looks up with a kind smile.

"Hi, I was wondering if Jen is in today?"

"Not until tomorrow."

"Thank you, I'll catch her then."

I start to walk away when she calls out. "Good to have you back, Autumn."

"Thanks."

I'm feeling a little lighter when I lead the way up the stairs to the burn center. Sandy is behind her desk, her eyes glued to her computer screen, but she shoots up when she sees me coming in. Unexpectedly she folds me in a bone-crushing hug.

"It's so good to have you back. I've been going nuts."

I gently untangle myself from her hold, grinning. "It hasn't even been two weeks."

"Felt more like two years. If I have to deal with one more grumpy patient, complaining about my cold hands, I'm gonna scream."

"Wash with warm instead of cold water before you touch the patients," I share my secret. Often times the burn scars are numb, but the area around them can be highly sensitized.

"Gotcha. By the way, talking about grumpy patients—you've got one coming in shortly. He just called not five minutes ago to confirm. That man has been the biggest pain in my ass."

"Who is it?"

"Jeff Youngman."

Just then the loud peal of the fire alarm sounds through the building.

"What the hell? Is this a drill?"

"Not that I know of," Sandy says, peeking out into the hallway, but Luna pulls her back inside.

"You two stay here. Keep the door closed. I'm going to check it out."

"Who is that?" Sandy wants to know when the door closes behind Luna.

It's a little awkward since I don't want to draw attention. "She's a friend. She's just keeping an eye out for me. Making sure I don't overdo it on my first day back."

The door swings open and I fully expect Luna to walk in.

But it's not her.

CHAPTER 27

Keith

"Check this out."

I stop on my way up the steps to knock at the front door and turn to see Tony peering in the rear window of the run-down vehicle.

"What've you got?"

He steps aside for me and I shield my eyes from the glare as I take a look inside. Half hidden by an old tarp and a battered jerrican, a compact pesticide sprayer is visible.

"Bingo," he says when I straighten up. "Although, I still can't see an old woman..."

"Who else lives here?" I ask sharply, looking up at the windows of the house. "Does she have children? Find out."

Ramirez opens the driver side door of my Tahoe and pulls out the radio while I march up the steps. My knocks go unanswered, as does the banging on the door that follows. Nothing.

"Mike Bolter is contacting the local post office. They might know. I also told him to check the local fire department about the burned-out shed. He'll call when he has something."

"Good. In the meantime, let's take a look around."

"There was definitely another vehicle here not too long ago," Tony says, brushing the toe of his boot over the dirt. "Tracks, wide ones, I'm guessing a pickup truck."

"I'm gonna check around back."

I spot the strange high mound of piled wood as soon as I turn the second corner. A stepladder sits on the grass beside it. When I get closer to investigate, I notice a faint odor of decay coming from the pile. Making sure the ladder is stable, I climb up a few steps until I can see over the edge and am greeted by the death grimace of a corpse. About two weeks, I'm guessing. Left out to bake in the sun. Amabel Jones, would be my guess, judging by the gray hair and floral blouse.

"Ramirez! I found her!"

Carefully I make my way back down, without disturbing the rather precarious structure, realizing as I go; I'm looking at a rudimentary funeral pyre.

"Jesus," he says when he rounds the corner. "Is that what I think it is?"

"Her body is laid out on top."

I watch as he clambers up the steps to see for himself.

"I'm calling this probable cause, I'm going in. Radio Bolter, see what the fuck is taking him so damn long!"

The lock on the back door is flimsy and it only takes a single well-aimed kick to open. The wave of hot putrid air coming from inside is almost worse than the stench of decomposition. Dead flies litter what is visible of the kitchen counter and table, the rest is covered with dirty dishes and rotting food. I quickly walk through and into what looks to be the living room.

An old TV cabinet against the wall beside the window,

across from a couch that dates back to the mid-seventies; it looks like the home of a hoarder, with junk covering almost every surface. Except for the coffee table. It looks clean and my attention is immediately drawn to three labeled white jars, lined up precisely in the center. I pick one up and the first thing that jumps out at me is the hospital name—Mercy Regional Medical Center—and by the time I read the patient's name, Jeffrey Youngman, cold fear is already crawling up my neck. I've seen that name.

I pull out my phone, but before I can dial out, it starts ringing.

"Luna," I answer with a quick glance at my screen. "I was just about to—"

"He's got her." She sounds out of breath like she's running. "The fire alarm went off, I told her to stay put with her assistant, Sandy, in the office while I checked it out. When I came back Sandy was trying to get up off the floor—bleeding from a head wound—and Autumn was gone."

"Son of a goddamn fucking bitch!" Hauling out with my foot, I upend the coffee table, the remaining jars flying through the room, but Luna doesn't stop talking.

"...seen leaving with a Jeff Youngman, age forty-eight, and getting into a silver newer model Ford Ranger. I'm getting in my car now."

"On my way," I bark, "call when you have a visual."

"What the fuck?" I storm out of the house and almost plow Ramirez over, who was running toward me. "What happened, I hear you yelling and cussing—"

"Jeffrey Youngman." I shove the container I'm still clutching in my fist at him. "He's one of Autumn's patients," I clarify, having pulled the pieces together. I never lose stride as Tony hustles to keep up. "He's got her."

"Hold up." He yanks at my arm. "Where are you going?"

"Didn't you hear me? He's got her. Caused a distraction at

the hospital and snatched her right from under Luna's eyes. I've got to get out there." I try to shrug loose, but Ramirez holds on tight, and I swing around sticking my face in his and yell, "Let go!"

"Think, goddammit, before you go off half-cocked. Where would he take her?" His question gives me pause and I take a step back. "That pyre out there is not an accident. That woman has been dead for a week or two. My guess is he was waiting for Autumn. He's bringing her here. Think about it—what if he already knew she was here only temporarily? What if he was trying to find a way to keep her here?"

"By supplying victims?" My tone is mocking, because it's almost too farfetched to conceive, but my friend is poker-faced.

"Absolutely. You're trying to bring rationale into the equation, but you know there's nothing rational about the way this guy's brain works. He was angry when he saw you got the jump on him with Autumn, lashed out in anger at her. Maybe lashed out at this poor woman. My gut is telling me he's bringing her here."

"He'll see the Tahoe," I consider, warming up to Tony's logic.

"Give me the keys, I'll pull it back here, behind those trees." He points at a small grove bordering one side of the yard.

I toss them at him. "Grab the Remington from the clip in the back. Extra ammo in the glove box." As soon as he jogs out of sight, I call Luna back. "We're at his house, Ramirez thinks he's coming back here. Head west on the 160. Right before the 140 cutoff, there's a dirt road on the left side. About half a mile down, there's a fork. Hang left. If you pick him up before you get here, give me a call."

Five minutes later, my Tahoe is mostly out of sight, Ramirez is crouched down on the far end of the porch, and

I'm inside hiding in the small hallway. I'm able to keep an eye on the driveway through the narrow window in the front door.

It doesn't take long before I see the sun bounce off the hood of a silver pickup truck speeding toward the house.

* * *

Autumn

I sit quietly with my hands clenched in my lap, as far away from him as I can get within the confines of the pickup truck. The barrel of his gun remains pointed at me, and I'm still trying to process what got me here.

At first it was shock when he barged into the office, immediately hitting poor Sandy in the head with the butt of the gun he was carrying. She was knocked to the ground, but I didn't get a chance to check on her because he was already dragging me out of there and into a waiting elevator. The whole thing couldn't have taken more than a couple of seconds. By the time the elevator doors closed, I got angry—yelled at him—but he never said a word. He quietly held up his phone, showing me a picture that froze every combative cell in my body.

I still battle the sobs that want to escape at the sight of Boots and Ziggy, chained to a cinderblock. They looked to be at the bottom of an old well, a thin stream of water coming from the green garden hose hanging over the edge.

He didn't need to tell me, I understood completely: I put up a fight; my cats will die a horrifying death.

I keep telling myself Keith will find me. I'm sure Luna has discovered I'm gone by now and would've been in contact, but when he turns onto the 160, driving away from Durango, that hope gets thin. Any escape scenario I can imagine means my cats perish, and I honestly don't know what I will do when the time comes I may have to make a choice—their life or my own.

"Your hands—they're soft. Caring."

I almost jump out of my skin when his low voice fills the cab, my heart thundering in my chest.

"I've never felt touch like that. Special—or at least I thought it was."

Keep him talking. The thought swirls persistently through my mind.

"Why?" I turn my eyes to him and he seems surprised at my question. "Why the fires?" I push.

"I couldn't let you leave. Not when I just found you. They were burning for you, a gift—for you. As long as you have patients, you can't leave. Then I saw you with him."

The gentle timbre of his voice stands in terrifying contrast to the madness contained in his message.

"You were responding, I could tell. You smiled at me." His voice crescendos as he turns his head toward me. I struggle not to heave when I see the insanity in his eyes. "I thought you were my salvation, but you are nothing but a seductress." Spittle flies from his lips as he hisses the words at me.

I can do nothing but stare back at the pure hatred twisting his face, when it suddenly morphs back into the quiet, placid mask as he turns back to the road.

His voice, soft once again, he continues his soliloquy. "It's an honor, you know? Being blessed by fire. The Vikings honored their loved ones with fire. Even to this day, there are cultures and religions that use fire to send their dead to a higher realm."

He falls silent, focusing on the road ahead. Just a minute or so later, he slows down, turns on his blinker and turns left onto a dirt road. I look in the side mirror and watch the highway disappear farther and farther from sight. Then he makes another left turn. My instinct for self-preservation is too strong, and I make the decision in a split second.

Reaching for my seat belt clip at the same time I pull on the door lever, I launch my upper body toward the opening door. I'm already thinking about rolling the moment I hit the ground, when my body is suddenly yanked back into the truck by my hair. I can't stop the scream flying from my mouth, as the truck comes to a stop with screeching tires in front of an old ramshackle farmhouse.

He drags me by the hair over the center console and out the driver's side door. With my legs still in the vehicle, my body plummets, my legs fly, and I hit the ground hard, knocking the air from my lungs when I land flat on my back. His body leans down over me, one hand still tangled in my hair and the other pressing the barrel of the gun against the side of my head.

"Get up," he hisses, pulling up on my hair. Still gasping for breath, I scramble to get my feet under me.

As he's dragging me up the steps of the porch, I see movement to my right, and the next moment I hear a yell.

"Red! Down!"

With the sound of Keith's voice a rush of adrenaline surges through me, and I instantly let my body drop down, ripping hair from my head.

Shots are fired, more screeching tires sound as chaos ensues, and all I can do is cover my head with my arms. I hear one last shot, and then a heavy silence settles around me.

"Jesus, baby…are you hurt? Talk to me, Red." I feel Keith's hand on my back as he brushes away the hair covering my face with the other.

"I'm okay," I whisper, following it immediately with, "Is he dead?"

Keith doesn't say anything as he helps me to my feet, immediately turning and pressing my head to his chest, and I already know the answer. Relieved and shaky, I grab onto his shirt and bury my face, willing away the tears that want to fall. Suddenly I stiffen in his arms.

"Oh no...my cats."

"What do you mean?"

I tilt my head back and my eyes well when I see the confused concern in his beautiful face. "Boots and Ziggy. He had them all this time. He's slowly killing them, and I don't know where."

It takes me a minute to explain about the picture on his phone.

"Stay right there," he orders as he steps around me.

He should know by now I don't take orders well, and I turn around to find him bent over the body of Jeffrey Youngman, rifling through his pockets. He's dead. It doesn't take a genius to see that. A large pool of blood has formed under his body, and as unscathed as it looks from this angle, I know there's a good-sized hole in him somewhere to cause such a large leak.

I'm surprised at how unmoved I am at the sight. It's not the first time I've seen a dead body, but it's the first time I've seen someone who died a violent death.

"Is this them?" Keith holds up the phone and the first tear starts rolling when I realize they may not even be alive anymore. I swallow hard and nod sharply.

"Show me," Tony, who I'm surprised seeing, steps up and takes the phone from Keith. "That's a well."

"That's what I thought," I agree.

"I think I know where it is." He turns to Keith. "When I

was moving the Tahoe behind the trees, I drove over a garden hose just like that."

Keith is already running before Tony even finishes talking.

"Where are they off to?" I just start moving after them when Luna appears by my side, watching the guys disappear around the corner. She looks at me and her face softens. "Are you okay? I'm so sorry—" Without slowing my pace, I hold up my hand to stop her.

"I'm fine. He had my cats. Stuck them in some hole, chained them down and it's filling slowly with water. Tony thinks he knows where it is." Beside me, Luna picks up her pace.

Behind the house, I spot the hose Tony was referring to and we follow it into the trees. That's where we see the guys, Tony is lifting a lid from the crumbled wall of what appears an old well. Luna sprints past me, and by the time I reach the well, Keith is already lowering her into the hole.

CHAPTER 28

Keith

I died a thousand deaths.

I never understood the concept of that phrase until today.

Luna's call started the count. When I saw the door swing open on that speeding truck and caught a glimpse her red hair swinging toward the opening, before being violently yanked back, I swear it felt like I'd never draw my next breath. Seeing Autumn with a gun pressed against her temple, it was all I could do not to storm out of my hiding place and tear that fucking miscreant limb from limb with my bare hands. One last remaining fiber of common sense is all that held me back from what likely would've ended in a loss I can't even begin to conceive.

Not with Autumn beside me in the Tahoe, alive, breathing, and tending to her two half-drowned cats while I speed to the nearest vet.

It was actually Luna's bullet that killed him. She pulled up just as I burst out of the front door. Both Ramirez and I were firing, and when he went down, my focus shifted to Autumn lying in a crumpled heap on the porch. I didn't see his gun come up until it was almost too late. Luna did and took him out with a single shot to the head.

We'd been just in time. I initially thought we were too late —only two little cat faces barely sticking up from the rising water—but Luna yelled at me to lower her. With a strength that still amazes me in that small body of hers, she somehow managed to pick up the heavy cinderblock, scoop up the cats, and lift all three up into our waiting hands.

"How are they doing?" I peek over at the sorry pile of fur on Autumn's lap. It had taken until the first emergency vehicle came down the driveway, to get the damn chains off the cats' necks. Both had nasty abrasions from trying, God knows how long, to pull out of those makeshift collars.

"They'll be okay." Autumn's words are confident, but the tone of her voice is not.

I go a little faster. I'll be damned if I let that monster take one more thing from her. She's lost enough at his hands. And I almost lost her.

I love her.

I'm actually surprised I'm able to identify this feeling of having your heart so deeply connected to another person's, you can actually feel every one of their emotions. It's both amazing and terrifying.

"I love you," I blurt out. Not exactly a romantic declaration, given the circumstances, but one I feel compelled to make nonetheless. "I can be an idiot, I have a temper that gets the best of me, and I have no fucking idea what I'm doing, but I'm doing it anyway because I love you."

Her eyes—big, shiny green orbs behind those red glasses that miraculously survived the ordeal—find mine, and I don't need to hear the words, I can see them clear as day.

I'm not a fool. I know love alone does not solve every problem. We've got a lot of shit going on, a lot of things to sort out, but I'm sure we can battle through them—one by one.

"You wait," I instruct her when we pull into the emergency veterinary clinic. "I'll come around and take them from you."

We'd wrapped the cats in the windbreaker I keep in the back of the Tahoe, and I scoop the whole bundle from her lap. She hustles ahead and pulls the clinic door open for me.

It's not until I hand both cats over to the vet, that Autumn grabs onto my arm, shaking like a leaf. Delayed reaction. I quickly wrap my arms around her before she hits the floor, and an alert assistant shuffles us into a small examination room, giving us some privacy.

"Let it go," I mumble in her hair, after sitting down on a plastic chair and pulling her onto my lap. "Let it all go."

I know what it's like when adrenaline wears off. It leaves you feeling emotionally raw and physically exhausted. Adrenaline can sustain you under dire circumstances but there comes a time, when the immediate pressure is gone, that the full impact of all you've been through hits you full force. I've seen men break under that wave. Hell, there've been times where I've been so overcome; I buried myself in a bottle. Downside of that option is waking up the next day feeling like the crap stuck to the bottom of your boot.

Unsure how much time has lapsed, her shaking has subsided some, and she lifts her face from where it was buried in my neck.

"Thank you." Her already smoky voice sounds even raspier, and I brush a soft kiss to the crease between her eyebrows.

"Always," I promise.

* * *

Autumn

When we walk through the front door, it's hard to imagine it was only about eight hours ago I left to go to work.

Keith disappears into the hallway to his office and I collapse on the couch. Both Jack and Gizmo come over, sniffing me up and down. They can smell their buddies, I'm sure.

The vet assured us both cats should be fine, but since they're both at risk for infection, they were put on IV antibiotics and will be kept at the clinic for at least forty-eight hours. I was able to see them before we left, and almost started bawling when Ziggy actually purred when I scratched her behind the ear.

Almost, but not quite. I've done enough of that in the past twenty-four hours to last a bloody lifetime.

"Come with me."

I open my eyes and find Keith standing over me, his hand stretched out. I let him pull me up and lead me to the guest bathroom, where water is filling the tub. Without a word, he starts stripping me, carefully examining every square inch of my body. I let him. I get what this is about. I can tell him a million times I'm fine, but he'll still need to see for himself.

"You're starting to bruise here," he says, whispering his fingers over my shoulder and down to the swell of my butt. "Here too."

"Probably the fall out of the truck," I suggest.

"Hmm. Get in, Red. Relax. I'll be right back."

He holds my hand as I step into the tub and groan with pleasure when I slowly sink down in the water. He rolls up a towel and props it in my neck before leaving me alone.

I'm almost asleep when he walks back in, carrying a

bottle of cold water and a plate with cheese, rolled up lunchmeat, and slices of apple.

"No wine?" I joke to hide the sudden swell of emotion at his gentle care for me.

"Not until you properly hydrate and get something in your stomach. You haven't eaten since breakfast."

"I bet you haven't either," I return.

"You didn't think this was all for you, did you?" He hands me the plate, sets the bottle on the edge of the tub, and promptly starts stripping out of his clothes, and sinking into the water facing me.

It's kind of amazing, really: just being with someone. Not much talking, not necessarily doing anything other than feeding the body, and nourishing the soul.

I could easily stay in this moment, oblivious of the passing of time, if not for the insistent buzz of Keith's phone in his pocket. Setting the almost empty plate on the floor, he reaches for his jeans.

"Blackfoot," he snaps into the receiver, but his soft eyes never leave mine, holding on to that connection a little longer. "Make it here, and make it half an hour." Ending the call, he tosses it carelessly on the pile of clothes. "Come here."

This time the order is gentle enough to sound more like an invitation. I scoot over, turning so I can fit myself between his cocked legs, my upper body against his chest. His arms come around me and his chin leans on my shoulder. I can feel the heat of his swollen cock in the small of my back.

"My plan to get you so relaxed, you'd have no trouble falling asleep in my arms later, has hit a glitch." Even as he's talking, his hand slides down between my legs, cupping my sex. "I have exactly twenty minutes…" He moves his feet between my stretched legs, slowly spreading my knees as wide as they can go. "…to make you come…" Fingers slide along my crease, already slick with arousal. All it takes is the deep vibration of his voice behind me. "...and leave you enough time..." First one, and then a second digit slips inside, slowly pumping in and out. Already my hips undulate and soft groans escape under his ministrations. "...to get dressed before..." His other hand slides through my curls, finding my clit easily. Blood rushes in my ears, my mouth falls open as my own fingers pluck mindlessly at my nipples. "...they get here."

"Oh God...ahhh," I groan, as I'm washed away by a deep throbbing climax that sends tingles down to the tips of my toes.

"Hmmm," Keith hums against the shell of my ear, sending an added shiver through my body.

"Who gets here?" I half slur my words, my body limp and sated, and my brain barely firing.

"Ramirez, Roosberg, Gomez, and Stan Woodard."

I'm out of the tub faster than a bullet, dripping water all over the floor. He has the fucking mayor showing up? I bend down to rifle through the now soggy pile of clothes to find mine.

"Are you shitting me? How much time do we have?"

"Five, maybe ten minutes. Just enough time to—"

I don't wait around to hear him finish. With my soggy pile of clothes under my arm, I dart out of the bathroom, sprinting butt naked across the living room, just as headlights hit through the window, catching me like a spotlight.

I think I've used up every conceivable curse word, in a multitude of languages, by the time I come out of the bedroom. My eyes find Keith's and I shoot him the dirtiest look I can muster, before I turn a smile on our guests.

Apparently they're here for some kind of briefing. Piecing together our collective experiences to form a cohesive whole. The urgency, to make sure all the pieces fit, is the press showed up at the scene shortly after we rushed off to find a vet. So far, no one has given any statements, but things tend to come out, and with so many first responders showing up at the scene, something is bound to slip at some point.

That's why the mayor has offered a press conference with Special Agent Damian Gomez, Luna, Ramirez, and Keith in attendance. He also urges me to attend, insisting the public will be able to identify best with the victim's experience. I'm relieved when Keith adamantly refuses subjecting me to any questions, and accuses the mayor of trying to use me as a token mascot to build his next campaign on.

Needless to say, there was some heated back-and-forth, before Damian—who like Keith, also appears to be quite outspoken—jumps in to referee, by verbally knocking some heads together.

There are a few moments where I find myself embarrassed, in particular the discreet details Keith shares of the times we may have been unwittingly observed. I get that those private moments have become an important part of the overall timeline, but sharing those memorable intimate experiences somehow stains them.

I'm surprised to find out the nature of the weird woodpile I'd seen in the back of the farmhouse. I didn't pay it much notice, too preoccupied with the rescue of my cats, and I'm glad I didn't after hearing the details. The poor woman apparently had been an elderly aunt, who took Jeffrey in as a teenager after his parents died in a house fire, while he was staying at a friend's. Something happened—perhaps she suspected what he was up to when he showed up with the cats and confronted him—but at some point he snapped and killed her. Presumably by strangulation, but the coroner would have to confirm.

I shiver when Tony outlines his suspicions around the

pyre, but as I recount his weird rant about honoring loved ones with fire, I realize he's probably not far off the mark.

I have little to say about the actual confrontation, since I was hugging the porch floor at the time, but at the end the mayor, as well as SAC Gomez, are satisfied the shooting had been a just one.

Keith doesn't waste time shooing them all out the door, but it's already past eleven when he locks it and turns off the porch light.

"You look tired," he says, his voice much gentler when he addresses me. Funny how I just notice that now.

"Exhausted doesn't even touch it."

"Why don't you head to bed? I'll just clean up and meet you there. You can sleep in tomorrow."

"No, I can't. I start at nine."

"Like hell you are."

Just like that we're back on quicksand.

* * *

Keith

I know I fucked up the moment the words leave my mouth.

She visibly shuts down, her lips a thin line and her shoulders pulled up to her ears.

"Can I please rephrase that?" I plead, rubbing my hands over her shoulders. "Before you shut me down, please hear me out."

I walk her backward into the kitchen and lift her to sit on the counter, wedging myself between her knees. At least that way I'm sure she can't run off.

"We already know there are a few hot-button triggers in

our relationship. Me tending to be overbearing in my concern for you, and you being sensitive to anything you perceive as control, is one. We also still have the housing situation, as well as your ongoing status in Durango to contend with. Am I right?"

Her lips are still tight but I still get a nod. I'll take it.

"We're both strong personalities, Red. We're bound to butt heads quite a bit, but we're also incredibly fucking good together, and I'm not just talking about the sex. If we could wrap our heads around this relationship being more of a joining of forces, than an endless compromise of our own identities, can you imagine how strong we could be?"

Her hand comes up and hooks around my neck, the other planting in the middle of my chest, and she nods again, but this time with the beginnings of a smile.

"What I meant to say was, after the news conference tomorrow, I would like for both of us to take the rest of the week off. Use that time, without circumstances driving us, to see if we can't make a start on those hot-button triggers." I tilt my head to find her eyes. "What do you say?"

Her eyes now smile too and she takes my face in her hands.

"I think I love you too."

CHAPTER 29

Keith

I would've preferred staying the last night of our self-imposed exile from the world at home as well, but Autumn was hell-bent on a game of darts and a Guinness.

For all our good intentions, we didn't spend too much time talking about the future these past days; we were mostly enjoying the moment. Or moments. There were many, most of them while naked, but a few others were memorable as well. Like yesterday, when we picked up Autumn's other two cats from the vet and brought them home.

I never was much of a cat person. Actually, that's not true: I was mostly indifferent to them. Autumn's cats have grown on me. I'm getting used to being woken up by Gizmo, who sits on my chest and meows in my face, butting her head on my chin if I don't move fast enough. A real little diva. I'm also learning to appreciate Jake's more aloof approach: when you pet him, he behaves like you should consider yourself lucky he even allows you to. He's a cool customer. I'm already picking up some personality traits from Boots and Ziggy. On top of that, I actually remember which name goes with each cat.

The one subject we did discuss was making her stay in Durango permanent. It was actually a call with Sophie on Friday that started the conversation. Apparently Autumn had mentioned something about her contract with Mercy expiring, and Sophie encouraged her to talk to them now. Put a bug in their ear that she might be interested in making it a permanent position. See how they respond.

The moment she ended the call, she dialed the hospital and set up a meeting for Tuesday afternoon. Just like that.

"Honey, are you ready?" I look up to see her coming down the hall from the bedroom, looking hot as fuck in a simple pair of jeans, a black tank top under some flowing kimono thing, but paired with some high-heeled contraptions on her feet with lots of straps and buckles. That red mane of hers all brushed out, cascading down her back and just a hint of gloss on those lips I love so much. For a woman who doesn't put a lot of stock in fashion or fancy things, she sure knows how to pull off feminine in a major way.

"I like when you call me that," I admit, folding her in my arms.

"What?"

"Honey. That's the fourth time in the past couple of days you called me that."

"You're counting?" she asks, a saucy little smile playing on her lips.

"Damn right I am."

"You'll lose count in no time."

"I'm hoping," I confess, and her smile deepens warmly.

* * *

The first person we see walking into The Irish is Evan Biel, sitting at the bar. He takes one look and turns his back, much like he did at the funeral. Fuck. I probably owe the guy an apology. I've been all but crawling up his ass since this whole mess started.

Autumn pulls on my arm. "Let's go talk to him." She clearly caught that cold shoulder too.

"Since I'm the real asshole here, give me a chance to talk to him one on one."

"Are you gonna piss him off?" she asks, an eyebrow raised.

"Probably." I grin down at her. "But we'll sort it out."

I order her a Guinness and get her a set of darts so she can practice. She elbows me in the gut when I suggest it.

"Got a minute?" I interrupt the conversation Evan is having with a fellow firefighter. He reluctantly turns around.

"Here in official capacity? Should I call my lawyer?" he taunts sarcastically.

"Knock it off, Biel. Let's find a quiet spot." I order us a couple of drinks, and with a quick glance at Autumn—who apparently found a willing victim to practice her skills on—I lead the way to the same booth I sat in when I first saw her. I wait for him to slide in across from me. "Here's the thing; I suspect if not for that gorgeous redhead over there, you would be more inclined to understand my position. By the same token, any victim other than Autumn, I might have been a little less…confrontational in my investigation." He responds with a snort, but I ignore it and push on. "Durango is not that big, Evan. You can turn your back on me in here, or anywhere else we see each other outside of work—but you know as well as I do—our professional paths cross all the time. I'd much rather do my job knowing I have you at my back than having to watch my back. I'm sure you feel the same way." This time it's a grunt, which I guess is a moderate improvement, but he's still not talking, so I decide to go balls to the wall. "I love her. She's working on moving here permanently, and I want her to be happy here." His head comes up and he first eyes me curiously before looking off over my shoulder, and I know he's watching her. "She could use all the friends she can get, and she considers you one. Now I regret like hell you ended up as a suspect when you were innocent, but I will not apologize for doing my job, I just hope you don't take your anger out on her."

His eyes come back to me and he pointedly drinks down his beer, sets down his glass, and leans over the table. "Was that all?"

"It's all I've got."

Without another word, he heads back to the bar, but instead of sitting back down, he walks to the other side where Autumn is just picking her darts from the board. When she turns around, he's right there, leaning down to kiss her cheek. A smile spreads on her face and her eyes quickly dart my way, gratitude clear in their depths.

I give them some time, head into the bathroom—and when I return—Biel is back on his seat by the bar and Autumn's victim has disappeared.

"Up for a game?" I offer when I walk up.

"What do you think?"

It's not until she's wiped the floor with me twice and we've ordered our last drink for the road, that she brings up our next hurdle.

"So...about that apartment..."

* * *

Autumn

I let my statement linger, waiting anxiously for his reaction.

He looks down at his beer before meeting my eyes, and I

take courage from the fact I don't sense any hostility from him.

"First of all," I start hesitantly, "I want you to know I adore your house. I love it there."

"But then—"

"Let me finish. Please?" He nods once, his full attention on me. "I like being there with you, I feel at home there, but I need a chance to get myself back on my feet. It's important to me to come to you whole and independent—the way I know myself." He moves to interrupt me again, but this time a lift of my hand is enough to have him sit back again—listening. "Staying feels like we're taking a shortcut, and I don't ever want either of us to think the other considers them a convenience. I want that step to be a conscious choice for both of us."

He's quiet. His eyes still on me, but he seems to be considering my words.

"Okay," he finally says. "I get that. Don't get me wrong, I don't relish sleeping without you right beside me, or waking up and not having you be the first thing I see, but I get it. I'll miss having you around—and believe it or not, I'll miss those damn cats as well—but I can wait."

I lean over the table and weave my fingers with his. "Not like I'm disappearing. I don't want to stop seeing you, or even slow it down, I just want to do this right."

"Perfect!" I hear over my shoulder and swing around to see Luna walk up to the table, a tall smiling blond guy right behind her.

"Tell me this wasn't planned," Keith groans, but before I can ask him what he means, Luna pulls out a chair and plops down.

"This is a happy coincidence," she says, smiling. "Autumn, this is Jasper." She indicates the blond man who pulls out his own chair, lifts his chin at Keith in greeting, and sticks out his hand across the table for me to shake. "He's the colleague I was telling you about? The apartment?"

Suddenly I clue in to what Keith was asking, so my first, rather sharp words are to him. "I obviously had no clue." Then I turn to Jasper, smiling wide. "Keith here seems to think I had some kind of hand in you showing up here, since we just happened to be discussing living arrangements."

The man just grins, shaking his head and holding up his hands. "I know nothing."

"Don't be an idiot," Luna says, punching Keith's shoulder. "Jas and I just stopped in for a drink before heading home. But…" her face twists into a calculating smile. "Since we apparently arrived at such a fortuitous moment, why don't we go see the apartment now? It's just across the street. You've got the keys, right, Jas?"

"You're pushing," Keith growls at her, but she just grins back.

"I know."

Twenty minutes later, Jasper opens the door to a gorgeous, loft-style apartment with large windows, lots of brick and stainless steel. Very industrial-looking. The first thing I notice is the furniture.

"It comes furnished?"

"It does. My in-laws use it from time to time when they come to town."

"But then are you sure you want to rent it out?"

"Yup." That's all he says. Not a lot of information, but I guess I don't need to know more.

We take a look around, Keith dragging his feet a little, and by the time Jasper locks the door behind us, I've come to a decision.

"I love it. Do you need me to sign a lease? Luna mentioned you'd be happy with shorter term?"

"I'm happy just going month to month. No fuss."

"That would be perfect. When can I move in?"

"Any time. Tomorrow if you like." Keith growls and throws Jasper a death look, but the guy doesn't seem impressed much and just grins back. "Never thought I'd see the day, Blackfoot. I've gotta say, feels real good to be on this side."

"Ignore them," Luna stage-whispers to me. "Your boyfriend loved poking fun at his buddies when they met their significant others. Guess he had this coming."

"No real rush," I tell Jasper, but my eyes are on Keith. He gives me a barely perceptible nod. "Next weekend is soon enough."

Half an hour later, we walk into the house and he doesn't even stop to turn on the lights, he keeps a tight hold on my hand and marches us straight to the bedroom. He stops by the side of the bed and turns to face me, the only thing visible: the reflection of the sparse light in his eyes. Wordlessly he reaches out and brushes my top off my shoulders, letting it drop on the floor at my feet. Slowly undressing me, he keeps his eyes on mine. Even when he goes down on his knees to unbuckle the straps of my sandals, easing them off my feet, before stripping down my jeans.

It's not until he takes my glasses off my nose and sets them down on the nightstand, that he speaks.

"Get in bed, Red."

His voice is rough and an involuntary shiver runs down my spine. I do as he asks, and watch from the bed as he strips out of his own clothes before joining me.

For the longest time he just holds me, and at some point I wonder if he's fallen asleep, but when I lift my head from his chest, I see the glint of his eyes, still looking down at me.

"I love you, Autumn."

I push up, swing a leg over his body and cover his body

with mine, chest to chest and nose to nose. "I know, honey, and I love you. So much."

Sitting up, I lift my hips and slowly slide down over the soft steel of his erection.

His eyes never leave mine.

-

Keith walks into the kitchen of my new apartment, bringing in the last of the bags.

It's amazing how much a person accumulates in a very short time. A few weeks ago, I had nothing but a garbage bag with a handful of outfits. Thanks to the wonders of Internet shopping and a couple of trips to the Durango Mall, I now have enough clothes to fill the closet, and some small household items to turn this place into a home.

"I've gotta run." Keith puts the bags of groceries we picked up on the counter. "With Benedetti taking over after next weekend, I've got a shitload of unfinished paperwork to clear before he gets here. Some of it predates my stint as chief. Gotta get things halfway in order, otherwise I'm afraid with one look at his office, he'll hightail it right back to Denver."

"Of course." I manage to sound understanding—and really, I am—but I'm suddenly not so sure this was a good idea.

Probably sensing my mood, he rounds the counter, hooks a hand behind my neck, and pulls me into his chest.

"You'll be fine, Red."

"I know," I mumble on a little sniffle.

"It'll work out."

"I know it will."

He tilts up my head and kisses me deeply. My hands curl in his shirt and I hang on, prolonging the kiss as long as I can. This is exactly the reason I need this distance. My need for him—his touch, his presence—is more like addiction. I need to know I'm still the same person underneath.

"I'll call you later, okay?" he finally says, rescuing his shirt from my clutches.

"All right."

I watch as he walks out the door, take a deep breath, and put away my groceries.

CHAPTER 30

Autumn

"How did it go yesterday?"

Sandy is waiting for me in the office, an expectant smile on her face.

Luckily, other than a small cut on her head that required a couple of stitches, she doesn't seem to have any lingering effects after being pistol-whipped last week. Just like me, she reported back for work Monday, and we've both been scrambling to get caught up.

"Well. I think. They'd like me to finish out the contract as it is, but apparently were already talking about making this a permanent position. They just assumed I would return to San Antonio, and hadn't bothered approaching me. Knowing I plan to stay in Durango, regardless, seemed to pique their interest."

"That's fabulous. I'm so glad you decided to stay."

"Me too. I really like it here."

Sandy grins at that. "I just bet you do."

Yesterday morning, I'd walked into my office to find a

large bouquet of flowers waiting for me. The card simply said: *Good luck today. K.*

Sandy said he'd actually delivered them himself when I was downstairs meeting with a young patient and her family. I was pretty bummed I'd missed him, since I haven't seen him since Sunday night when he walked out of my new place. Oh, we've talked on the phone every night, but between his workload—trying to get his office in order—and mine, trying to get caught up, there simply hasn't been much time.

When I mentioned last night this is harder than I thought it would be; he reassured me that it's just a temporary situation. With Benedetti in office, he would have more downtime, and once I get on top of my own work, the same would apply for me. He even suggested getting away for Labor Day weekend, maybe fly down to San Antonio and see our friends. Head down to the River Walk and eat some hot churros from one of the street vendors, listen to live music.

It helped. I can be patient. Sort of.

I spend the rest of the morning plugging away at the pile, but when my stomach starts growling for food, I walk out into the reception area to see if Sandy wants to come grab a bite.

"Hey—what are you doing here?" I ask Evan, who is leaning on a slightly flushed Sandy's desk.

"Came to see if I could interest you in lunch. Both of you," he quickly adds, looking at Sandy who is now full-blown blushing.

I should probably warn him that although Sandy is highly intelligent and undoubtedly pretty, she also has stars in her eyes, and in that respect is still very young.

"I was actually just going to suggest that, but let's grab something quick downstairs, Sandy and I have a ton of work left to do this afternoon."

Apparently Evan is quite well-connected, every five

minutes someone else stops at the table to say hello. At some point, he waves a pretty dark-haired woman in an EMT uniform over.

"Hey, Bella, come say hi to Autumn."

"Oh my God, you're Jasper's new tenant," she says, enthusiastically shaking my hand. "I had totally planned to be there to meet you when he handed over the keys this weekend, but I got stuck with a double shift. I'm so glad to get a chance now. Luna speaks highly of you too. Even my brother mentioned you. Actually he said it was about damn time Keith met his match, but he was talking about you."

I'm a little taken aback at the waterfall of kind words, but I deduce Bella is Jasper's wife, and therefore Damian Gomez's sister. I'm starting to get the sense that this community is smaller than it looks.

"Happy to meet you too." I smile back, as Evan pulls out a chair for her to join us.

By the time I get back to my office, I've been introduced to more new people than I did in the months previous, and I have an invite for a movie night this Saturday with Bella and her sister-in-law, Kerry, Damian's wife.

Already I'm starting to feel solid ground under my feet again.

* * *

Keith

"I wasn't expecting you until tomorrow. Eager to get a head start?"

I glance over the desk at the large man unexpectedly sauntering into my office. Or, what will be his office soon enough. Joe Benedetti sits down heavily in the chair across from me.

"I'm looking for refuge," he says, looking a little rough around the edges.

"Here?" I snort, looking around at the new stacks piling up on my desk as quickly as I'm able to process the old ones.

"Trust me, compared to packing up fourteen years and two kids' worth of living, seven hours in a car with my hyped-up offspring, while trying to keep up with a moving truck intent on breaking every kind of speed record, followed by two days of utter chaos in the new house, this place is an oasis," he groans.

Benedetti got to town last Thursday, taking up residence in a nice three-bedroom place not too far from the college. He's scheduled to be sworn in tomorrow at noon, and I hadn't expected to see him before.

"What did you do with the kids?"

"Trial run with the new babysitter. I left them beating the snot out of each other on their PlayStation. All three of them."

"Sounds like the babysitter will work out fine then," I observe teasingly.

"A seventeen-year-old neighbor with purple hair, combat boots, and enough metal in her face to set off security detectors from fifty feet, but she came highly recommended. I just hope my new flat-screen TV will still be there when I get back."

We spend the next few hours going over the schedule, open cases, staff, and administrative obligations. It helps that Joe, having led a division larger than our entire police department here, seems to be more familiar with the workings of the office than I was when I got thrown in the deep last year. Mike Bolter is on call, so I have a chance to introduce him, as well as a few other officers wandering in and out of the station over the afternoon.

When six comes around, Joe gets up and runs a hand through his deceptively silver hair.

"I should go and make sure my two terrors and their gatekeeper have left the house standing. The natives get restless when feeding time is near."

"Check out J. Bo's up on Florida Road. They have great pizza and rib deals. Two blocks from your place."

"Perfect, that way I can silence them the moment I come in the door. Good plan."

I'm still grinning when he walks out the door with a half-assed wave goodbye. For all his bluster, I can tell his family is priority in his life. As it should be.

I think I'm gonna like working with this guy.

My mood sours when I walk into my own place less than an hour later, carrying my own takeout. I haven't really had any interest in cooking since Autumn left and have regressed to my college days, eating quick and easy crap every meal. Sonic is on the menu for today.

I quickly turn on the TV to fill the silence, only wishing I'd have a noisy house to come home to. Kicking off my boots, I collapse on the couch, eating my burger and fries straight from the bag. At this rate, my love handles will turn into truck-sized spare tires in no time.

Tossing the remnants of dinner on the coffee table, I prop up my feet, find a Rockies' ball game on a local station, and try to get into it, but end up turning it off. I should be celebrating tonight, my last day as interim Chief of Police. Something that seemed so important, just last month, seems pretty insignificant now. Still, I remember promising myself I'd get hammered.

Walking into the kitchen, I grab the bottle of Jack from the cupboard, and bring it out on the deck off the bedroom. I wince when I take the first swig straight from the bottle. Damn, it's been a while since I've indulged in hard liquor.

The last trails of sunlight dissipate in the sky, while the moon makes an appearance on the other side. The view below is already cast in dark shadows. It's a hot night. Just a little breeze hitting my face every now and then. Inevitably my thoughts drift to the one person who would make this night perfect.

I haven't seen Autumn at all this week. We've talked on the phone daily, but every time we tried to plan a date, something would come up. By Friday, I'd had enough and told her —come hell or high water—I'd come see her Saturday. That's when she mentioned she'd made other plans. That was unexpected, and frankly a bit of a slap in the face. Here I am pining for the woman and she's off making friends and going out. She did offer to cancel, but I told her not to.

I've struggled the past few days, wondering if maybe this was not meant to be after all. I certainly don't seem to be doing too well with this distance thing. It's entirely possible I'm just not cut out for this.

I take another swig of Jack and already it goes down a lot smoother.

Closing my eyes, I lean my head back against the log siding and just listen to the sounds of the night. Crickets, an occasional screech from a bird of prey, and in the distance, the faint sound of two coyotes call out to each other across the canyon.

I must've dozed off because my eyes fly open when a rustle of clothes brushes my arm. For a second I wonder if I'm dreaming.

"Hey." Her raspy warm voice slips from her smiling lips. "I was wondering where you were."

"What are you doing here?" I ask, more curt than I intend, I'm still trying to process her sudden appearance. Instantly the light in her face dims as she leans back against the railing. "I didn't mean—"

"I tried," she interrupts my apology. "Seven nights I've tried to sleep by myself—like I've been able to do for most of my forty-two years—but I can't. I can't sleep. I can get through my days, staying busy and distracted, but the moment I walk through the door of the apartment, not even the cats can make me feel less alone."

I push myself up from the chair and take a step toward her. "I get it."

"I'm finding my feet, but it's not enough," she continues as if I hadn't spoken. "I don't want to be independent and alone in my apartment—I want to be here, with you, talking about our day while we share a meal at the end of it. I want to wear your shirt after we've made love on the couch, because we can't keep our hands to ourselves. I want to trip over your boots when I walk in the door, and smile just because you make my coffee just right. I want to go out with my friends to the movies, so I can come home to you. I want—no—I need to be with you, because I don't like who I am without you."

Every negative thought, every insecurity, every doubt I've had this past week disappears. I'm struggling to keep my composure as my face twitches with barely contained emotion. Even in the sparse light of night her heart is visible, clear as day in her eyes.

"Turn around," I instruct her, forcing the words past the lump in my throat. A slightly quizzical look on her face, she does as I ask, before swinging back around.

"The cats," she whispers.

"What about them?"

"They're in my car. Along with the rest of my things."

Jesus, this woman can lay my heart bare.

"Keys," I growl and she hands them to me. "I'll get them. When I get back, I want you naked in the moonlight."

It takes me five minutes to round up the cats and put them safely inside, haul in her bags that I drop beside the front door, and strip buck naked on my way through the bedroom.

I can see her leaning on the railing, her back to me, looking at what I know is a stunning view even in moonlight, but nowhere near as breathtaking as the view I have.

I step through the French doors, and see from her reaction she hears me, but she doesn't turn around. I walk up behind her, pressing myself against the soft swells of her body as I wrap the length of her hair around my fist, pulling her head to the side. Her eyes meet mine for just a second before I cover her lips with mine in a bruising kiss, pouring all my emotions in every stroke of my tongue in her mouth.

My other hand cups and lifts her breast, rolling the tip between my fingers with a firm pinch as my mouth runs along the exposed tendon in her neck, marking at the junction of her shoulder with a nip of my teeth. Her body shivers in response, and as if orchestrated, she raises up on tiptoes, tilting her hips up in offering. I don't need more encouragement—sinking through my knees—I line the crown of my cock up with her slick sex and pull her to me as I surge up inside her. The moan that escapes her: music to my ears.

Releasing her hair, I cross that arm in front of her, holding onto her opposite shoulder, while my other hand settles low over her stomach, controlling the tilt of her hips. With my thigh muscles driving, I power myself into her, feeding off the sounds falling from her mouth. I feel primal, marking her for the world to see—mine.

She doesn't hold back and screams out her release, the sound echoing back from below. Shaking with the force of my own orgasm, and still rooted deep inside her, I lean my chin on her shoulder.

"This spot here—that view—it used to be my world. My dream, my existence, the end of my day—everything. Now, it means little, unless it includes you."

EPILOGUE

Keith

"This is unreal."

I glance at Autumn, sitting on a rock beside me, looking down on Upper Bear Creek Falls. The view is stunning.

We arrived in Telluride around midday. Well over a month later than originally planned, but I'd forgotten about the influx of bikers from all over the state for the annual Labor Day Bike and Car Parade. Generally a peaceful event, but there have been years when stuff got out of hand with one biker group or another. In any event, it wasn't the right time to take time off, so we postponed it until now.

She's been officially living with me for two-and-a-half months, give or take a couple of days. As much as we've settled into a daily routine, every day I wake up with her beside me I wonder what on earth I've done to be this lucky. Even when we argue—which we do regularly—she captivates me with her intelligence, her tenacity, her fire.

I never expected loving someone could be so completely consuming, leaking through in absolutely every aspect of your life. I also never understood the concept of the term 'becoming one,' but I get it now. There isn't a thought, a plan, an idea that doesn't somehow involve the one you love. You become completely aware of each other.

Which is why I've noticed this morning on the drive here, and even on the hour hike up the mountain we decided on for this afternoon, my Red is out of sorts. I tried earlier, when I caught her wringing her hands in her lap on the drive, but she waved it off.

We're out on a rock, just the two of us in the middle of nowhere, and I'm not about to let her brush me off again.

"Are you ready to tell me what's on your mind yet?" I ask, tucking a strand of hair behind her ear. She doesn't flinch at my question as she did earlier, so I assume she was expecting it.

"Not really, but I will." Her answer is straightforward, which is one of the things I love about her. She's not in the habit of beating around the bush. "Let me preface it to say I am totally freaked out. I mean, my stomach is in knots and I could puke on the spot, because I have absolutely no clue how you're going to respond."

Well. I wasn't worried before, but I am now. My mind immediately goes to the worst-case scenario, and I'm wondering if there've been signs I've missed. Is she unhappy? She didn't strike me as particularly unhappy, but maybe I'm not reading her as well as I think I am.

"Stop thinking," she admonishes me, brushing her thumb over the crease that formed between my eyebrows. "It makes me even more jittery." I bark out a nervous laugh myself.

"Spit it out then," I urge her, and she grabs hold of my hand.

"Remember that night when I came home? Out on the deck? You went and got a washcloth to clean me up after, remember that?"

"Fuck, Red. Not a night I'll ever forget, of course I remember."

I remember every detail about that night. The way she looked leaning naked against the railing, the way her moans bounced off the rocks below, the way her body pulsed around me as I emptied myself...

My blood rushes to my extremities all at once, leaving me dizzy and breathless. I scan her face for the answer and see it in the soft smile on her lips, the shine of her eyes.

"Mid-April," she whispers.

Here I thought my life was already complete.

THE END

ABOUT THE AUTHOR

Freya Barker loves writing about ordinary people with extraordinary stories.

Driven to make her books about 'real' people; she creates characters who are perhaps less than perfect, each struggling to find their own slice of happy, but just as deserving of romance, thrills and chills in their lives.

A recipient of the RomCon "Reader's Choice" Award for best first book, "Slim To None", and Finalist for the Kindle Book Award with "From Dust", Freya continues to add to her rapidly growing collection of published novels as she spins story after story with an endless supply of bruised and dented characters, vying for attention!

Freya
Website
Goodreads
Facebook Page
Reader Group
Twitter
BookBub
Instagram
Book+Main
or mailto:freyabarker.writes@gmail.com

ALSO BY FREYA BARKER

ALSO BY FREYA BARKER

CEDAR TREE SERIES:

SLIM TO NONE

HUNDRED TO ONE

AGAINST ME

CLEAN LINES

UPPER HAND

LIKE ARROWS

HEAD START

PORTLAND, ME, NOVELS:

FROM DUST

CRUEL WATER

THROUGH FIRE

STILL AIR

SNAPSHOT SERIES:

SHUTTER SPEED

FREEZE FRAME

IDEAL IMAGE

PICTURE PERFECT (coming soon!)

NORTHERN LIGHTS COLLECTION:

A CHANGE IN TIDE

A CHANGE OF VIEW

A CHANGE OF PACE

ROCK POINT SERIES:

KEEPING 6

CABIN 12

HWY 550

(coming February 19)

There are many more books in this fan fiction world than listed here, for an up-to-date list go to www.AcesPress.com

You can also visit our Amazon page at: http://www.amazon.com/author/operationalpha

Special Forces: Operation Alpha World

Denise Agnew: Dangerous to Hold
Shauna Allen: Awakening Aubrey
Shauna Allen: Defending Danielle
Shauna Allen: Rescuing Rebekah
Shauna Allen: Saving Scarlett
Shauna Allen: Saving Grace
Brynne Asher: Blackburn
Jennifer Becker: Hiding Catherine
Julia Bright: Saving Lorelei
Julia Bright: Rescuing Amy
Victoria Bright: Surviving Savage
Victoria Bright: Going Ghost
Victoria Bright: Jostling Joker
Cara Carnes: Protecting Mari
Kendra Mei Chailyn: Beast
Kendra Mei Chailyn: Barbie
Kendra Mei Chailyn : Pitbull
Melissa Kay Clarke: Rescuing Annabeth
Melissa Kay Clarke: Safeguarding Miley
Samantha A. Cole: Handling Haven
Samantha A. Cole: Cheating the Devil
Sue Coletta: Hacked
Melissa Combs: Gallant
KaLyn Cooper: Rescuing Melina
Liz Crowe: Marking Mariah
Jordan Dane: Redemption for Avery

Jordan Dane: Fiona's Salvation
Riley Edwards: Protecting Olivia
Riley Edwards: Redeeming Violet
Riley Edwards, Recovering Ivy
Riley Edwards: Romancing Rayne
Nicole Flockton: Protecting Maria
Nicole Flockton: Guarding Erin
Nicole Flockton: Guarding Suzie
Nicole Flockton: Guarding Brielle
Casey Hagen: Shielding Nebraska
Casey Hagen: Shielding Harlow
Casey Hagen: Shielding Josie
Casey Hagen: Shielding Blair
Desiree Holt: Protecting Maddie
Kathy Ivan: Saving Sarah
Kathy Ivan: Saving Savannah
Kathy Ivan: Saving Stephanie
Jesse Jacobson: Protecting Honor
Jesse Jacobson: Fighting for Honor
Jesse Jacobson: Defending Honor
Jesse Jacobson: Summer Breeze
Silver James: Rescue Moon
Silver James: SEAL Moon
Silver James: Assassin's Moon
Silver James: Under the Assassin's Moon
Becca Jameson: Saving Sofia
Kate Kinsley: Protecting Ava
Heather Long: Securing Arizona
Heather Long: Guarding Gertrude
Heather Long: Protecting Pilar
Heather Long: Covering Coco
Gennita Low: No Protection
Kirsten Lynn: Joining Forces for Jesse
Margaret Madigan: Bang for the Buck

Margaret Madigan: Buck the System
Margaret Madigan: Jungle Buck
Margaret Madigan: December Chill
Rachel McNeely: The SEAL's Surprise Baby
Rachel McNeely: The SEAL's Surprise Bride
Rachel McNeely: The SEAL's Surprise Twin
KD Michaels: Saving Laura
KD Michaels: Protecting Shane
KD Michaels: Avenging Angels
Wren Michaels: The Fox & The Hound
Wren Michaels: The Fox & The Hound 2
Wren Michaels: Shadow of Doubt
Wren Michaels: Shift of Fate
Wren Michaels: Steeling His Heart
Kat Mizera: Protecting Bobbi
Mary B Moore: Force Protection
LeTeisha Newton: Protecting Butterfly
LeTeisha Newton: Protecting Goddess
LeTeisha Newton: Protecting Vixen
LeTeisha Newton: Protecting Heartbeat
MJ Nightingale: Protecting Beauty
MJ Nightingale: Betting on Benny
MJ Nightingale: Protecting Secrets
Sarah O'Rourke: Saving Liberty
Debra Parmley: Protecting Pippa
Lainey Reese: Protecting New York
Jenika Snow: Protecting Lily
Jen Talty: Burning Desire
Jen Talty: Burning Kiss
Jen Talty: Burning Skies
Jen Talty: Burning Lies
Jen Talty: Burning Heart
Megan Vernon: Protecting Us
Megan Vernon: Protecting Earth

Fire and Police: Operation Alpha World

KaLyn Cooper: Justice for Gwen

Aspen Drake: Sheltering Emma

Barb Han: Kace

Reina Torres: Justice for Sloane

As you know, this book included at least one character from Susan Stoker's books. To check out more, see below.

Delta Force Heroes Series

Rescuing Rayne (FREE!)
Rescuing Aimee (novella)
Rescuing Emily
Rescuing Harley
Marrying Emily
Rescuing Kassie
Rescuing Bryn
Rescuing Casey
Rescuing Sadie
Rescuing Wendy
Rescuing Mary
Rescuing Macie (April 2019)

Badge of Honor: Texas Heroes Series

Justice for Mackenzie (FREE!)
Justice for Mickie
Justice for Corrie
Justice for Laine (novella)
Shelter for Elizabeth
Justice for Boone
Shelter for Adeline
Shelter for Sophie
Justice for Erin
Justice for Milena
Shelter for Blythe
Justice for Hope
Shelter for Quinn (Feb 2019)
Shelter for Koren (June 2019)
Shelter for Penelope (Oct 2019)

SEAL of Protection Series

Protecting Caroline (FREE!)
Protecting Alabama
Protecting Fiona
Marrying Caroline (novella)
Protecting Summer
Protecting Cheyenne
Protecting Jessyka
Protecting Julie (novella)
Protecting Melody
Protecting the Future
Protecting Kiera (novella)
Protecting Dakota

SEAL of Protection: Legacy Series

Securing Caite (Jan 2019)
Securing Sidney (May 2019)
Securing Piper (Sept 2019)
Securing Zoey (TBA)
Securing Avery (TBA)
Securing Kalee (TBA)

New York Times, USA Today and *Wall Street Journal* Bestselling Author Susan Stoker has a heart as big as the state of Tennessee where she lives, but this all American girl has also spent the last fourteen years living in Missouri, California, Colorado, Indiana, and Texas. She's married to a retired Army man who now gets to follow *her* around the country. She debuted her first series in 2014 and quickly followed that up with the SEAL of Protection Series, which solidified her love of writing and creating stories readers can get lost in.

If you enjoyed this book, or any book, please consider

leaving a review. It's appreciated by authors more than you'll know.

www.stokeraces.com
www.AcesPress.com
susan@stokeraces.com

Made in United States
Troutdale, OR
11/05/2023

14324786R00166